Rob Thurman lives in Indiana, land of rolling hills and cows. Lots and lots of cows. *Nightlife*, *Moonshine*, *Madhouse*, *Deathwish* and *Doubletake*, the previous novels in the Cal Leandros series, are also published by Penguin. Visit Rob at www.robthurman.net.

BERKLEY OR

SLASHBACK

By the same author

Nightlife

Moonshine

Madhouse

Deathwish

Doubletake

Slashback

ROB THURMAN

BERKLEY UK

PENGUIN

BERKLEY UK

Published by the Penguin Group
Penguin Books Ltd, 80 Strand, London WC2R 0RL, England
Penguin Group (USA) Inc., 375 Hudson Street, New York, New York 10014, USA
Penguin Group (Canada), 90 Eglinton Avenue East, Suite 700, Toronto, Ontario, Canada M4P 2Y3
(a division of Pearson Penguin Canada Inc.)
Penguin Ireland, 25 St Stephen's Green, Dublin 2, Ireland (a division of Penguin Books Ltd)
Penguin Group (Australia), 707 Collins Street, Melbourne, Victoria 3008, Australia
(a division of Pearson Australia Group Pty Ltd)
Penguin Books India Pvt Ltd, 11 Community Centre, Panchsheel Park, New Delhi – 110 017, India
Penguin Group (NZ), 67 Apollo Drive, Rosedale, Auckland 0632, New Zealand
(a division of Pearson New Zealand Ltd)
Penguin Books (South Africa) (Pty) Ltd, Block D, Rosebank Office Park,
181 Jan Smuts Avenue, Parktown North, Gauteng 2193, South Africa

Penguin Books Ltd, Registered Offices: 80 Strand, London WC2R 0RL, England

www.penguin.com

First published in the USA by Roc, an imprint of New American Library,
a division of Penguin Group (USA) Inc. 2013
Published in Great Britain by Berkley UK 2013
001

ISBN: 978-0-718-19880-0

www.greenpenguin.co.uk

MIX
Paper from
responsible sources
FSC
www.fsc.org   FSC™ C018179

Penguin Books is committed to a sustainable
future for our business, our readers and our planet.
This book is made from Forest Stewardship
Council™ certified paper.

ALWAYS LEARNING   **PEARSON**

To Chelsea

ACKNOWLEDGMENTS

To my mom, who suggested why didn't I give my old dream of writing a go? If I become a victim of artistic Darwinism, I blame her. Also to Shannon—best friend and sister with a black belt in tough love; to my patient editor, Anne Sowards; Brian McKay (ninja of the dark craft of copywriting and muse of a fictional disease we won't discuss here . . . but did discuss at length in *Roadkill*); Agent Jeff Thurman of the FBI for the usual weapons advice; brilliant artist Chris McGrath; Lucienne Diver, who astounds me in the best possible way at every turn; and great and lasting friends Michael and Sara.

A bad neighbor is a misfortune. . . .

—Hesiod, b. 800 BC

History repeats itself. That's one of the things wrong with history.

—Clarence Darrow, 1910

If I cannot move Heaven, then I will raise Hell.

—Latin proverb

1

Niko

Twelve Years Ago

"Our neighbor is a serial killer."

It was that kind of day.

There had been tutoring no-necked football players lacking enough in brain cells that I was surprised they didn't have calluses on their knuckles from walking on them. It would've gone well with their gorilla grunting. Following that had been the food poisoning caused by a casserole brought in by Mrs. Dumpfries. The teachers' lounge had been liberally labeled a biohazard. The color of which is not orange like they tell you, but the bile green of nonstop vomiting. I stood witness to that. I'd gone through three mops.

And now we had a serial killer.

Or so said my little brother.

I closed the door behind me and locked it, not because I was immediately on board with the serial killer comment just issued, but we rented in a bad neighborhood. For us, an average neighborhood would be a more truthful way to put it. We'd not lived in better and we'd sometimes lived in worse. This cramped little house with a pronounced lean, no insulation, and cracked windows in east New London, Connecticut, was nothing special in one way or the other. When we didn't stay anyplace longer than five or six months, thanks to our mother's "occupation," it was all the same. I put my duffel bag containing my schoolbooks and janitor uniform by the door and took off my worn, but warm, Salvation Army coat to hang it from a rusted hook by the door.

With everything in its place I moved to the kitchen table, which wobbled, where my little brother with pencil and paper sat in a chair, which also wobbled. I lightly ruffled his black hair, shaggy in length but with a gloss like silk. Thanks to Cal being a good brother, he let me without complaint.

"Where's Sophia?" I asked. She had given birth to us and I used the word "mother" sometimes, but the truth of it never quite fit in my mouth.

"Gone. With her suitcase." The pencil kept moving and he didn't look up.

With her suitcase . . . that meant she would be gone anywhere from three days to three weeks. If business was slow in the area, she went looking for it elsewhere. She told fortunes, picked pockets, ran scams, whored herself out if the price was right. There was only so much whiskey you could shoplift before the local liquor store owners became suspicious and you had to actually start paying for it. Yes, life was hard for Sophia. I swallowed my anger as I'd been taught. I wouldn't let Sophia have that kind of power over me.

And truthfully, the times she was gone were the best times.

"Are you doing your homework?" I asked with a little disapproval for him to hear. It was six p.m.—although I couldn't make it home at the same time he did, I made it there before dark. Always.

The homework—he should've been done with it by now. There was also a pan crusted with burned SpaghettiOs in the sink, some less scorched fake pasta in spots on the cracked linoleum floor, and a purple handprint, grape soda probably, on the door of the groaning refrigerator. Cal was a good brother, but there are all sorts of definitions for good when it came to an eleven-year-old.

"Yes, Nik. I'm doing my homework. Watching the serial killer made me get behind." I didn't have to see his eyes to know they were rolling with the disdain and sarcasm only an eleven-year-old could manage, and I gave him a gentle swat to the back of the head.

I took the other chair and sat down. "All right. Tell me why our neighbor is a serial killer," I said with a patience I didn't have to fake. I listened to Cal when he had something to say. I always listened to him. I had even when he was three and thought a monster lived under the bed, because in our world . . .

In our world, there was every chance that he wasn't necessarily wrong.

I also listened to him as he'd had to grow up very fast and deserved the respect and dignity that came from surviving a harsh road that I hadn't been able to change nearly as much as I wished. There were times I could close my eyes and see the small bloody footprints on that blackly grim path. That my larger ones were beside his every step of the way didn't help. Didn't absolve.

I was fifteen and I was smart. More than smart. I could admit that because it wasn't boasting. Being more than smart meant knowing too much. If I'd had a choice, I would've chosen to be less smart. I would've chosen not to know all about absolution and how hard it was to come by.

Impossible on some days.

As for right now . . . I'd grown up as quickly as Cal, but if I hadn't—if I'd been a normal fifteen-year-old, I would still know this: you show respect to a warrior. For Cal to have survived our childhood, he was a warrior. I gave him his due. Anything else would've made me less of a brother.

He put down his pencil and raised his eyes from the carelessly rumpled paper. I swallowed the sigh and reminded myself that there were worse things than a messy nature. Cal was a good brother and a good kid when, if they'd lived his life, other children would be feral as wild dogs and amoral as sharks at dinnertime. Cal was amazingly, painfully human in comparison and not once did I overlook that.

I reached over and gave him an encouraging tap on the back of his hand as he hesitated, something he rarely did. Cal knew his own mind about generally everything under the sun and all the other suns in at least half our galaxy. "Go on, grasshopper. Tell me."

Gray eyes, the same as mine and that of our mother, Sophia, blinked; then he shrugged. "I smelled it. On him."

That's where the discomfort entered the picture. Cal didn't like admitting he could do something other people couldn't. He didn't want to be different. I told him that sometimes different is good, sometimes it's better. It was one of the few times in his life he hadn't believed me.

"Okay," I said, calm as if that was something I heard every day. I pretended not to see the flush of shame behind his pale skin. He wouldn't want to talk about it and if I tried, it would make it worse. On certain matters Cal was determined that no positive spin could be put on it and that was that. Stubborn, so stubborn. "What exactly did you smell?"

He shrugged again. "I got off the bus at the corner with the other kids." To say that Cal could take care of himself better than your average eleven-year-old was something of an understatement, but I made certain he played it safe all the same. That he stayed with a crowd or a group of other people if he could. "I was walking home and he was at his mailbox by the sidewalk. When I passed him, I smelled it. He smelled like blood. A lot of blood. After he went inside, I snuck around to his backyard and got close to the house. There are tiny kinda half windows to the basement. I think they're covered up with cardboard on the inside or painted because I couldn't see anything." He made a face. "But I could still smell. It's like roadkill. His basement smells like a mountain of roadkill."

He gave a third shrug, a habit I was going to have to break and soon while I was still sane. "He has a basement full of dead bodies," he declared, "and that means he's a serial killer."

End of story. Which was my brother's way. If he became a lawyer when he grew up, he'd have the most succinct closing arguments in any court system in America.

He had already picked up his pencil again and gone back to the math problems. It wasn't that he liked math or homework of any kind, but he knew no homework meant no TV. That motivated him to no end . . . normally. What motivated him now was the amount of trouble he knew was coming his way.

"You went prowling around the man's windows? Cal, how could you do something so stupid? He could've shot you. If he'd seen you, he *would've* shot you," I snapped. This was the type of neighborhood where everyone, little old ladies included, had guns, and if they saw a shadowy shape that remotely looked as if it was trying to break in a window, they would shoot first and not bother to wait long enough to register the shape was the size of a child.

"I was careful. I was sneaky. You know I'm good at that," he replied matter-of-factly, pencil moving to write a sadly sloppy number. Cal's handwriting wasn't all it could be and that extended to numbers as well. That he was actually smart, if not "freakishly smart" as he labeled me, but lazy as the day was long made my back teeth grind enough that I thought I'd be in dentures by the time I was twenty. Now, however, my teeth were grinding for a different reason.

"Yes, I know you're good at that," I echoed and the urge to destroy my molars disappeared just that quickly. I only wish I didn't know why he was so good at it. Cal was talented at being careful and sneaky as that was the best way to not be hit by one of Sophia's bottles. The malicious verbal abuse she gave him, that was harder to dodge. She'd slapped me more than once when I was younger and smaller, but I was five eleven now, taller than she was. She didn't slap me anymore. She had never slapped or hit Cal. She didn't have any desire to touch him physically and if she accidentally did, she rubbed her hand against her skirt as if she'd touched a toad or a snake.

Cal noticed that more than her words. Cal noticed everything that I wish he didn't.

Although she didn't use skin on skin in a fit of temper, a drunken rage had Sophia quick to throw a whiskey bottle at the nearest moving target. It was fortunate for her she didn't come close to hitting anything or anyone. Very fortunate for her. "But Sophia can't hit anything when she's drunk," I pointed out to Cal as if that was something to be thankful for, tasting the blood of a bitten tongue for my punishment.

I did the best I could. I did the best I could in a very bad situation.

Didn't I?

"And you know Sophia is a big difference than a sober man with a gun. Don't go over there again, all right? Promise me," I finished.

Cal snorted. At times despite my skipping a grade, reading books thick enough that he casually used them as stools, and being at the top of my class, my little brother thought I was incredibly slow when it came to common sense. He kept me humble. "He's a *serial killer*, Nik. Why would I go back? He could get out his chain saw and chop me up into pieces. Except I'm a virgin so I might get away." Not-quite-under his breath, he added, "You don't watch enough movies. You don't know anything."

"Fine. You're the expert on all things serial killer," I said dryly, less than glad to know my birds-and-bees talk had ended up as nothing but misinformation about murderers letting the abstinent escape. "But I still want to hear you promise."

He exhaled, obviously aggrieved at my dense ways. "I promise." He drew out "promise" until it lasted as long as if it had twice its normal syllables.

"Good." And it was good. I'd put Cal's first diaper on him the day he was born. Fed him his first bottle. Imagining him shot dead in some asshole's—damn, keep the language clean for impressionable minds—some *person's* backyard wasn't a picture I wanted to take to bed with me that night.

"Now that's taken care of," I continued, "let's talk about what this man could be other than a serial killer." Cal knew there were monsters in the world. He'd seen them. He searched the window every night for them. So did I. He didn't need to think he was sleeping next door to a serial killer on top of that. The shadows hid enough already.

"First, he could work at a slaughterhouse," I started the list. "Even if he changed and showered at work, you're special. You could still smell the blood. And his basement might be full of bloodstained aprons with pieces of rotting meat on them. He's lazy—like you, little brother." I couldn't resist a teachable moment. "He doesn't do his laundry. That would explain all the blood and the smell of rot. Wouldn't it?"

I was trying for logical. Cal would know in a heartbeat if I tried to pull the wool over his eyes, especially if the wool was made of bullshit. *Bullshit*, damn. Hell, impressionable minds. I had to remember that: impressionable minds. My thinking words like shit were the next step to saying them and once Cal heard one of them slip from my mouth, it was all over. I couldn't stop what he picked up at school, but I could set the example here at home. Sophia said the filthiest of words all the time, but that was Sophia. Cal knew nothing good or right came out of her. But his big brother, although slow in serial killer mythology, could do little wrong and more importantly he was not above using that big brother worship to his advantage the first chance he got. *Nik* did it and if Nik did it then it wasn't bad and Sophia didn't count.

Cal folded his math paper and stuffed it in a folder bulging with papers from two grades ago. Lazy beyond lazy, but while I could nag him about it until I wanted to bang my head against the wall, I wouldn't force him to clean it up. I could spend my entire life fighting that battle. I had to pick them carefully. And messy or not, Cal needed to be independent, had to be. I'd taught him so. Surviving Sophia, ignoring the monsters when they did show up to gaze in the window with lava-red eyes. Cal had to be able to handle that. I couldn't be with him every minute of every day. If sloppy but independent was the best I could manage, I'd be more than happy with it.

He rested his elbows on the folder and cupped his small chin in his hands. He was small for his age, looking at least a year if not two younger. He was due a growth spurt anytime now. "Slaughterhouse? Maybe," he said. "What else could he be?" Only eleven and serious as a soldier going to war. Gathering intelligence. Listening to theories—not that it meant anything. Cal's mind was made up. The intelligence was wrong. The theories bogus. Cal knew what he knew. Changing his mind had never taken less than an act of God.

But I was trying all the same. I went for number two on the list. "A butcher." There weren't many butcher shops open these days. You bought meat, when you could afford it, at Kroger or K-Mart or Wal-Mart; it all depended on the city we were squatting in at the time. "He could work at a grocery store, wrapping up meat behind the counter. He'd come home with blood and brisket on him. It makes more sense than him being a serial killer. They're pretty rare in smaller towns like this. He either kills animals or he packages meat. We already have monsters. What are the odds we'd get a serial killer too? That would be winning the worst lottery of all time, right? You get that, don't you, Cal?"

He tilted his head, staring at me. I saw emotions roiling behind his eyes. Some I recognized: worry, resignation, and others I couldn't make out. I hadn't failed to read Cal's feelings, any of them, in his short life. This was the first time. "Cal? You do see?"

"I can see how *you* see that." He shook his head, long bangs flopping. "But that's not the way it is. He doesn't work at a slaughterhouse and he's not a butcher. He kills people and puts them in his basement."

"Why?" I demanded, frustration peaking as hard as I was trying to hold it back. "Why are you so sure of that?" Why are you so sure that it's all bad? Everything? I couldn't let myself believe that, because how could I hope to find us lives someday, real lives, if he was right?

He echoed my finger tap to the back of his hand. This time his finger, almost as white as his homework paper, tapped and clashed with the dusky brown of my skin. This touch didn't hold reassurance like mine had though—it held pity for me that I didn't know. That I was four years older, but I was the one who couldn't see, not him.

"Because this is the real world," he said almost apologetically.

Plain and straightforward as it came.

"And this is just the way things are, Nik."

He picked up his folder and headed for the bedroom. "I'm sorry. I know you don't get it. That you don't see."

He paused to smile. I'd seen that smile before and it never failed to make my chest ache. It was touched with a near-adult bitterness that looked to have been carved into his face with the blade of that fictional serial killer. "But maybe monsters and half monsters are the only things that can see."

Eleven years old and that's what he thought of the world. What he thought of himself.

He closed the bedroom door behind him, leaving behind emotions that this time I could read. Disappointment that I didn't automatically accept and trust in what he thought. Worry for me that I didn't know enough about the real world. Worry for *me*—a kid that could've been shot crawling around the back of a stranger's house and it was me that he spent his concern on.

I pulled the black rubber band out of my hair to let my short ponytail fall free, a few dark blond strands hanging in my eyes. It didn't help my headache like I'd hoped. I could take Tylenol for that, but there wasn't a pill for the guilt. Guilt that I couldn't convince Cal the world wasn't like that, not all of it. Guilt that I couldn't believe him and possibly ruin a man's reputation with an anonymous call to the police—not without proof first.

Which meant I'd have to get proof—proof that our neighbor with his cologne of blood *did* work in a slaughterhouse or a meatpacking plant. I would show Cal that not every corner, not every house, not every street, and not every minute of our lives was touched by hungry shadows. There was sun. There was normal. You had to know only enough to look for them.

Proof, then. It was a plan. I liked plans. I liked order. When everything was sorted and in its place, the out-of-control became routine and the routine became tolerable. I heaved out of the chair and moved to the sink to work on the pot crusted with blackened pseudo-pasta. Self-pity was a luxury I didn't have and it rarely made a bad day better. Besides, now I had a plan . . . for one problem at least. I looked over my shoulder at the bedroom.

"Half human," I said quietly, trying to erase his last words. "Not half monster. Not a 'thing.'"

He didn't hear me through the closed door.

If he had, after a day of smelling blood and rot that no one else could . . .

He probably wouldn't have believed me anyway.

2

Cal

Present Day

"There's a serial killer in the city."

Yeah? Really?

And rain was wet, grass was green, the sun set in the west; also, reality shows caused brain tumors.

None of it was precisely fucking news.

"Thanks for the info, boss," I drawled, bored as I mixed a mojito for Elegua, a dark skinned, cat-eyed African trickster, and slid it across the bar. Yes, a goddamn mojito. He used to drink straight rum while smoking his foul-smelling cigars, but once he started visiting Cuba, he became high maintenance. It was getting a little too fancy in the Ninth Circle lately. I missed the days when beer and whiskey were all we had and haul your furry, scaly, or prehensile tailed self elsewhere if you didn't like it.

Auld Lang Syne.

"But guess what, Ish?" I wiped my hands on the black apron tied around my waist. "There are probably at least three serial killers in New York. That's why there's police. Let them deal with it. And why do you even care? It's human business, not *paien* business." *Paien* was the pagan world, the supernatural world, and half human or not, the world I'd chosen to live in for five or so years now.

It had been gradual, that. From thinking I was a human with a fraction of monster in him to knowing I was a monster with just a little human seasoning the soup.

I couldn't say I'd changed sides either. Humans didn't know monsters existed and damn sure didn't know about the particular monster I was. If they did, they would run screaming, piss themselves, or be caught up in enough zombie apocalypse movies to try to grab an ax to fight back—the latter never ended well. Then there were the ninety-nine percent of the *paien* who hated me for the Auphe I carried in my blood. But I went with the *paien* anyway the majority of the time, despite the fact I could've pretended with humans and they wouldn't have known.

But pretending every minute of every day can be tiring. And . . .

Boring.

With the other monsters I could be myself, no matter how much they oh-so-profoundly wished I wouldn't be.

Sheep aren't the only ones to piss themselves came the gleeful inner mutter.

I really had to stop thinking of humans as sheep. I'd picked up that bad habit in the past month or so, from the other monsters on the outside, yeah, but primarily the one on the inside. If I said it out loud, my brother would do more than kick my ass. He'd remind me I had human in me too by dunking me in the East River, holding me under for a good three minutes, and calling it negative reinforcement training instead of the overgrown swirly that it was.

Sheep versus human . . . yeah, that might very well point to an identity crisis on my part.

When it comes down to it, I'm a monster. There was some human in me, true, although less all the time. I'd tried to hold on, but life is life. Love it or leave it.

It's simple. I am a monster.

And I kind of liked it—which *is* the definition of an identity crisis.

Oh Jesus. Was Ishiah still droning on and on?

Hell. Of course he was. Serial killer. Serial killer. The guy could not take a hint if they were giving them away free with a hooker and a six-pack.

"Because, Caliban, while this serial killer preys only on humans, from what I hear it is not human itself. Very much not human and is skinning people alive. The police will not know what it is, much less be able to catch it." The peri's gold-barred white wings flashed into view, disturbed, and then disappeared as he continued to stack glasses. "That makes it your business, doesn't it?"

It did. If it was supernatural and you were willing to pay enough to make it dead—then go ahead and pick out the coffin. If there were some annoying issues of conscience to be assessed, I let Niko figure that out these days. Not that I didn't have a conscience. I did. Smaller than average, okay, but there. Unfortunately for most, it tended to be as lazy and rebellious as the rest of me. It was better for everyone to let my brother handle the moral issues while I played to my strengths:

Violence, sarcasm, and a respectable collection of pornography.

"If there's someone forking over the fee, sure." I reached over the bar, grabbed a handful of passing fur, and slammed the Wolf's head on the counter hard enough to hear something crack. It could've been the polished wood surface or a lupine skull. I wasn't concerned which. "Leaving, Fido?" I asked cheerfully. "But you haven't settled your tab yet. We don't like that. It hurts our feelings."

Long teeth bared at me in a spittle-spraying growl and snap, but the twisted combination of a hand and paw, a member of the All Wolf caught between wolf and human—neither nor, slid across the rumpled green. I counted with my free hand and frowned, all that cheer draining away. "Tips are not mandatory, but they are appreciated and guarantee you'll be greeted with a sunny disposition next time you're back." I demonstrated said sunny disposition with a grin that wasn't that different from his Nice-to-see-you, Grandma snarl—except more effective. Several more bills were shoved across. After an assessing glance, I grunted, and let him go. "Thank you, *sir*. Now get your cheating, cheap ass out of here, tail between your legs just the way I like."

I watched the werewolf slink out of the door, smelling like the last-in-line Omega that he was. The other Wolves hunched over the scarred and stained tables in the bar grumbled, but let it go. We had an understanding of live and let live or, more accurately, if they fucked with me, I would goddamn *bury* them. "Puppies. They do try the patience, don't they?"

"You make enough money with you and your brother's true business. You could quit the bar." As it was Ishiah's bar—he'd been blackmailed into giving me a job—and I had a tendency to play rough with the clientele, he had to wholeheartedly wish that I would focus on my other higher-paying career.

"Nah. Nik says it's good for me. Keeps me socialized."

Apparently, just like with pit bulls rescued straight out of dog-fighting rings, socialization was job one when it came to me. I polished a glass with a towel and yawned. "And I still haven't heard about a client willing to foot the bill for running this supernatural serial killing fuck-head to the ground."

"Socialization. Of course. I see the improvement daily," he muttered, fingers sheathed tightly in light blond hair. Maybe he had a headache; allergic to his own feathers. That had to be it. It couldn't be me and my winning ways. "You and Niko have done free 'exterminations' before. You'll be saving lives. What better time than now to do some charity work?"

"Yeah, we've done free . . . when Nik knew about the problem and as I don't plan on telling him, there's no need for him to know about this one."

Nik had other worries right now and as usual they were thanks to me. I had no plans of adding to them. "Why don't you hunt down whatever bogeyman this is in *your* spare time?" I goaded. "I've seen you with a sword." It wasn't a sight I'd be forgetting either. Conan the Barbarian would think twice about going up against Ish. "I think you can manage."

Ish, massaging his temples, said absently, "Peris are discouraged against killing *paien*-kind . . . other *paien*-kind, I mean. We're tolerated here in New York, but that could change if the others thought we rose above our station."

"Station?" I snorted. "You have a station? You kick Wolf, vamp, and every other kind of supernatural butt in the bar on a daily basis. If you could wear your station on your foot, you'd have broken it off in someone's ass a helluva long time ago."

"Fighting is different than killing." He let go of his head and pointed toward the door. "Go home. Your shift is close enough to being over and you are as bad for my mood as you are for business. I curse Goodfellow every day for convincing me to give you a job. *Go.*" He loved me like the brother he never had. I mean, didn't everyone—when they weren't trying to kill me?

I gave him an evil grin and drawled, "You do something to Goodfellow every day all right, but I don't think cursing is it." He grabbed the first thing at hand—

an unopened bottle of whiskey—and threw it at my head. Déjà vu. I ducked easily, some childhood habits you never lose. I then tossed my apron under the bar, pulled on my jacket over my shoulder holster, and made for the door. I didn't want to be around if he did bring out the sword.

Did I mention it was a flaming sword? Angels were a myth, but the seed that had started the myth, the peris, were close enough for shagging your ass toward the Promised Land without stopping to think maybe a map and a timetable would be good things to ask for first.

In this case, the Promised Land was a street shrouded by the cloying breath of dangerous night and the less poetic ammonia stench of were-cat urine sprayed on the curb. I didn't care what anyone said. No one moved to New York for the ambience—except for monsters and they had considerably more leeway when it came to ambience.

I checked my watch. I had thirty minutes before the end of my shift. That meant I could do my brother a favor and try to keep his love life from going down in flames. Or at least toss him a fire extinguisher because he was already in the doghouse and that, too, was my fault. I walked toward the next block. Cabs didn't come down this street, unless a monster shrouded in human clothes was driving one. You could call this street the point of no return, the edge of the earth like the old days, and it was for oblivious humans. Luckily, nature kept most humans from wandering onto a feeding ground. Some subconscious sense of ill-ease had them veering off to safer streets where shadows were only that.

But sometimes you run into something different. With monsters there was always something different, but with humans, open book—open, harmless pop-up kiddie book. Except for Nik, who fell in a category all his own, there were rarely any surprises with humans.

Tonight I was surprised.

They lined up on both sides of the street, barely an inch from where open season on sheep began. They knew. They were human and they *knew* and not just subconsciously. Not that the inch was more than a suggestion. Nearly any creature would kill a human anywhere in NYC, much less an inch or so off pure monster-ville territory. But, the fact these men knew there was a territory at all . . . huh. Suddenly I wasn't quite as bored as I had been.

There were eight of them, four on each side until four walked over and it was eight on one side—my side. I smelled the youth on them. It made it past the stink of living on the streets: filth, and rotting food, cigarette smoke and decaying teeth, but oddly no alcohol. No scent of heroin, a sleepy smell, or meth, tinfoil and edgy. They were homeless, but not too old and not too young. In their twenties it looked like under the hoods of their identical white hooded sweatshirts and the scruff of beard. What kind of homeless managed to team up to wear white? That's what it was under the patches of grime and it made no sense. Their world was a dirty one and white had no place in it. It was odd as was the fact that they were all in their prime, as much as the underfed and unsheltered could be.

It was interesting.

This wasn't a mugging. I hadn't had anyone try to mug me since I was sixteen. Pit vipers and me, we both gave off an unspoken, "You want to screw with me? Really? Because I would fucking *love* that." We had the time and the tools and we were more than happy to put them to use. Muggers tended to veer off for easier-appearing targets.

No, this wasn't like that. This was different entirely. For one, there were eight of them. Even for this city that was more than your usual dose of daily violence aimed at a single source.

I stopped and let them circle me, catching another smell as they came closer. Metal. On every one of them was the sharp, sweet singing whiff of a good chunk of metal. Knives or guns. I didn't smell cordite or gun oil. Only knives then, but all armed, and that made them more interesting.

Interesting.

Fun.

Playtime.

No, no. I was bored, but there were other ways to entertain myself. None were coming to mind, but there had to be at least one or two. And these were humans, not sheep. Humans.

"You guys here for some exercise?" I checked my watch again. "You should probably look elsewhere. I'm having identity issues right now, which is frustrating, and I tend to express my emotions with bullets. It's so much cheaper than therapy."

I needed an outlet for my monster, a specific one. One that would challenge me and take all my effort to put down. I hadn't had a distraction like that in a month now, which meant things tended to spill over in all directions. Then, wham, I was all "put the lotion in the basket" and no one, but no one was happy with that attitude.

I was doing my best, trying to hold back. I gave them one warning, which was one more than I usually gifted unto any jackass. All they had to do was take it . . . quickly, if they were smart, but they had an out.

Years ago I tried to avoid killing people if I could—whether they deserved it or not. It seemed like an important distinction. Monsters go down, humans go to the hospital. Sometimes I couldn't get around it, but most of the time I managed to wound instead of kill. Recently I'd begun to wonder if that was bad decision making. There were human monsters that were every bit as bad as the real deal, some worse. I'd known that my whole life. Did they deserve a free ride?

Nope, I was thinking they did not.

Their genetic makeup didn't come into it at all. I treated all monsters equally. After all, that was only fair, right?

I was one step off the Ninth Circle open buffet invitational, but the streetlights were out, the shadows dense. This was a human street, but it wasn't a safe one by any means. One of the men, this one wearing the same white sweatshirt as the others with the hood up,

almost like a monk, with filth-covered jeans, and ratty
sneakers, stepped closer to me. He had reddish stubble,
a pockmarked face, and remarkably clear eyes. Too
clear. Eyes that focused, that bright, that *shining* usually
meant there was one thought and one only in the gray
matter behind them. When you have only one
thought—a single unwavering incandescent unshak-
able goal—that made you generally ape-shit. The ape-
shit could rarely be reasoned with.

People: can't live with them. Can't destroy them
with the power of your mind.

Oh wait. I *could*.

"Heaven says you should pray." His breath was
what I expected and forevermore would the word
"heaven" be linked to the rank stench of tooth decay in
my mind. Joy. His knife was out now and swinging
toward my throat. I took it from him with a simple
block and twist, slammed it into his chest, punching
through the bony crunch of sternum into his heart, and
used his momentum to flip him over my shoulder. It's
an amazing world when a dead man can fly. I'd given
him an out, and he'd chosen it. Too bad it was the
wrong one. That left seven knives slashing at me and
seven more foul-smelling huffs of exhaled air carrying
the same word and then more of them.

"Last chance for the rest of you." I looked around
the circle. "I am both ethically and morally challenged
at the best of times. And you annoying me with your
festive little homicidal ways doesn't come under the
category of best of times."

"Child of God, on your knees and pray."

"Pray for deliverance."

"Pray for mercy."

"Pray." "Pray." "Pray." "Pray."

I was praying all right. Praying for a round of breath mints. Jesus Christ.

"I should pray, huh? Hate to tell you assholes, you should've prayed for better directions. This is not a part of town for a good churching up." I grinned, sharp and gleeful. "Not a steeple in sight."

Seven men, young but malnourished. No problem. Seven knives out and slashing if not with trained efficiency, then with wild enthusiasm. More of a problem, but it could be handled. Seven sets of eyes burning with the fire of the martyr. Seven psychos willing to die for something, who the hell knew what, willing to die like their buddy if they could take me with them. Seven knives against two guns and more rounds stashed on me than World War II would've needed. It was doable. Even as close as I'd let them get, to see—you know— just to see what could happen. Did that make me a bad boy? Yes, it did. But all in all, the entire situation still very doable. But eight bodies to clean up, and they were too close to me to be anything but bodies now, that was different.

Fun was in the execution of some easily justifiable violence. Fun was not in the cleanup. Not that I should think that. I shouldn't.

Really, really shouldn't.

I could leave. I could go—in the way the Auphe did—and leave them behind, but, entertainment aside, I needed to do more than exercise my skills. I needed to stretch them. I had someone after me who could do the same as I could, only better, quicker, years ahead of me in experience. If I was going to survive him, I needed to level the playing field. I had to catch up. I needed the practice. Practice made perfect. But did I need to use seven men . . . homicidal, but still men . . . as an exercise? Was that right?

Playtime. Playtime, playtime, playtime.

What the hell.

I sent them away. All of them.

Nice and tidy.

As I said—skills.

The world screamed, my attackers screamed along with it. Reality ripped as my gate opened, and the night itself came alive as ravenous gray light ate them. Eight hungry mouths made of lightning and death tore through the shadows turning them the purple of co-agulated blood and took the men to where they could pray to their hearts' content. Not that it would do them any good and not that they would last long, depending on how much time had passed in that particular hell and how much radiation lingered there. Then the mouths closed and the night was only the night again.

Well, shit.

Chances were you were supposed to be worried about identity crises, not embrace them. If I were the hugging type, I'd say I'd just given my slow and grad-ual defection to the monster side a big one.

I couldn't say I hadn't meant to do it. I didn't know what I'd meant to do, but I had planned on thinking about it for at least another fraction of a second. Debating the right and wrong of it, the thousand shades of gray, the thousand hues of justification, as there was a chance . . . a small one . . . that I was wrong.

I sighed and brought them back.

It had only been a second, but they looked as if they'd been gone a while. Time ran oddly in the Auphe world. A day here could be two years there—I knew that all too well. The seven of them appeared a little thinner and were curled up in moaning, whimpering fetal balls on the street. I knew that feeling too. Tumulus wasn't Hell—no, it was Hell's big brother. Not a pleasant place to be. My best guess was they'd been there a few days in Tumulus time.

That was enough that I didn't think they'd be attacking anyone else anytime soon. Someone official would eventually come scoop them up and stick them in the real world's version of Arkham Asylum. After what they'd seen on the other side, they'd be lucky to regain enough coherence to use a spoon again, much less a butcher knife, in the next few months.

Now, though, it was time to get on with what I was doing before a bizarre street cult thought I didn't look holy enough, that I needed to pray more. That was New York for you. Not many Jehovah's Witnesses jumping you on the street, but Jehovah's pseudo-ninjas willing to kill you to save your soul, those we had. Pretty presumptuous ones too. How did they know what I did or didn't do? I could pray. I could be holy. They didn't know.

My grin widened despite my uncertain conscience. It felt like a tangle of razor wire decorating my face.

Yeah, I guess maybe they *did* know. Apparently my ability to blend in with your average, harmless humans wasn't all it'd once been. Of course I wasn't all I'd once been. I was more or I was less, depending on your point of view.

Either/or, I'd have to work on passing for a little more normal. I still had to shop. Beer and porn didn't buy itself.

I checked my watch again. Still on schedule. For good or bad, right or wrong, eight wannabe psycho-killers had been taken care of in less than a minute. I had plenty of time left to deal with Nik.

Although I did wonder how they had known precisely where the theoretical line of the danger zone ran between monster versus human New York. Knew consciously instead of instinctually, unlike most humans, and knew to the inch. That was peculiar. But as none of them were remotely close to coherent, there was no point in asking. Plus, they were no longer my problem or the problem of any annoying innocent bystanders. As my curiosity on most situations was fairly nil once the potential violence was over, I let it go. Maybe I'd think about it later, maybe not. Psychos in my world were a dime a dozen. Who had the time to think about them all?

Besides, Nik came first.

Soon enough I was waiting at the third landing in the stairs of Promise's building. A very rich and exclusive building it was with a condo board that would reject the queen of England for not keeping a low enough profile. They liked their privacy here, their quiet, and a certain appearance. I made it past the doorman only because Promise, who was Niko's love life I was there to save, graciously slipped . . . I mean, tipped him two hundred bucks a month for me sully- ing the atmosphere.

Leaning against the wall I waited for Niko to climb down the twenty flights of stairs, which he would be doing, I knew for a fact. For the past four weeks he had shown up nearly every night I worked at the bar at closing to make sure I made it home in one piece. Sadly for his sex life, this was not new behavior for him. Not at all. My nearly getting killed inevitably turned him into a hybrid of babysitter/bodyguard/and human Terminator. It was past time to break that cycle. For his sake.

As for the walking instead of the elevator, it wasn't all about the cardio. Never take the elevator. Ask any- one who's killed someone in one of those steel boxes— yeah, that'd be me holding up my hand—they're nifty death traps with limited opportunity of exit.

"You should be at work."

I'd been waiting for him, but naturally I hadn't heard him. Nik was too good for that, too good for me. I had smelled him though. The faint tang of oiled metal and the farm fresh smell of goat-milk soap. The man could slice out your heart and hold it in his hand before you even noticed he was there, but he was addicted to goat-milk soap because it was "all natural." It was embarrassing as hell is what it was. The fact that I used it as I was too lazy to buy my own soap wasn't embarrassing at all. That was just practical.

"Cyrano, it's been a month now. Nothing's happened. You need to take a break. I'm here to make sure you take it," I said with exasperation as I looked up at him moving halfway down the stairs from the fourth floor and waited for him to join me. He did need a break, although I hadn't had much luck convincing him of that. The guy deserved a life of his own that was more than rolling out of Promise's warm bed at three a.m. to look after me, but once a big brother, always a big brother. That his little brother was a monster in his own right didn't put a dent in his determination.

Promise had been patient about the protectiveness issue several times now, but everyone's patience runs its course. Promise with her knowing eyes, fields of lavender under moonlight, and her ability to snap a neck as gracefully as the movement of any Renaissance dance, was good for Nik. She was a mirror of his calm and control, and being a vampire helped if our work spilled over into our private lives. Promise had no difficulty taking care of herself. I didn't want him to lose the sanctuary he had in her because of me. The very reason he needed a sanctuary was thanks to me after all.

"Grimm waited twelve years to find you," he pointed out, stopping beside me. "I doubt a month of laying low will be much of a strain for him."

Grimm was the problem I'd gifted Niko with, the reason I'd blown off Ishiah and his serial killer. Grimm was actually my problem, the outlet for the worst part of me—he did double duty. He was not Nik's trouble, but brothers, like company, loved misery. Or was that the other way around? Whatever. Grimm was half

Auphe like me, the result of the same experiment in genetic engineering spawned by a race that had once ruled and ravaged the earth long before man had yet to be the next best thing to a tadpole. Now, thanks to Niko, some friends and myself, the Auphe were extinct, but part of their experiment remained. Grimm and me.

Grimm wanted to kill me and he wanted my help in fathering a new race to replace the Auphe. And being half Auphe he saw no reason he couldn't have both things. It was something of a blind spot, but not a surprising one when the Auphe had been the worst of the worst when it came to monsters. They had lived only to murder and mutilate and do so as frequently as possible. Our childhood name for them, Grendels, had fallen damn short of the reality.

Now Grimm thought he had the balls to step into their jockstrap—and he was right.

As problems went, Grimm was a big one. I was a monster, no matter what Nik said to the contrary, but there were degrees of monster. Grimm was the better monster. A month ago I'd sent him packing with a chest full of bullets, but I'd been able to do it only because I'd set my human part to one side and let all my monster come out to play. A dangerous thing that.

A fun thing.

That too, but my kind of fun came with a price tag. Every time I let it off the leash, there was more to chain back up when I was done. More monster equaled less room for the human in me—the sanity in me. There were monsters and then there were *monsters*. I didn't want to become the latter . . . if I had a choice . . . at least not this soon.

What I'd done to the eight killers on the street—that was nothing to what I could do. *Nothing.* I could have done so many things. . . .

Not the time nor the place.

No longer a member of the human race was the singsong rhyme in my head.

I snorted at the childishness of my own subconscious before shoving it down hard and slamming the lid on its box. I had once made a mental box when I was a kid to store bad thoughts, bad memories, bad desires. Now I had thousands of boxes. That was good, in my opinion. It meant that I was in control. I would fight to my last breath to keep it that way—identity crisis or not.

Not that it mattered now, because this was Niko time. I needed to make the most of it. Niko deserved a personal life that didn't involve playing bodyguard to me and I wasn't giving up on that.

"If Grimm shows up," I said, "I'll gate the hell away to parts unknown"—at least to Grimm—"and he's screwed."

Gating or traveling was a nice way of saying I'd tear a bleeding hole in reality, wounds of rippling tarnished light, and step through to end up a block away or a thousand miles away. My choice, although not to where I'd sent my eight attackers in questionably fashionable hoodies. I'd never go to that place. Never again.

The ability to gate came with the Auphe blood and though I hadn't been able to use it well or often at one time, now I was cooking with gas. The Traveling King. All bow before me. Grimm could gate too, but as long as he didn't know where I was going, he couldn't follow.

"Ah yes, the gating," Nik said with grim bite. "The gating that you think gives you an edge when we hunt the supernatural now. Fighters who think they have an edge often get sloppy." A light smack to the back of my head accompanied each following word. "Do . . . not . . . get . . . sloppy." He dropped his hand and added with a growl, "Especially with Grimm."

There I stood, carrying the two guns I hadn't used earlier, a fancy new garrote, and four knives concealed in various easily accessible locations—all of which I could wield as automatically as I could breathe, and yet I was being schooled like a three-year-old thrown into a mixed martial arts caged death match. Did Dirty Harry have to put up with that? Nope. Then again all Dirty Harry's partners died on him. Nik stuck around and had all my life. That was worth a smack or two.

Plus as Nik was the one who'd taught me to use any and all weapons, he could and would kick my ass if I tried to smack back. Affectionately kick my ass of course . . . with brotherly love. Not that brotherly love made it sting any less. Which was not why I didn't tell him what I'd done only a half an hour ago. I didn't tell him because he already worried about my getting careless. He didn't see that using the gates as often as possible helped me catch up with Grimm, whose experience in that was years and years longer than mine. Grimm—the better monster.

When it comes to living versus dying, you want to be the better monster. But . . .

Nik's not always practical.

That wasn't the voice of my inner Auphe. That was the voice of a much younger Cal who had learned at the age of four that being practical was better than behaving, because practical kept you alive. Behaving wasn't as effective that way. Practical was a definition in a black bound dictionary, the words written in the scarlet red of fresh blood. Practical was the code I survived by.

Not that I brought that up either. Nik had worries enough now, and Nik was ruthlessly practical when he had to be.

That was the key: when he *had* to be. I didn't mind being the practical one if it let him keep his hands clean. I didn't have to think about it like he did. It was as natural as breathing to me. I was good at being a monster and Niko was good at being a man, the very best of them. I wanted him to have the chance to stay that way.

But, sooner or later, we would have to talk about the gates. Sooner, most likely. Niko was going to have to accept my practicality in this.

"Don't get sloppy. Got it," I said with a good nature I reserved for a very few. I didn't smack, but I did aim an elbow at his ribs. He avoided it without seeming to move. "Now go back upstairs and bang"—his eyes narrowed and I immediately amended my sentiment— "and crochet passionately while drinking Metamucil or whatever you geezers do in bed. I'll see you in the

morning. Bring me a love-stained afghan." These
words would come back to bite me in the ass, because
while I could deal with it when it was out of sight, out
of mind at Promise's place, the reverse was true when
it was closer to home.

His eyes narrowed further to slits as he gave my out-
of-luck elbow a disapproving glance. "You're not inspiring faith in your fighting abilities or even your
ability to bully on the playground."

Fortunately, no one else other than Niko was standing on that landing waiting for inspiration or faith as
neither of us proved much good at providing them in
the next moment—the moment the body fell out of the
sky.

All right, there was no sky, but it fell far—at least ten
stories if not more. It plummeted to land on our feet . . .
literally. Or it would have if Niko hadn't jumped back
up the stairs and I'd jumped back down, both of us with
weapons drawn. The flash of descending red, gray, and
white had had my Desert Eagle in my hand just as it hit.
The fall hadn't been silent. I'd heard the cacophony of
bangs as it hit the metal handrails, bouncing its way
down. The landing wasn't quiet either. There was a wet,
heavy thump. "*Shit*," I breathed. "Where the hell did it
come from?"

I hadn't seen anything. It had come down out of thin
fucking air as far as I could tell. It hadn't been from one
of Grimm's gates. Those I could feel in my gut, twisting
and adrenaline-packed, and invisible they were not.
No, this wasn't him. I'd already looked up to see nothing. Now I looked back down and saw why the impact

had sounded as if the body had fallen into mud instead of on once-immaculate marble tile.

It had been skinned.

I hadn't seen that before. I'd seen people gutted, their throats cut; I'd seen mutilated corpses and even dismembered remains. Parts of a meat puzzle. You could put those kinds of puzzles back together, but they weren't ever the same. And neither were you. With every new horror, you thought that was the end. You'd seen enough. Nothing, no matter how new under the sun it was to you, would be able to rattle you again. You always thought it. And you were always wrong. I probably should've been grateful for that. That was the nature of being human. *I* was still human, some of me anyway, no matter what the depths of me said.

I moved back toward it and studied the god-awful mess at our feet, trying to feel gratitude for my spoonful of humanity. I tried and failed. Right then I would've preferred a monster's indifference.

There was leaking red flesh, patches of rippling fat like small clumps of yellow grapes, the smooth shine of muscle in the stairwell light, dead veins and arteries the color of ash, and the pale flash of bone from surgically clean slashes over the chest between small scarlet mounds. The eyes weren't gone, but they were burned to the black of charcoal. The lips, the only skin still intact, were the smooth pink of a woman's lips. They were peeled back from the teeth in agony, showing she'd been alive when the skinning started.

No, no fucking gratitude in me at all.

Goddamn it. I kept the Eagle ready and used my

other hand to run over my face, quick and hard. Coming to terms. All right. As much as we had on our plate already with Grimm planning to remake the world in His image—could I get a Hallelujah—I was forced to admit Ishiah was right. There was no way around it now. Something had to be done, especially as we were obviously subjects of special interest. Nothing says "Hi! Nice to meet ya!" like a dead, tortured woman crashing on top of you. A basket of muffins and a balloon bouquet couldn't match that for the goddamn personal touch.

I exhaled and ignored the pungent smell of death with long practice. "Oh yeah. I forgot to mention: Ishiah says there's a serial killer in town." I checked the stairs rising up and up above us again. "And it's not human."

Niko wasn't pleased I'd planned on holding that information back. He was less pleased about that than about being targeted by a supernatural serial killer for reasons unknown. To be fair to him, that wasn't new. We'd been targeted by another supernatural serial killer a few years before—Sawney Beane. But we'd attracted his attention by chasing him first—a case for which we *had* been paid. Whatever this son of a bitch was, why he had a hard-on for us, I had no idea.

We'd checked with Promise to make sure she was all right. The body was too tall to be her, but on the inside I couldn't tell vamp from human, except for the teeth and they retracted at death. I didn't blame Niko for calling her. It was quicker than running back up twenty flights to make sure you weren't off on the height by a few inches. She would also arrange for the police to be called as they already knew about the bodies and a killer, just not a supernatural one, but she'd give us a few minutes until we were done. With his katana still in one hand, he used his other to take pictures with his cell phone to better research what type of monster was into skinning people alive. He'd remarked on the three cuts in the chest. All three crossed each other, but whether it was supposed to be a mathematical shape or a letter, I had no idea. The murderous asshole must not have made it past kindergarten in monster school.

I left my phone in my pocket. I didn't want pictures, I sucked at research, and if I had pulled it out, Niko would've most likely inserted it in a place I was saving for my colonoscopy when I turned fifty. My caution didn't help. Once we were out of a cab and home, my plans for the whole Niko having a life having taken a nosedive, he used words instead. The second we made it through the door, it was all over for me.

"You somehow thought in your minuscule mind that it was a good idea to keep the fact to yourself that another Sawney Beane is turning the city into his hunting ground?" he demanded.

Although it had been only a lie of omission and an extremely short omission at that, I gave him the truth now. "It was for your own good."

"My own good?" he echoed, not impressed with my logic. "That is what an adult tells a child, an *impatient* adult, and it's certainly not what I told you when you were young."

He was right. He'd always explained exactly why things were the way they were or why things had to be done. He hadn't once brushed me off with an "it's for your own good." Even as a kid he'd been a better man than I was now. It didn't bother me a bit. Watching out for Nik was more important than being a better man.

"You were a good big brother. Still are, which is why I wasn't going to tell you. It really *was* for your own good." I dumped my jacket on the battered couch. "If the dickhead hadn't dumped a body on us"—less metaphorically than I'd have liked—"it would still be for your own good."

"It would be for my own good to let people be slaughtered when we might be able to stop it?" His duster went neatly on a hook he'd hammered into the wall beside the door the day we'd moved in. He'd done the same at every place we'd lived since I could remember. I had an image flash through my brain of a solemn blond nine-year-old hitting a nail into a stained plaster wall, using the heel of a shoe for a hammer.

Everything in its place. I felt the corners of my lips quirk at the memory. We all developed coping mechanisms. Niko imposed order on chaos. I imposed chaos on those not fast enough to get out of my way. Whatever worked.

I flopped on the couch and propped my feet up on the cheap coffee table. "This is New York City. Someone is always being slaughtered. We're in a big enough mess as it is. If our calendar was wide open, I'd have told you."

Possibly, but I wouldn't have dropped a fifty on that

bet. It wasn't exclusively the big brothers who leaned toward the overprotective range. Little brothers, we gave as good as we fucking got.

With the Wolves, revenants, boggles, lamias, succubae, incubi, and on and on in the city, slaughter was on the menu every day. Although they killed to eat. They just happened to eat people. What we called slaughter they called dinner. The *paien* serial killers were different. They might take a nibble here and there, they might play at having a snack, but when it came down to it—they killed because they liked it. It got their supernatural dicks hard. No other reason. That made them less predictable, which made them harder to catch. They also tended to be—at least Sawney had—batshit fucking crazy. And that had made him almost impossible to catch.

To me it didn't make much difference. Slaughter for food, slaughter for fun—NYC was one giant combo buffet and toy shop and it was always open for business. We could work for free twenty-four/seven and that wouldn't change. If it was selfish not to want my brother to join the body count, then I was fine with that. Selfish was good. Selfish was great. Stamp it on my forehead. God knew the Peace Corps wasn't calling my name.

"But our calendar *isn't* open thanks to Grimm and his Bae kiddies." The new Auphe—if fully grown maneaters could be called kiddies. "We're full up. You're full up. So, ream me out all you want. You're not changing my mind: *it was for your own good*," I emphasized with all the stubbornness I could scrape up. And that was a lot. "If we could whittle your conscience down to a normal size, you'd agree."

My feet were pushed off the table with a light swat. "What about Ishiah's conscience? Our two to your one." He frowned down at me.

"Ishiah has enough conscience to tell me about it, but thanks to some peri rule that sounds like bullshit to me, he doesn't have enough to do anything about it himself." I took off my holster to lay it and the guns on the duct-taped cushion beside me. I raised my eyes to the narrowed ones fixed on me. We had the same gray eyes, but I hadn't to this day managed to pull off that look of solar-flare-heated annoyance yet. I grumped and put up my hands to preempt a further teachable moment about consciences. "Hey, I get it. The asshole threw a body at us. That's not random. Booked calendar or not, we've been called out. He's after us for some reason or another. Grab the hip waders because we're in the shit now. I'm on board, okay already?"

He was silent for a moment, arms folded, blond hair pulled back so tightly to fall in a braid down his back that it gave me a headache just looking at him. "The body . . . it was a woman."

"I know." I wasn't blind. Sawney Beane had killed women too . . . pregnant women, young women, little girls. Being the more reasonable sex didn't exclude you from an early death. And every one of their bodies had been a nightmare, the same as the body tonight. "Even though I'd like to keep your anal-retentive ass alive doesn't mean I don't feel when I see them." Innocent bystanders weren't always annoying. Sometimes they were slaughtered lambs, bleeding their lives away in crimson pain, horror, and despair.

"I know," I repeated, picking at a corner of the duct tape. I wasn't defensive. I knew my brother. That's not what he was thinking.

"I realize that." His jaw tightened. I wasn't defensive, but he was. "That little girl Sawney killed. I remember that you found it . . . difficult, although you tried to hide it. Now on top of that, we have your gates making you overconfident combined with your pathological need to guard me like an entire pack of attack dogs against even the *knowledge* of a new supernatural serial killer."

That wasn't the pot calling the kettle black, not at all. I let it go as I summed it up for him. "Be careful?"

He relaxed. "Yes, Cal. Be careful."

On two of the three, no problem, I'd go along with them. On the attack dog issue, that wasn't going to change. Sawney hadn't been that long ago. He had come close to killing all of us, Niko included. The memory had stuck with me. The little girl had stayed with me, too. I still had her sunshine-colored barrette tucked away in a drawer, I thought with a sharp pang.

It wasn't a good idea. Sentiment for unknown victims either made you miserable or got you killed in our line of work. I should throw away that barrette. Yeah, I would.

Someday.

There was more of my lingering human. More of

that identity crisis. Huh. I was kind of surprised. Maybe I needed a new T-shirt to join my banned supposedly offensive ones: 30% HUMAN. FDA APPROVED.

No sense in worrying about it either way. I yawned and levered up off the couch. After another jaw-cracking yawn, I said, "Bed. Make me a happy-face pancake for breakfast. Put me in the mood for serial killer hunting tomorrow."

"I have one use for a spatula and you and it does not involve pancakes. Would you like me to explain it in detail?"

"I'm lazy, Cyrano, not stupid." I grabbed my holster, left the jacket on the couch and automatically tugged Niko's long braid as I circled him and headed past the kitchen on one side, the training area on the other and down the hall to my bedroom.

I heard the snort from a nose seen on many a Greek statue. Hawklike and noble in size. It came from a stray Northern Greek horn-dog who sweet-talked a girl from our Rom clan centuries ago. That's also where Niko's dark blond hair entered a dusky-skinned, black-haired gene pool. Just as my decidedly non-Rom pale skin came from the Auphe swimming in my blood.

The difference was Nik would be considered pure Rom to the Vayash clan—if he turned his back on me . . . or, as they'd said, preferably put me down like a rabid dog. Put *me* out of *their* misery, because I would never be Rom. They'd made that clear. I would never even be close to human, never anything less than an "abomination."

Too bad they didn't know sooner or later if Grimm

had his way there'd be a new hybrid race of Auphe sweeping the earth, worse than the originals, and all wearing—if the universe had any sense of humor—T-shirts of their own that read ABOMINATION NATION.

One could hope.

3

Cal

Present Day

The next morning there were no smiley face pancakes waiting for me. There was only Niko wearing sweat-pants and already finished up with his two-hour-long workout over in the gym-designated area of the space. As he toweled the sweat off his neck and chest, one of the heavy bags still swinging from what had probably been a roundhouse kick, I went to the kitchen cabinet to dig out a box of cereal. Ignoring the high stools, I boosted up to sit on the breakfast counter, my usual spot, and ate a handful of Captain Crunch dry. Cooking was for wusses who couldn't fuel homicidal fury on pure sugar alone.

"Why aren't you at the university?" I asked while

chewing. Manners and me, we weren't much on a speaking basis. "Don't you have an eight a.m. class on Tuesdays to teach about boring dead guys?"

"Normally. I'm surprised you knew. It means so much to me that you take an interest in my work," he said dryly, dumping his towel in the workout hamper.

"As often as you've kept me from being one of those boring dead guys, I feel I should give a little back." I tossed down another handful of sugar. That was the great thing about the life span in our career: you rarely lived long enough to develop diabetes from poor nutrition. "So? What's up then?"

"We have a business appointment, which naturally you've forgotten as your brain has all the retention qualities of a sieve. We've twenty minutes before we have to leave. I get the first shower since you're still grazing your way through endless vistas of sugarcane."

"You used to say I was smart." Sieve, my ass, and what was wrong with Captain Crunch? It was the perfect food.

"You are smart when you can be bothered. You, little brother, can rarely be bothered," he said with a Death Valley dryness to his voice.

He had me there. As the bathroom door closed behind him, I slid down, my feet hitting the floor, and moved to check the calendar, the note taped to my door, and then down at the neat marker writing across the box of cereal in my hand. Yeah, Nik tried to keep me updated on these things, but I was hopeless.

I finished up the half-full box of cereal and thought

about it. There was Grimm, a jack-in-the-box you never knew when was going to pop up and spill your guts on the floor. There was this new serial killer who dropped bodies like kids dropped water balloons. Now a job too?

I checked the calendar and the notation again. Eh, what the hell? This wasn't like me telling Ishiah to forget a freebie-of-the-week on Jack the Rippers. This was only the Kin. Granted, they could lick their own junk and run the supernatural crime in NYC at the same time, but they were still the Kin. The day we couldn't handle the werewolf mafia with one hand while jacking off with the other was the day it was time to hang it up and get out the walker. Our multitasking beat theirs every time.

Twenty minutes and thirty seconds later—Niko loved his schedules; he'd have made a great fascist— we were moving down the sidewalk. He was looking for a cab. I was looking for something more important and I spotted mine first. The blessed hot dog cart. If Leonardo da Vinci had painted it, light would've spilled from the heavens to radiate around it in an ethereal luminous glow . . . and the guy hawking the dogs would've looked a little like a woman under his beard, but art was art.

That is to say, I didn't give a crap about it. I just wanted my dog.

"More onions," I told the man as he spooned them on top of the mustard and relish. "Seriously, dump them on there." The guy huffed in annoyance but loaded it up with triple onions and handed it over.

As we walked on, I took a bite. New York may be low on ambience, but it knew how to do a dog right. As I took an enthusiastic second bite, Niko asked, "Why? I don't have anything approaching your sense of smell and even I am offended."

I loved onions enough that my enhanced scenting abilities had accustomed themselves to the smell over the years. They didn't bother me at all now. "First, I like onions. Second, it pisses off Wolves. Third, I like pissing off Wolves."

Almost as much as killing them.

I tightened the choke chain on my inner darkness, gave it a mental smack, and a "naughty bastard" with my usual resignation—maybe even fond resignation. It was the same reaction you'd show your pet great white when he brought back half of a surfer instead of the beach ball you'd thrown into the water. He was a bad boy, true, but he was also only doing as he was created to do. How could you hold that against him?

Just keep your grip tight on that leash and make sure it didn't happen for real.

I took a third bite of the hot dog and it was as amazing as the first two. "Tastes good and pisses off Wolves. There is no downside."

And I proved that when we arrived at the office of the Beta Ivar. Alphas were too high up to muddy their paws with Niko, a human sheep, or me, a sheep deepfried in Auphe Hell with his own bogeyman squatting in his brain. That meant poor Ivar, icy blue eyes watering copiously from my onion breath, had to deal with hiring us. When it came to Wolves, I was used to the lack of respect and the occasional yellow squirt of fear from the ones who'd actually seen an Auphe before they were erased from the earth. Except for my pale skin, I didn't look anything but human—slate eyes, black hair—but I *smelled* like Auphe to those who had the noses sharp enough to tell.

Even under the onions, to a Wolf it would come through as easily as a scalpel slicing flesh. Fortunately for Ivar, he, like many Wolves, had never come across a true full-bred Auphe. He'd only heard the legends and he only knew my smell was wrong. I saw it in his face twisting in disgust. *Wrong*. Didn't belong in this world . . . didn't belong in *any* world. It was a battle-field scent—a legion of marching grim reapers shoved into one body, and Ivar didn't care for it, didn't care for any of this at all.

But you had to be smart to be Beta in your pack, especially if your pack was Kin, and that had him concentrating on other things—things that were an-noying. Things that he could react to while he ignored the rest and did as his Alpha ordered.

He growled, "A sheep who grazes in an onion field is not a very smart sheep."

Ivar sat behind a battered desk in the office of what I liked to think of as a CAW—conveniently abandoned warehouse. Movies were full of them. Reality was as well . . . except they weren't genuinely abandoned; they only appeared to be. The Kin bought up the ones on the edge of being condemned and used them for various purposes. Members of the pack not high up enough to have their own place slept in them. Drugs and prostitutes from other cities sometimes were un-loaded there. A location to hire non-Kin sheep that weren't good enough to see where Ivar or his Alpha actually lived—another good use. And sometimes the Kin used them to store food. Fresh food. The kind that was still capable of screaming.

You never knew though. Some packs ate people and some would consider that on par with stealing creamed carrots from a baby's spoon. Too easy. A humiliation to a predator. Until we saw differently, we'd assume Ivar's pack were predators with the ballsy taste to hunt only those that challenged them. If we didn't, we'd have to do extensive background checks on every single job we took—checks that would take longer and cost more than the job itself. The strong survived, sure, but it was the practical that let you put the food on the table, that kept you upright and mobile.

Ever see a starving man kick a monster's ass? Me neither.

"I doubt Niko said I was smart when he agreed to a meet." I slouched in a chair as battered as the desk, the morning light a hazy glow through the dirty window. "I'll bet he *did* say we could take care of your business if you didn't screw around with us. Satisfaction guaranteed or your next of kin gets your money back."

Nik didn't bring up the fact I'd started the back and forth, irritating Ivar with the hot dog. He didn't like to waste time on petty insults. He wanted the facts, the money, and to get to work. He didn't see the entertainment value in baiting the clients. Later, when he un-sheathed his sword, he'd find amusement enough. Not that he'd admit that. Not even on the inside, and, on the outside, he was always setting the example. One day he was going to realize it was a lifetime too late for that. He could make a katana dance and defy gravity like no man on earth, but there wasn't a damn thing he could do about genetics, mine or his. When he realized that, then I hoped he'd realize something else. . . .

If you were a born warrior and your career was basically combat, you might as well enjoy it. He'd be happier for it.

Hell, I knew I was.

Where I slouched, Niko didn't sit at all. He stood perfectly upright, back straight, alert and ready—a general facing his troops . . . or one criminally minded Wolf who might or might not want to give us some money. He suggested, clearly short of patience, "May we move this along past the interview stage so that we can find out the exact nature of the job?"

That's when Ivar did screw around with us. But this kind of screwing around was expected. It was the annoying part of dealing professionally with Wolves. It was the pack way. You had to prove you were tough enough to deserve their business. And "interview" was defined as Ivar and three other Wolves doing their level best to rip us apart.

Beginning as a fairly average-sized man with average brown hair and average blue, if watering, eyes, Ivar flowed over the desk to end up as the next best thing to a grizzly bear. Muscles bulged under the thick spiky coat of fur as blue eyes rounded and shaded to the yellow of a scorching desert sun. The gaping jaws were large enough to crush my skull while puncturing the bone with fangs nearly seven inches long. Ivar wasn't a big man, but he was one damn big Wolf. The rags left from his shirt were snagged on his claws as he landed on me . . . almost. I lunged out of the chair a split second before it shattered into splinters.

One roll and I was up, Eagle in hand, and burying a round in Ivar's chest as he spun in the wreckage of the chair to face me. Then I flung myself flat and put a second round in the stomach of the black Wolf that sailed over me. A flash of gray and silver, Niko and his katana whirled with a spray of blood whipping in the wake as two large red Wolves howled in near unison. Their blood was darker and more scarlet than their fur, hitting the floor in heavy splatters. Following that Niko swiveled again and using one hand to grip fur combined with a little applied physics and the smaller of the Wolves was tossed through the window. The explosion of glass rang like funeral bells as I heard it hit the pavement below followed by a loud thump and an even louder yowl of pain.

Back on my feet in a crouch, I faced the black Wolf who'd flipped head over tail from the shot to his stomach but was ready for more. I threw myself to one side and then the other. He mirrored my movements, which landed his neck right into the jaws of Ivar, who'd been leaping in our direction. With his head in profile, I planted the muzzle of the automatic between the Beta's eye and the pointed tuft of ear. There was the thud of a metal blade cutting into flesh and Nik's voice drifting over my shoulder. "Is the interview done? If not, you'll want to forget the mops and call for a fire hose to handle the extra blood."

Ivar, who'd managed to stop short of tearing out the throat of the black Wolf, eased his jaws away from it and my gun. In a shimmer of fur and a ripple of flesh, he was that average man again. But this time he was naked with a bullet wound to the right of his chest. I hadn't aimed for the heart. This was, after all, just the testing ground, not the war. "The interview is done," Ivar agreed with a begrudging lift of his upper lip. We passed, but we weren't Wolf and we weren't Kin. He had to respect our skill, but he didn't have to like it or us.

The faint breathlessness to his voice, the result of a bullet-nicked lung—a very familiar sound—would fade quickly. Probably before we left. Wolves healed fast. He waved off the other Wolves, still in lupine form and snarling with displeasure, and they limped from the office. Ivar sat back down behind his desk, unbothered by his nudity—Wolves have no sense of modesty. Why would they? They were Wolves first, people a very distant second. "One hundred thousand for the job." His nails extended to the thick blunt ones of the Wolf and he tapped them on the desk. "We have someone whose ambition has become . . . irritating . . . to the Kin. We respect the way of the pack, the order of domination and submission. Alphas rising, falling—same as it has been since the beginning of time. But this one, she cheats. She denies the honor of the Wolf. That cannot be tolerated."

She. That answered any question we might have had on what the job was. There was only one "she" that the

Kin would subcontract out on. Delilah. Delilah definitely did cheat and considered honor something puppies cowered behind. Not to mention stupid. Last I'd known my ex-fiend with benefits had taken over half the Kin with her all female pack. The Kin allowed females membership in the Kin, but it didn't allow female Alphas.

Delilah didn't give a rat's ass what the Kin allowed. She wanted to be head of the Kin and given enough time, she would be. Ivar and his three Wolves . . . she'd have eaten them alive literally—howling, screaming, and all—as a lesson to others who dared get in her way.

Niko had put his katana away. "We do not get involved in politics. Assassination is a slippery slope that tends to rebound with endless blood feuds and vengeance-vows. We prefer to keep our killing clean."

That was Niko's line and I stood with him on it. Although I had to admit it was a tempting offer. I wanted Delilah dead anyway. We hadn't had friendship. We hadn't had love. But we'd had companionship, acceptance, and unbelievably wild sex. The never knowing if she'd try to hang the head of a half Auphe on her wall as a trophy had been a price I'd been willing to pay for that. Acceptance for a half Auphe was a rare thing, even more rare among sexual partners. Bottom line: I didn't trust Delilah, but she had liked me as I was. I didn't get that often.

Then she tried to kill another Wolf friend of mine, her first ploy to rise in the Kin. I didn't have many friends. I could count them on one hand and have that all-important middle finger left over to put to good use.

Trying to kill me was one thing—my eyes were open when it came to Delilah's sociopathic ways. But trying to kill my friend; I wasn't letting that go. I had one rule. She knew it, and she'd broken it without regret. Killing her was on my list; being paid for it would've just been a bonus.

But this was between Delilah and me alone. The Kin wasn't invited to that party.

"Don't worry," I told Ivar. "She *is* dead. It's only a matter of when my vacation time comes due."

Ivar didn't like it. I didn't blame him. However, he did have something to add before we left. "We've heard about the body from last night—the skinned one." His upper lip wrinkled in distaste. If a Kin Wolf found a piece of violence to be excessive, that was something indeed. "Don't come to the Kin with questions about it. We want no part of it."

"What? You afraid?" I was more incredulous than anything else. Ivar was a Kin Beta. Admitting he was afraid, or insinuating the rest of the Kin were, would have ended up with him dead a long time ago. The Kin took their reputation seriously.

"We want no part of this trouble," he repeated flatly. "No Kin will speak of it. Don't bother asking. Don't bother us with *anything* right now or we'll decide we want you as dead as Delilah."

I didn't like having the Kin put me in my place, but if the word was out to keep quiet, they'd die before they broke with the edict of the Alphas. Whatever this thing was flinging bodies around, it had to be one truly evil, badass son of a bitch to have the Kin lying low.

It was annoying. As was having to go through an "interview" for nothing. Okay, the second wasn't true. I had liked the fighting. What was life without your daily dose of exercise? And this exercise was more enjoyable than Niko's preferred ten-mile run. It put me in a good mood for the rest of the day.

The night was a different story.

I'd brushed my teeth, for the third time. That onion breath was persistent as hell. The towel covered the bathroom mirror as always. I could manage quick glances when I needed to. That was enough for me. It was a phobia I'd come by honestly. I didn't waste time trying to overcome it or being embarrassed by it any longer. Life was too short.

One last rinse and spit of toothpaste and I was in my bedroom. I changed into sweatpants and flopped on my back on the bare mattress of my bed. I'd been forced two weeks ago to wash my sheets and blanket at knifepoint, Niko's knife, but I'd forgotten them at the Laundromat. I had a short attention span if carnage wasn't involved. I'd wandered off to find some. By the time I remembered what I'd been doing, the sheets were long gone. I'd have to end up buying new ones. Whenever I got around to it. Or I'd wait for my birthday. Nik was a practical gift giver.

It was late, hours past midnight. Not that it mattered. Early, late—I could sleep anytime, anywhere. A lifetime on the run taught you that—among other less legal skills. Ten seconds after I hit the mattress I was gone.

A medium-length pornographic dream following that, I was catapulted to consciousness by the shattering of glass, something slicing into my stomach, the sharp spiking stench of ozone in the air, and fingers or something like fingers fisted painfully tight in my hair. And a voice, one that bubbled and flowed thick as tar, words from lungs dead and drowned. "Black hair. Like the dark within you. I covet it. I covet the skin that binds it within you."

Our skin-loving serial killer hadn't waited long at all after dumping that body on us. Serial killers are bad, but impatient ones—they're the worst.

"I've waited for you and your skin," the voice spilled on. "I shall take your darkness, wicked creature. I shall save you."

Lying in the warmth of my own spilled blood, I gathered his understanding of "save" was a hop, skip, and a fucking minefield away from my definition. Unless he meant save a chunk of my flesh like a nowhere mint condition stamp—a trophy of his raving psychosis. It was a good guess. Those who mixed their raving and their potpourri bag of psychotic issues loved trophies.

I may have misheard though. Save was only my best guess as to what the jackass said. I had to catch the words between the sounds of the breaking glass. The window was gone, but impossibly the sound went on and on all around me—an endlessly flowing, then crashing, waterfall of fracturing crystal. Amidst that were the gunshots of the Glock I kept under my pillow. The gun had a silencer, but they're not as quiet as they make out on TV. The shots did get louder as I neared the end of the clip. Nothing happened other than my running out of ammunition. He didn't move except to keep cutting me and slamming my head up and down by my hair. With my left hand, I pulled the combat knife from under my mattress and took a swing. Other than a shimmer running through blackness, I would've sworn he didn't move, but the knife didn't connect. He was quick, too damn quick for me and that was quicker than most.

Son of a bitch.

The thing wasn't made of mist, no matter first appearances—more like surrounded by it, concealed by it. The pounding in my head and the pain in my stomach would've made the inner solidity clear alone, but I could see, as well. The room was dark, and what squatted on top of me almost as dark, but inside of the smoke I could see serrated razors of midnight obsidian slicing through the haze. A multitude of overlapping angles, sharp and deadly, just barely visible, but they were there.

Hell's own geometry.

There were shards upon shards stabbing out from the core, each two to three feet long. Hundreds of pieces of volcanic glass come to life. Jagged pieces of . . . what? How had my knife missed him, a hunchbacked creature practically *made* of primitive blades?

Then there was a hint of movement, a shadow growing within the shadow, as if the crystalline daggers shifted in unison, spread, and fanned out above me like wings. There was a sound that set my teeth on edge, the hollow chime of shattered glass pieces scraping and breaking as they ground ominously against one another. It had me gripping my own useless knife even tighter against the threat of the phantom blades articulating in the murk above me.

A clot of the shadowed mist came up and electric blue-white eyes flared to life, studying the blood, my blood, that dripped out of the sharp-edged darkness. There was a hiss and if hisses could be disappointed, this one was. "You are not mine to save. Not of my keeping. You are not of the Flock."

I was a lot of things, but this shithead was right—part of a flock wasn't one of them. Not a sheep for a monster to prey on and damn sure not a pelt to be saved and nailed to a supernatural whackjob's wall.

I couldn't gate him away. Hell, we were a little too attached at the moment for that. I was about to gate myself out to the hall instead and hope not to take the most dangerous part of him with me when I heard the explosion of my door being kicked open. The weight disappeared from on top of me, taking its sharp blade or talon and what felt like a handful of my hair. I was out of bed in an instant to see Niko knocked backward out of the doorway and against the hallway wall with his katana flung to one side but remaining in his grip. My brother didn't lose his weapons. But what happened next was quick enough that he didn't have a chance to use his sword. It was also quick enough that I barely saw it.

There was an impression of a long-fingered hand . . . no . . . the *shadow* of an impression wrapped around my brother's neck, a ripple of the darkest of shades and then nothing. It was gone. If I wasn't bleeding, head aching from the vicious jerking of my hair and mild whiplash, and Nik didn't have a bright red handprint around his neck, I wouldn't have been able to swear anything had been there at all.

"You're bleeding."

The cut, a familiarly clean surgical slice, the same kind Niko had pictures of on his phone from the body that had fallen into the stairwell, was about six inches long. It started a good four to five inches to the left side and barely above my navel and ran in a perfectly straight line to the right. And, yeah, it was bleeding, but it wasn't gushing. That meant it wasn't too deep, which was a good thing. That was the area I kept my guts and they tended to work better on the inside than out. "Some," I dismissed, wiping a hand over it. All that did was smear the blood to cover my stomach. The new blood that welled out of the slice was steady but fairly slow. "It's not bad. Whatever it used, knife, talon, extra-sharp press-on nail, it didn't go any more than half an inch deep, I don't think."

"Not deep enough to skin you," Nik said. "But enough for a start."

"There is that, the asshole." I covered the wound with my hand. It'd do for the moment. "What the hell did it do to your neck? I can see its handprint." Long, knifelike fingers etched in red.

"It's a burn." Niko touched it lightly. The smell of ozone, the crackle of lightning in its eyes. If all Niko had was a burn, he was lucky. "Between first and second degree, I think." He'd already started to check out the rest of our converted garage, but neither of us had seen which way it had gone. Back out the window that sat almost two stories high among the steel beams? Through the front door, locking it behind it? Down the damn kitchen sink drain? It had moved so fast I had no idea where it had gone or what it looked like, other than impressions. There was only the sense of a black wraith hovering around a mass of smoky glass knives appearing and disappearing out of the corner of my eye. That couldn't be right. I'd been attacked by many monsters in my life, but nothing that looked so . . . inorganic . . . inorganic and maybe with wings. That was some crazy shit indeed.

Nik was scowling up at the window. It had been a problem in the past and we'd probably put iron bars on this time, but that would have to wait for the glass replacement people to wake up and get to work. As often as this happened, we might want to invest in a two-story-tall ladder.

There wasn't anything to be done about it now and Niko gave my shoulder a light shove. "You're dripping on the floor. Stitches. Go." As I turned toward my room to give him something to bitch about—that always cheered him up—he nudged me again. "To the room without the bubonic plague–ridden mounds of filthy clothing on the floor."

I stood in Nik's sterile room of Zen and did my best not to bleed on his equally sterile floor. I didn't lie on his bed and wait. I'd ruined enough of his bedding over the years to actually feel guilty when I did now. "Everything in its place" wasn't a motto that worked as well for your brother when your bloodstains were on his sheets. When Niko, arms filled with supplies, walked in two minutes later he frowned. "Why aren't you in bed?"

"I'm waiting for the plastic. I told you last time to get a plastic mattress cover. You spent half your teacher's salary on sheets this year alone." Not that part-time teaching at NYU paid much.

"Idiot. Get on the damned bed," he ordered as he deposited the medical supplies on his spare and Spartan dresser. "I'll invest in red sheets if you're that concerned."

I gave up on the plastic and on trying to be considerate. I wasn't much good at it anyway. Once I was flat on the bed, a gloved hand pulled my bloody one away from my stomach and wrapped it around a damp towel. I used it to wipe the blood from my palm, fingers, knuckle creases, pretty much every millimeter of skin. It didn't distract me from hissing at the cold swipe of Betadine across the cut. Six inches long. Lots of stitches, but Niko was quick. It wouldn't take too long. I glanced down at the sliced flesh. It was in a different spot from long ago, a lifetime ago, and longer and deeper, but similar enough that it reminded me . . .

"You remember when—"

"We don't talk about that," he cut me off instantly, a little more sharply than I thought he meant to. That was a sign that he was certainly remembering it too. Hell, how could he forget? But talking about it?

No, we didn't. There are life-changing events and life-ruining events and sometimes there is something that falls between. Twelve years since it had happened and we still didn't talk about it. For two entirely different but equally valid reasons, but the result was the same. I blamed the disorientation of having a fairly decent sex dream interrupted by a monster who'd tried to skin me, was impervious to hollow-point rounds, and so fast as to be almost invisible for having let the comment slip at all. Nik was right.

We definitely did not talk about it.

"He was right on top of me, the son of a bitch, and I hardly *saw* him," I said, changing the subject. "I shot him. There was no way I could miss, and nothing. He didn't flinch. I didn't even see him when he hit you. It was just . . . shadows of something already gone. Shadows and knives. He was that goddamn fast."

Niko had already injected the area with lidocaine and was using a probe to see how deep the incision actually was. He looked up at me, face somber. "I'm sorry."

"No big deal. I'm not feeling a thing." Probing the cut wasn't why he was apologizing. We both knew it and we both let it go. I didn't want to talk about it either. The past was the past. Neither one of us wanted to dig up that mental childhood grave. It was ancient history and it was best to stay that way, especially for Nik.

If not for the reasons he thought.

He gave a faint but thankful curve of his lips, then went back to work. "It's barely half an inch deep. If it wasn't so long, I wouldn't bother with stitches. But with your . . . energetic lifestyle"—kicking ass any chance I got—"you'll constantly be ripping it open if I don't." He applied more Betadine. "Whatever he is, you were correct, he wasn't serious. Not this time. He was simply playing." He began stitching. "The ones that like to play are never the easy kills. Still numb?"

"Yes, Mom. Still numb," I snorted. "And I'm not sure it was play. He looked at my blood. Just, hell, looked at it and said basically I wasn't his to take. I don't know if I wasn't good enough a specimen. Too many scars to make a nice rug or if it's because I'm not human."

Niko gave me the look, the one I'd lived with my whole life. I changed it up a bit. "Not completely human. Ishiah did say it was only killing humans and Edward Scissorhands said I wasn't a sheep. But playing or not playing, bullets, knife, sword, and neither of us touched him. He could've had us on a silver platter with a frigging caviar garnish if he'd wanted." Hard to say if it was for real or just a dry run. I gave in to the inevitable. "I never thought I'd say this with your giant brain, but you might need help with the research. The next time he comes back and is serious he'll have his choice of which of us he wants to wear as his summer jacket and which his winter coat. We need the info on this thing now. Or preferably a half hour ago."

"My cell is on the table beside you. Call Goodfellow." Robin Goodfellow was our go-to guy on all things *paien*. What he didn't know, chances were you didn't want to know. Niko kept stitching while I called. He'd trained for this when we lost our last healer back to the home country. Niko could go to the hospital if worse came to worst. He was human inside and out. I wasn't. One scan, one blood test, and that was something else not worth talking or thinking about. Nik had been taught by the best healing spirit around. He could handle most serious trauma. If it was critical . . . with ventilators, heart-lung bypass machines, lacerated livers, kidneys, a nicked heart—then, hey, nobody lived forever.

By the time Goodfellow arrived Niko had finished with me and had rubbed ointment on his neck. The burn looked painful, but not serious. That had me in a slightly better mood when Robin picked our lock, walked in, and dumped a Styrofoam container on the sand-colored kitchen counter. Nice kitchen, big apartment, flat-screen TV, and all the weapons money could buy. We'd moved up in the world since the bad old days. "As requested," he said. "Why such a request, I don't want to know."

I lifted the lid immediately and grinned. He had brought me a smiley face pancake. "That puts you one up on Nik." Hell, it even had "Cal" incised across the happy, syrup-drenched forehead.

"He's an actual adult?" the puck asked Nik with a large helping of disbelief in his snake-oil smooth voice. "You're quite sure about that?" It was five in the morning, but as always Goodfellow was dressed like he was heading for a photo shoot at *GQ*.

In sweats of his own, although considerably newer and less bleach stained than mine, Niko shrugged. "Some jump developmental hurdles. Some scale them slowly but with determination and success. And then some, like Cal, are laziness incarnate and run around them. I consider it a miracle he doesn't eat with his hands." All this was said at the same time he set a bottle of Tylenol on the counter by me and tapped it meaningfully. Lidocaine doesn't numb forever and he knew it would be wearing off about now.

I took a closer look at the pancake and scowled. "What exactly is that hanging from the bottom? Right under the smile?"

"Sausage link," Robin answered promptly. "Smallest they had for authenticity. I toothpicked it there myself. You can thank me at any time." I would've thanked him by throwing it at his head, but I was hungry. Sometimes pride takes a backseat to an empty stomach.

While I ate, Niko described the skinned body, showed Robin the pictures, told him about the attack on me and then him, the speed involved, the smell of a lightning strike—my cut and his burn in the shape of a hand. Goodfellow listened, studied the pictures, the handprint, and gave a speculative hum. The entire thing had taken three minutes total. Pucks were not known for being slow or bringing up the rear—unless it was in a sexual context. He knew, I could tell. Already, he knew.

He'd taken off his suit jacket and now slouched on our beat-up sofa that I refused to give up as it was shaped perfectly over the years to my lazy ass. There was an unhappy look in the usually sly green eyes. He was a fox faced with an empty henhouse. A barn cat who'd already eaten all the mice and had nothing left to entertain him. "It appears to be . . . but no, it couldn't be him. He's been absent for over a hundred years. The real one anyway. I doubt seriously it could be him."

"Who? Who the hell can't it be?" Finished with breakfast, I sat on the coffee table to face both of them. Robin was a puck. Pucks lived long lives. Thousands of years, hundreds of thousands, some even more. Robin Goodfellow, as far as we knew, was the oldest puck alive. If anyone knew everything about absolutely anything, it was him.

"Did he say anything about your hair?" he asked abruptly. "Cal, did he say anything about that shaggy mop of yours?"

Absently, I pushed my hand through the mess. Thick, black, and straight, it hung almost to my shoulders. I could get it into a ponytail, barely, to keep it out of my face for fighting. "How'd you know that? He said he liked the color. That it was black. Something about it meaning I was wicked and he wanted it. Hell, I think he took a good hunk of it with him." Lucky it *was* thick. I didn't care about my hair, not like Robin with his six-hundred-dollar haircuts to keep those Great God Pan brown curls just as they'd been drawn on temple walls. But I didn't want a bald spot over my ear either.

"Ah, *skata*." He ran a hand over that expensive haircut and turned it into a tumbleweed. "Dark hair. He likes dark hair. More importantly he likes to kill or 'save' people with dark hair. He thinks it's a sign of evil. Wickedness. At least goes the rumor. If it's him." He shook his head. "I'm not certain. It could be or it could be other things. This is a diagnosis I do not want to commit to without more information. Truthfully, I'd rather not commit to it at all."

He was looking less and less happy by the moment. "Niko? Did he mention your hair? The rumor also goes that he tends to associate blond hair with whores and whores also with wickedness. Red hair too. Whores, whores everywhere. It's a theme with him. He is a judgmental bastard. He cannot abide wickedness. Odd in a killer, isn't it?"

Niko gave a forbidding frown. "You wish to know if he called me a whore? Is that what you're asking?"

"Yes, yes. Don't be so sensitive. There was a time when next to Caesar that was the highest position in the land. I myself had a franchise of fertility temples—" Niko's expression darkened and Robin returned to the point. "In deference to your prejudicial ways, let me rephrase: did he mention the color of your hair or call you immoral?"

"We will go with immoral. Yes, he may have mentioned it." Niko folded his arms. "What of brown hair like yours? Would he consider you free of corruption, as pure as the driven snow?"

"No, wicked as well, only slightly less so. He'd still kill me, but I wouldn't be his first choice like the darkly depraved and the wickedly wanton." He glanced at both of us, but the usual humor was lacking in the barbs. "But with what Cal has said and his victims in the past, apparently it's only full-blooded humans he's after—if it's him. Being me has always had its advantages, even with serial killers." He gave a grin, but it also wasn't the same, not his customary con-man special. He made the effort though. Robin was worried, but Robin was also still Robin. If he had but one finger out of the grave he'd still be using it to yank our chains.

"If this creature is what I think he is, he's killed before. *Paien* history says almost forty people, in the eighteen hundreds in England. All human. History rounded down by about a hundred. Someone, no doubt the Vigil, did an excellent job of covering up the murders and the skinnings from the populace. It was passed off as a few high-strung people startled by an obvious prankster leaping about in the manner of a seven-foot-tall frog while spitting blue flames." He curled his lip. "Intentionally described to be ridiculous. Supposedly nothing damaged but dignities. This monster became a mere idiotic urban myth to them after the fact. Now it seems the lethal truth he's always been is back for more. It's too early for news this bad." The disdain for bad storytelling was gone. He rubbed the heels of his hands over his closed eyes. "Offhand, I know of no way to stop him as he *wasn't* stopped. He simply disappeared. Oh, and those slices to the bone of the victim in your cell phone picture? That's a J. He likes to sign his work."

"Who then?" Niko demanded. "Who is he?"

"Spring-heeled Jack. Spring-*hell* Jack." He gave a laugh, but I didn't hear any amusement in it. "One and the same. Either way if it *is* Jack, then he has brought Hell to New York. And I don't know if there is anything we can do about it."

4

Niko

Twelve Years Ago

Hell.

I'd wondered off and on if the monsters came from Hell. But I didn't believe in Hell. I never had. It seemed too easy. Do whatever you want, say you're sorry, and then you're lifted unto Heaven. Do whatever you want, don't say you're sorry, and be cast down into Hell. The people in Hell probably didn't think it was easy, but I had more problems with the Heaven part. If you did wrong, no matter how sorry you were, you still should pay . . . not burning in hellfire. That was over the top.

But you should pay somehow. Learn your lesson and learn it well. That's why I leaned toward Buddhism. I borrowed books about it from the library. If you did the crime, you still did the time, but you learned from it and in another life you'd be a better person. Then better and better again in each new life—if you were capable of learning. That made sense—the same as physics made sense. There was a balance to it. For every action there is an equal and opposite reaction. As energy is never lost, you are never lost . . . only improved.

Then I saw the Grendel and I didn't think Hell was that unbelievable after all.

It was under the car parked in front of the house across the street. The flame-red eyes, skin so transparently pale it almost glowed at night, a fall of white incredibly fine tendrils masquerading as hair and an inconceivably wide stretch of sly smile filled with a thousand metallic needles. If Lovecraft and Clive Barker had collaborated to come up with a soul-eating Cheshire Cat, that was what its smile would be. Not of this world and more effective than a wood chipper at stripping flesh from bone.

I'd searched every mythology book I could find and hadn't found a description that came close to matching our pale shadows. As I couldn't find their real name I'd ended up calling them Grendels from the first time I'd read *Beowulf*. Grendel, one of literature's most well-known monsters. It was good enough for our own. And it helped to label your nightmares.

I pulled the faded curtains and was grateful it was across the street and not peering in the window as they often did. This was the first one I'd seen since we'd moved here two months ago. Sometimes we'd go four months without seeing one. Five months one time. But never longer, not since I'd seen my first one when I was seven. Cal had seen his when he was five.

They didn't do anything. They didn't try to get in the house. They didn't come up to us if we were outside at night. They only watched. And although I'd been seven when I'd first seen one, I imagine they'd been watching all of Cal's life. One of them was what Sophia said she'd whored herself to for gold and a child. Sophia had sold herself to a monster—a human monster for a genuine monster. Cal had been the result. Proof that two wrongs could make a right.

And he was as right as they came.

Not that Sophia saw it that way. She'd called Cal a monster all his life, an "experiment" that didn't pay nearly enough, but Sophia was Sophia: a drunken liar on her best day. So Cal took it with a grain of salt. He didn't believe her then . . . not completely. It wasn't until he saw his first Grendel that he knew for sure.

What he saw that day, leering through the glass . . . that was in him. It was half of him. Sophia didn't always lie. When it hurt worse, she would tell the truth. Cal lost his innocence at the age of five and for six years I'd been trying to get it back for him. But innocence wasn't like a lost dog. Once innocence was gone, it wouldn't find its way back home again.

"Grendel?"

Cal was already in his pajamas, lying on his stomach on his mattress, and reading a comic book. He'd lost his innocence, but he'd lost his fear too. For six years he'd seen Grendels watching him. If it doesn't hurt you, it's funny how quickly you can get used to anything—no matter how horrific it appears. If you were going to rank them, Sophia was far above the Grendels in the cruelty and caution categories.

"Just one." I said it as if it were no big deal because that let Cal believe it *was* no big deal. At least on the surface. Deep down, he knew the same as I did. Monsters don't watch you without reason. Monsters don't make certain that a little boy, half human–half not, was born without a bigger reason. One day they'd let us know what they wanted with Cal. Given a few more years of training, and I'd be ready for that day.

Whatever they wanted from my little brother, they weren't going to get.

I changed into sweats faded and worn thin. Like my coat, they'd come from the Salvation Army, but one state away. I took the second mattress, the one between Cal's and the bedroom door, just in case. Thieves, Sophia in the mood to spew her spite, monsters who'd changed their minds—it paid to be ready for everything. Sophia didn't bother to buy us beds, used or not. I could have with money from my part-time jobs, but mattresses were enough when I could save that money for getting Cal and me out of here someday. And no separate rooms. The places Sophia rented didn't have more than two bedrooms. Sometimes they had only one. It wouldn't have mattered if there had been five bedrooms. Cal and I always bunked together. Another "just in case."

As I was sitting down, I spotted a black plastic handle tucked tightly against the bottom of Cal's bed, the blade hidden between the mattress and the floor. "Is that the butcher knife from the kitchen under your mattress?"

I'd taught him knives weren't for playing, but I'd also taught him how to use them. I'd taught him everything I learned, not that he was the best student. Discipline and hard work were a worse nightmare to him than the monster outside. But I kept trying and pushing to make certain he did pick up some. Where Sophia dragged us, there were predators other than Grendels or movie-style murderers.

"Uh-huh." He turned a page in his comic. "For the serial killer. He's probably not stupid enough to kill people who live right next door, but you don't know. Lots of people are all kinds of stupid."

There was no arguing with that. I didn't bother trying. But tomorrow, finding proof that this guy scraped roadkill off the asphalt for a living was my number one priority.

"Enough with the comic book. Lights out." I waited past the grumble and toss of the comic book to one side before I reached up and flipped off the switch. I pulled up the blankets and it was time for the nightly ritual. "All right, Cal, tell me one good thing that happened to you today."

There was an aggravated groan followed by the sound of a pillow being turned over and smacked. They were actually good pillows. New. Most everything we had was used several times over, but I'd learned that with sheets, blankets, and pillows, Cal couldn't tolerate anything used. It was a fact I hadn't much thought about, but found to be sadly true, most of those things came to the Salvation Army or Goodwill via family members whose relatives had died on them. And before dying on them they'd been sick on them for months if not longer. No amount of bleaching could get rid of the smell of terminal illness for Cal. With his sense of smell, which had to come from the nonhuman part of his biology, he'd vomit until he dry-heaved at a stench I could only imagine . . . not detect myself. I spent my savings on the cheapest they had at the nearest Wal-Mart.

Of course that didn't stop him from pretending the pillows were lumpy.

Kids. I wasn't sure I'd ever been one, but they were an interesting stew mixed of annoying and amusing. If there was a God, he was playing with fire with these recipes. "I'm listening," I prompted. "One good thing."

He gave a sigh so exaggerated that only an eleven-year-old could've pulled it off. "I didn't get chopped up by the serial killer next door?"

"*Cal.*" Despite myself, I smiled in the dark. He was such a smart-ass. I couldn't imagine the living hell my life would be when he hit his teen years. "Tell."

There was more rustling of covers and flopping of the pillow before he finally settled down. Cal was a restless sleeper. In the morning he'd be so wrapped in his blankets he would look like a human burrito. Or the blanket would be hanging from the nonworking ceiling fan. Mornings were not dull.

"Okay. Okaaay." There was a moment of silence, then words small and self-conscious. "I saw a mother pushing her little boy on a swing. He was four, I think. One big snot-ball, but he was laughing. It was like when you used to push me when I was little. I'd forgotten about that. Stupid kid stuff, but it was . . . fun. You know, then. It was like flying."

One good thing a day. It wasn't much in the face of the monsters inside and outside the house, but it was something. One stone in a protective wall that grew taller every night. "I remember. It was fun. We could still do that, you know," I needled. "Go to the park . . ."

I wasn't given a chance to finish. *"Nik!"* A serial killer next door was worth mentioning, although not worth fearing as long as you had your butcher knife. But having someone see him on a swing at his age, that was horrifying.

Smiling again, I said, " 'Night, little brother."

"You're pure evil." Another pillow thump, but he still said it because we always did. " 'Night, Nik."

I slept deep. I did when Sophia was gone. It wasn't unusual for her to stay up until three or four, shouting at nothing and no one. Throwing glasses to shatter against the walls. I studied those nights and Cal read too many comic books. The quiet was nice.

When morning came, with the first ray of sun, I was already at the window. I hadn't seen a Grendel in the daytime yet, but better safe than sorry. There was nothing but rusty cars and houses covered in peeling paint. I looked over at Cal. He was a mound of blankets. You could guess there was a kid under there, but that's all it would be—a guess. "Cal, up. Time for a shower."

The covers were tossed to the side and Cal got up in

stages. There was the "five minutes more," the "no," the whiny enhanced "nooooooo" with the "go away," and finally the "you're rotten" followed by him sitting up with a gloomy huff of outrage and despair. This morning his pajama top was gone. I looked up instinctively at the ceiling fan. There it was. That's when it hit me . . . what I'd seen.

The bruise.

It was just below his left collarbone, velvety black, and as big as an orange. "Cal," I said, using enough care to keep my fingers from breaking when my hands folded into tight fists. "What happened?" Guilt instantly washed over his face and he tried to cover the bruise with his hand. "It's too late to hide it, little brother. Tell me what happened."

I managed to unclench my hands and sat on the mattress beside him. I cautiously moved his hand away and touched the bruise. I examined it gently with fingers as careful as I could make them. With five years of daily different martial arts training, I'd felt a cracked rib after a sparring gone wrong before. I'd know it if I felt it again, but nothing seemed broken. I knew he hadn't fought at school. Cal had punched a bully's teeth down his throat when he was in the fourth grade for trying to take his backpack and sneakers. I'd made sure he knew he couldn't do that again, no matter how much the bully had deserved it. It was one mistake that wasn't fixable. The school might call in Social Services.

One surprise visit to Sophia and it would be foster care for us, if there was room, a state institution if there wasn't. Either way we would most likely be split up. It was a thought I'd had hundreds of times. Sophia was bad, worse than bad—especially for Cal, and I knew that. I also knew Cal without me beside him, knowing how special he was, wouldn't survive. He might live, but he wouldn't survive. And telling anyone else how special Cal was would make sure I wouldn't see him again. That no one outside some government bunker full of medical equipment and autopsy tables straight out of *The X-Files* would see him again.

"Cal, tell me what happened," I repeated. "Now."

He ducked his head stubbornly. "It's no big deal. Just a bottle. Sophia wasn't as drunk as I thought she was. I can't believe I let her hit me."

Let her. *Let* her . . . as if it was his fault.

Last evening I'd told myself that I did the best I could in a bad situation. Now here was my best in vivid black and purple, showing me . . .

My best was worthless.

I bent my head, doubled over, linked my hands on the back of my neck, and stared blindly at the floor. Bile scorched the back of my throat. That's the cliché I'd always read. Over and over. But it wasn't bile that burned. It was vile. This was a thing so monstrous and vile that flesh should sear to ash at its touch.

When Cal was younger, he'd been quiet and careful around Sophia when she was drunk, the same amount of time she spent breathing, but by the age of seven he didn't care anymore about triggering her temper. Instead he put his energy into dodging. He was reckless, quick, careless, and brave. He was so brave it hurt me to see it. Bravery comes only with that loss of innocence. There's no need to be brave unless you're pushed to that line and Cal had been forced to find his line far too young.

This was the first time Sophia had managed to hit him.

This was the last time she would *try* to hit him.

I'd warned her although she hadn't ever come close to hitting me or Cal with her alcohol-blurred vision. I'd warned her often. She didn't listen and she didn't care. There was one thing to do.

Give her something to care about.

When she came back, I would break Sophia's arm.

There would be no coming back from that, not for me, but now it was my turn to not care. It was my line and, like Cal, I had to cross it. That would give her six weeks to think over the consequences of leading a one-handed life. And when the cast came off and if she wasn't convinced, if she threw a bottle at Cal again, I'd break her other arm. Anger like this, it wasn't good and what I was thinking wasn't right. But sometimes necessary was more important than right. It was a lesson I'd been slow to learn, too slow, but for my brother it was time to learn it. And hadn't he tried to teach it to me before, since he was four years old? Seven years, but I finally saw what he'd been trying to tell me.

Practical. Like Cal. It was time to be practical.

There was an old Rom saying I'd once heard Sophia mutter: teach a dog to bite once and it will bite a hundred times. When you cross your line, that line disappears. You couldn't retreat back behind it again if you wanted. You cross it, you erase it.

A hand patted my back, a patch of warmth. "It's okay, Nik. It is. I promise. I've been bruised worse when I used to play dodgeball."

That was a lie. As deep and purple-black as the bruise was, the bottle that hit him must have been heavy. Full. Sophia didn't throw full bottles of any alcohol no matter how drunk she was. She must have been furious. I straightened and wrapped an arm around Cal's shoulders. He was eleven years old. He was a child. If she'd hit him in the head, she could've killed him. She would be lucky if I broke only one of her arms. She would be lucky if I didn't break her neck. I closed my eyes, took a deep breath, opened them again, and tried for the discipline I'd been learning in dojo after dojo, gym after gym. Tried for calm.

It wasn't there.

I needed a distraction. "Why exactly was Sophia so angry?" Not that she needed much of a reason.

Now he flushed red, not guilty anymore; he was mad. Furious. "She was stealing your college money. You need that money. It's *yours*. So I called her a c—" His eyes slid sideways. "A dirty word. Like I said, she wasn't as drunk as usual or she wouldn't have tagged me."

"Cal, you don't provoke her. She's insane." She wasn't. She was worse—evil, the Old Testament kind. Grendels and Sophia, they did their best to change my mind about the Fire. "It's not worth it," I said, touching a light fingertip to his bruise. "This isn't worth it."

The rest of what he said caught up with me. "And you don't use that word. I know you're getting older and hearing words like that at school. I know you'll start using them sooner or later whether I like it or not, but never that word. Girls and women don't like it and I don't blame them."

He leaned his head against mine with an unconscious affection Sophia hadn't yet managed to tear out of him and considered. "I guess I could've called her what the old ladies down the street do. See You Next Tuesday."

I swallowed an unexpected laugh. *"No."*

See You Next Tuesday. That was as bad as when he'd bitten another kid in the first grade. The note he brought from school had said that was often a sign of acting out over issues at home—of which we had more than our fair share. A very unfair share in fact. When I'd asked Cal why he'd done it, he'd answered all innocence, "Because I wanted to know what he tasted like."

All right, we had different issues from most people. When I broke Sophia's arm, we'd have more, but that was life.

Our life anyway.

"Back in bed. I'll get some ice for your bruise and get Mrs. Spoonmaker to call us in sick. No school for us today." Whenever we moved, I made friends with the older ladies on the block starting the first day. They all ended up hating Sophia, but Cal and me, they felt sorry for us. And if I paid them five dollars, they'd pretend to be our grandmother and call us in sick if needed as Sophia was passed out most mornings.

He was back under the covers as quick as a cat finding a patch of sun and already yawning, looking forward to a lazy morning. "Mrs. Spoonmaker? She smells like kitty litter and Vaseline, but I like her. She always has Oreos. Bring me back some."

"If anyone can teach me to find the silver lining, it's you," I said. Cal didn't stop surprising me with his ability to bounce back from anything. And, yes, his ball bounced in strange, wild directions compared to everyone else's, but what did that matter? "Cal, this won't happen again. I'll take care of Sophia. I promise."

"I know that, Nik." He said it as if it were the most obvious thing in the world, with faith unbreakable in every word. He then pulled the covers over his head, blocking out the pale morning light and the chill that came with it. It made his next words muffled. "And it's the chocolate lining. Look for the chocolate lining. It's better than silver."

I snagged his pajama top off the fan and stuffed it under the covers with him. "Thanks for the lesson, grasshopper."

My instructors had given Cal the nickname when I'd first talked my way into free lessons at the age of ten. Whether it was karate, jujitsu, Krav Maga, kickboxing . . . every master took one look at a six-year-old Cal tagging along with me and he was grasshopper from then on. I picked up the habit. I even knew where it came from. It wasn't as if we could afford cable. They played a whole lot of shows made before I was born on the four channels our Sophia-boosted TV received.

I gave Cal ice wrapped in a ragged dish towel, locked the door behind me, and headed across the street. Mrs. Spoonmaker was sympathetic about Cal's "flu" and quick to take the five bucks. Cal had been right. Sophia had taken my money, but only some of it. I had several stashes. Sophia could smell money. I'd be an idiot to put all my eggs in one basket. Mrs. Spoonmaker also gave me Oreos without my having to ask. Cal was hitting her up hard and often. I should warn him not to take advantage, but if we didn't—if we hadn't, we wouldn't have made it this long.

I was walking back, plastic bag of cookies in hand, when I spotted our neighbor. Cal's serial killer. He was picking up his paper from the tiny scrap of front yard. He was in sweats like me and a ragged terry cloth robe, but slightly blue bare feet. It was going to be full-on winter in another month or so. No bare feet then.

I seized the opportunity. "Excuse me, sir." I didn't believe he was a killer, but there was no harm in being polite. Just in case. He lifted his head from the paper and blinked at me. He had soft brown eyes, drooping at the edges, like a tired old hound dog. Friendly and happy, but ready to leave the running to the pups while he lay on the porch. In reality he was likely in his mid-thirties. It didn't matter. Most people in this neighborhood looked at least ten to twenty years older than they were. They were either honest and worked far too hard for far too little or they were into drugs and nothing aged you like that, selling or buying.

This tired old dog also had a bit of a beer belly or fast-food flab and a receding jaw to match his receding hairline. He also had a small silver cross around his neck that looked like it had been worn to the brightest of shines from frequent fingering. He gave me a tenta-

tive smile that showed a gap between his two front
teeth. "Can I help you, son?" He had a slight stammer,
his eyes blinking more often as he spoke. Embarrassment, he hadn't outgrown. Obvious signs and easy to
read. Sophia was no kind of mother, but watching her
work taught you things that were helpful. Since I didn't
use those things to steal, I didn't feel guilty for using it
for other things.

"Yes, sir. I was wondering where you worked. I've
been looking for a job." Not true. I had two part-time
jobs already, but a harmless lie was the best way to
bring Cal around to the truth.

"Sir?" He blinked again, more of a hound dog than
ever. "I ain't sure anyone's ever called me sir. You can
call me Junior." He turned the paper over in his hands.
His accent was a little Southern. We'd been all over the
country. His wasn't as far south as Georgia, more like
Kentucky somewhere. His watery eyes looked me up
and down, wary. While Cal looked younger, I looked
older. I could pass for seventeen easily. And seventeen
in this neighborhood was more than old enough to
force you back in your house, take everything not
nailed down, and stab you with a rusty five-dollar
switchblade. I tried to look harmless, another trick I'd
learned from Sophia—who was anything but.

Junior seemed reassured. "Well, son, I work in the
hospital cafeteria. No openings there, sorry 'bout that.
But if you go by human resources, they post pages and
pages of jobs on a bulletin board outside the office.
Might find something there."

"Thank you, sir . . . Junior." I gave him a friendly

smile with no thought behind it. My mind was already elsewhere as I moved the fifteen feet over to our rented house. I didn't think orderlies took a shortcut through the cafeteria to the morgue with the deceased patients, but hospitals were all about the sick and the dying. Maybe Cal's nose had picked up on that. Or the smell of blood passing from a surgeon to this guy dishing up his mashed potatoes and gravy.

It was possible.

Cal didn't agree.

He'd already wolfed down a cookie while telling me with a full mouth that was bullshit at the same time I was telling him eggs first, dessert later. No teacher could instruct you in multitasking and how to fail at it spectacularly as raising a preteen. Cal had deserted his bed to follow me to the kitchen. Followed the bag of cookies rather as I started scrambling an egg. "So why is it bull . . . I mean, not true? And I told you about the bad language."

"You're such a grandma. It *is* bullshit." He shrugged, eyes fixed on the Oreos I kept close and safe while I pushed the egg around with a spatula. "I smelled dead people." Then he forgot about the cookies and grinned. "Hey, I smell dead people. Why don't I get a movie, huh?"

I snorted but didn't discourage the humor. It wasn't often Cal laughed about his other side. "You're too talented for your own good. Hollywood is jealous."

"Probably." His eyes went back to the cookies and his mind to our neighbor. "I didn't smell sick people. I smelled something, a lot of somethings rotting in his basement. Hospitals don't let dead people hang around their cafeteria and rot, do they? Even I might have trouble eating through that. Hey, can I have onions in my eggs?"

"We're out of onions. We do have half a piece of cheese left. How about that?" Junior, damn it, why couldn't your hefty, religious ass work at a funeral home? It would make convincing Cal much easier. And it would allow me to stop the internal cursing while getting Cal to stop his outer cursing.

"Cheese is good," he agreed. I looked at the ice pack lying on the table and when that didn't work, pointed at it with the spatula. Cal sighed but put it back up to where his shirt covered the bruise.

"Your 'serial killer' neighbor is also religious from the looks of the cross around his neck." I stirred the egg again, then scraped it onto a plate I'd set in front of him. "How many serial killers are devout Christians?" I was really hoping to slide this one past him.

"The Spanish Inquisition?" he said promptly.

"I'd be impressed if I thought that was from your history class and not Monty Python reruns." I handed him a fork. "He also has a gut on him. I doubt he could catch anyone if he tried."

"If lions are fat it means they're the best hunters." He took a bite of cheesy eggs.

I could not win. "You're *not* suggesting he's eating them?"

"Nope. If he did, his house would smell like barbeque, not roadkill. I just like lions. They're cool."

Absolutely could not win.

I sat down with my own plate of three pieces of toast. The last egg had gone to Cal. I couldn't keep him away from the SpaghettiOs when I was at work or school, but I could make him eat one healthy thing a day when I was home. "Cal, give me the benefit of the doubt on this one, would you? He's a flabby, churchgoing man who stutters. He's not a raging homicidal maniac. He is not storing dead bodies in his basement. It's simply not likely. Just trust me on this, all right?"

"I always trust you, Nik. But sometimes you're not practical," he said matter-of-factly. He also said it frequently. He didn't know as of thirty minutes ago when I'd first seen the spill of dark blood under his skin I was a true believer of the concept.

Cal's definition of practical had always both covered and absolved many sins. As he'd committed them on my behalf when I'd twice been sick enough not to be able to take care of myself, I had trouble getting him to see that his practical was most people's criminal. As my little brother came first with me, his big brother came first with him. I thought I was smart, but in some ways Cal was far more so than I'd ever been.

He popped in the last bite of eggs. "Just remember, don't get laid until we move again. Stay a virgin and everything will be okay. I told you, Jason Voorhees and Michael Myers wouldn't lie."

Watching the fake butter refuse to melt on the bread, I lost any appetite for the toast or life in general . . . if only for a second.

Laid.

Sophia had gone from verbally to physically abusive. The first inevitable Grendel had shown up. The serial killer issue still hadn't been solved, and now my eleven-year-old brother had just told me to not get *laid*.

Why me?

Honestly, why me?

5

Cal

Present Day

"Why me?"

The faux leather/duct tape combo squeaked as Good-fellow leaned back and covered his eyes with an olive-skinned hand. "I have a limitless number of people to lie to, cheat, and rob. I'm a trickster. I have a *calling* and no time for this. Sweet Fortuna, goddess of luck, tell me, why me?"

Let me fucking count the times I'd heard this song stuck on the radio. But, on the other hand, it was nice having a constant in a world of chaos. The brash ego, the bravery in the face of imminent death, and the accompanying bitching during the bravery in the face of imminent death, never changed. Which was good. Change was rarely for the better.

I tossed the now empty pancake container in the garbage. "Why you? Why us? Why Niko and me? What'd we do to him? Damn straight no one hired us to put him down. Hell, Niko didn't know he existed until a body fell out of the frigging sky. What's any of that have to do with you?"

"What's that have to do with me? Are you senile? When have the two of you *not* dragged my wit, wisdom, charisma, and impeccably formed ass along in the wake of your bloody misfortune?" he demanded.

He had a point.

"Lifetime after lifetime," he moaned on. "It never ends."

"Are you measuring months as lifetimes now?" Niko asked, deadpan, as always when it came to Goodfellow's exaggerations.

"I may as well," Robin complained. "It certainly does feel that way."

"Then since you know history repeats itself, try for a more positive attitude," Niko suggested, not bothering to hide his amusement when Robin dropped his hand from his eyes to glare at us.

"Positive attitude? Let me tell you about my opinion regarding certain death and a positive attitude. It's the same thing I told Dickens over ale and who despite his view on workhouses was a horrible tipper." He sat up. "I hate Tiny Tim. I hate his chirpy optimism. I hate his purity and goodness in the face of grinding adversity.

The nerve of the little bastard. It's unnatural. There. My personal view of a positive attitude."

Niko wasn't impressed. "When Cal was three he shot Tiny Tim on the TV screen with his finger. Six imaginary rounds if I recall. You are barely in the running on attitude. Now, why is this Jack concerned with wickedness and immorality? Those are not concepts with which the *paien* usually bother themselves. That is closer to a human judgment."

He groaned and dug in his jacket for a gold-chased silver flask. "Absinthe. It doesn't make the heart grow fonder, but it can make the frustration grow fainter. Sometimes." Draining the alcohol to the last drop in three swallows, he reached for a second flask and did the same. Looking marginally less annoyed, he rang the two containers together, an alcoholic cowbell. The silver note hung in the air as he said, "First, we don't know that it's Jack for certain. I said I wasn't committing to that until we have further proof and I meant it. He is that much of a nightmare." He gazed at the empty second flask mournfully. "Second, rarely, very rarely, mind you, a *paien* can become attached to a human or a certain subset of humans. Relate to them. Embrace them. Take them on as family or worshippers. That, in turn, can have human habits and prejudices rubbing off on them."

Something Robin had done in the past—except for the prejudices. He'd set himself up as a god. It hadn't ended well, but he hadn't given up on humans, which is why he hung around Niko and me. And humans long before us. He'd almost married one in Pompeii before the volcano blew. He was one of the few *paien* who considered humans worthy company.

"It most definitely wasn't you," Niko said, "or another puck. Besides you, vampires, and peris, I don't know any *paien* that associate with humans. What kind of *paien* is Spring-heeled Jack exactly?"

"Not me?" Goodfellow put away both flasks and gave a predatory grin. "Are you sure? I do have a preoccupation with licking the velvet-skinned throats of blond women and blond men. Blond anything really."

"Put it back in your pants." I snorted. "And even you couldn't leave a hickey the size of a hand."

Apparently I was wrong as he continued to grin. Niko frowned impatiently. "Goodfellow, we have a vicious *paien* serial killer roaming free skinning people alive. Focus. And if you continue with your lecherous behavior, I'll tell Ishiah."

Goodfellow stretched his arms, spread his fingers, then linked them to put his hands behind his head. "Feel free. He accepted me as I am and although I am giving monogamy a try, it wasn't a requirement. And I still talk the talk and look the look." The grin grew wider. "I'd have to be dead for that to stop. As for what Jack is"—the grin disappeared—"I don't know. I wasn't in England then. I've not seen him. Let me think on it." Rolling eyes in my direction, he continued, "I will need more alcohol. It's far too early to be thinking. Morning mounting is mostly muscle memory *and* a nice alliteration, but thinking . . . for that I'll have to bribe my brain."

I raided the fridge for two six-packs: one for him and one for me. Yeah, nice alliteration and one I was going to do my best to scrub from my own brain cells. As he looked down his nose at anything as common as beer, I was pouring Mountain Dew and Dr. Pepper into a glass with the beer on top of that. Beer for the amnesia, the rest for caffeinated coherence. I wasn't good with mornings either. I considered one or two p.m. still morning. I considered five thirty a.m. an abomination. If Hell had existed, it would always be five thirty there.

"Seriously?" Goodfellow asked dubiously as he watched me mixing the brew with the combat knife that had proved useless against Jacky-boy or what might be Jacky-boy as Robin remained on the fence there. At least the puck was distracted from his own horrifyingly domestic brew.

"Dr. Dew. Good for what ails you and a barrelful will decompose a body if you're out of sulfuric acid." I had no idea if that was true, but it sounded true. It also felt true as the first swallow hit my stomach and became a miniature nuclear explosion. I was back on the couch and guzzling. When I felt my eyes begin to burn and my nerves do a convulsive dance, I said, "Okay, I'm awake. For about forty minutes. Jack—our monster of the month. Maybe. Go."

Robin had finished his first, second—hell, he was on his fifth beer in less than a minute. "Black, fog or mist, possible wings, the ozone smell you said, I'm thinking some sort of storm *paien*. Too bad it's not a parasite, looking only to drain energy. They're more pests than anything. This one, however, sounds far above the pest category. Hopefully it's a creature or spirit and not a god." Yeah, we'd fought pseudo-gods before. Not fun. "Perhaps in earlier days he associated with uptight humans. Your people are quite good at that, labeling anything such as sex, gambling, and drinking as being depraved." All of which happened to be the puck's favorite activities. "Insanity beyond the pale. You said Ishiah was certain all the victims were human, yes? That would make sense if he clung to humankind for a pace. We hate what we love and love what we hate. Let me consider this for a moment longer."

All human victims. Or at least partly human when it came to me. Then once tasted, I was off the menu. That hurt my feelings.

As Goodfellow closed his eyes to concentrate, I finished my Dr. Dew. When I came back with a second one, my knife that had been on the coffee table was gone. I glared at Niko, who was drinking soy milk with the obvious delusion there was some sort of taste to it.

"When you stop twitching like a lab rat with electrodes in his brain, you'll get it back," he responded calmly. "Stir your poisonous concoction with your finger and if it eats the flesh from your bone don't come crying to me."

I stirred, drank, and growled. My finger turned slightly red but that was probably psychosomatic. When I said so, Niko told me I didn't have the depth of imagination for a psychosomatic disorder. I poured half of the Dr. Dew in his grass milk. He poured all his milk over my head. Normally he would've flipped me over the couch, but this was his way of being considerate of my stitches.

"This is what you do while I think?" Robin's eyes were now open. "Squabble like children in a sandbox?"

"No, usually I kill something when I'm bored, but there's nothing here to kill except you," I complained halfheartedly. "And Niko hid my knife." I tried to wring the milk out of my sopping hair.

"Lack of an immediately convenient weapon. Never was there a truer sign of friendship." He got to his feet. "I have an idea or two and someone to verify them. Fortunately, her business is open twenty-four hours a day. She'll be awake. Let us go."

"How about a shower first?" I complained.

"No, leave the milk." His lips curved in a way I long recognized as being at my expense. "She'll like you better for it. Apollo knows, you need all the brightening of your personality that you can get."

"But . . . milk?"

"Milk," he confirmed at the door before pausing.

"Oh. And a dead rat if you happen to have one."

"A cathouse? You brought us to a whorehouse?" Niko, arms folded and eyebrows furrowed, looked up at the face of the four-story brownstone built of warm-colored stone and accented with creamy white. Nice. Expensive. Classy. This wasn't the place if you wanted a quick fifty-buck suck-and-fuck.

"Now you sound as judgmental as Jack-the-skinner-

Sprat, if that's who it is. And it's not a cathouse. It is *the* Cathouse. It has existed for well over four thousand years in different locations. I have stock in it. It's quite profitable . . . except for the kilos of catnip they go through monthly. That does eat into the profit. But we all have our vices."

It had been a twenty-minute cab ride here and I now smelled like sour milk. I had two guns under my jacket and Niko had given me my KA-BAR knife back, but my mood was not good. There was the caffeine crash combined with the itch of new stitches and it was still too goddamn early for anyone or anything to be upright and viable for life.

Sometimes I hated my job.

I ignored the doorbell, a softly glowing button surrounded by a curved brass sleeping mouse, and pounded on the door. "We're three little kittens who've lost our mittens. Ah, the hell with it. It's a whorehouse." I pounded on the door again. "Kits who need tits. Open up."

"I wish I could believe he was drunk. But I know his Auphe metabolism better," Robin grumbled as he nudged me aside to press the bell. "Are you certain you raised him or did you let Hannibal Lecter babysit him? Genghis Khan? Attila the Hun? Please, enlighten me."

Niko was undisturbed per usual. "Cal is his own person. I learned at a young age to accept that or step in front of a bus and move on to my next incarnation."

Goodfellow gave a peculiar hum. "You always have been a glutton for punishment. Over and over and over again." It sounded, best guess, half smug and half melancholy and entirely more specific than his usual random comments on Niko's Buddhist philosophy. My general annoyance factor needed no extra commentary, apparently, but before I could ask him anything he was already ringing the bell again.

"Why are we here? You wanted proof. How are we going to find proof here?" I asked.

"A den of iniquity—Zeus, how I love them—is a prime source of every rumor in the wind. I plan on speaking with my good and formerly intimate friend to see if she's heard any such of certain *paien* being in the city." He held up a finger. "Their presence could rule out Jack. For example, Taranis."

"Celtic god of thunder. Usually associated with a wheel," Niko supplied.

"He didn't slice me open with a goddamn wheel. I'd have noticed that. And no more gods. We fought one god, that's enough," I countered.

"Lei Kung." Goodfellow held up a second finger.

"A Chinese spirit known as the Duke of Thunder. He supposedly punishes mortals guilty of concealed crimes and carries a drum, mallet, and chisel." Niko started to elbow me, remembered the stitches and accused, "You should know this. We discussed Chinese supernatural creatures three months ago."

"You might have discussed. It's safe to say I just nodded and watched whatever game was on TV. And neither of us was beaten, sculpted, or assaulted with a drum solo. You can probably cross off the Duke of Earl." I yawned and fished in my pocket for a lukewarm can of the last Mountain Dew I'd had in the fridge.

Robin already had his third finger up. Our back and forth was probably like white noise to him now or, as usual, he was more interested in listening to himself. "As much as I dislike talking trash about my own kind, there is also the Lakota trickster, Heyoka, the spirit of thunder and lightning. He—" The opening of the door cut him off. That was damn lucky for us because no matter what he said, talking trash about other tricksters and how they didn't measure up to his wild and wicked ways was one of Goodfellow's favorite pastimes.

I recognized the species of *paien* in the doorway although I'd not come across one in person until now. The air from inside the house that flowed around it carried the smell of oranges, honey, cinnamon, and some interesting spices I didn't recognize offhand. Oh, and sex. I smelled so much sex I was surprised the intense musk of it, as strong as a natural gas leak, didn't cause the brownstone to explode. Then there was the smell of our friend the doorman. Doorwoman. Doorperson. Blood and flesh and decomposition rank on her breath. Someone hadn't brushed since their last meal. The exhalation of a scavenger, the kind who made certain you were clinging to life when they started to eat you. Where would the pleasure be if you were already dead?

She stood well over seven feet tall, bending down to see us, and had eight arms, seven of which held swords. Wearing something consisting of numerous leather straps, she also had a split skirt of silk that fell to bare brown feet. Thick black hair fell nearly as far, black eyes with pinpoint white pupils, and the triangular teeth of a voodoo statue from B-movie hell in a mouth almost as wide as a bear trap. In addition, there were claws on the hands that held the blades—long, lethally curved and as black as the hair and eyes. No surprise in that. There were days the entire world was made of bloody claws and tearing fangs.

Just not today. It was way too damn early for that.

"Need appointment and card." The single unarmed hand with the ebony talons was held out palm up. The voice was surprisingly understandable considering the freakish size of the mouth and the equally freakish number of teeth, although she didn't have much to say. Couldn't blame her attitude there as I understood it. I wasn't doling out advice to the sad and lonely at my job, bartender or not. The less I had to talk to what passed for clients at work, the better.

"Ah, yes." Robin reached inside his jacket for a wallet, gave it a brief glance and returned it before fishing out a second one. "Actually I don't need an appointment and how you fail to recognize me time and again, I will never know."

"This puck, that puck, all fucks. Who can tell the difference?" Robin was told with bored indifference.

He stiffened. "You could not be further from the truth if you were the drooling picture of sub-intelligence—which you are. I have no difficulty seeing why you're working the door instead of upstairs as you have so little personality to work with, despite what you could do with eight hands." Flipping open the apparently extra-special wallet, Goodfellow had his mouth open for more insults, barely warmed up, when he said something else instead.

"Where's my card? I have a lifelong platinum-class come-and-go-as-I-please membership card. Wait . . . where's my card for Aphrodite's Pleasure Palace—best strippers in Greece? Godiva's Clothing Optional Hair Salon?" Replacement cards were pulled out, read in the light spilling from inside the house, and discarded as if they burned to the touch. "The Salvation Army? Big Brothers, Big Sisters? Soup Kitchen? Humanitarian aid in a trickster's wallet? *My* wallet?" The horror was clear and true in his voice. "I am tainted beyond redemption."

Niko squeezed his shoulder with false comfort and commented smoothly, "As you said, it's inspirational when your sexual partner accepts you for who you truly are."

"No hair salon, huh?" I popped the top on my soda. "It'll be hard to be a pretentious ass with an eight-dollar Supercuts' special."

"That pigeon will rue the day his mother laid that rotting, spoiled egg that hatched him," Robin gritted before pushing past the guardian, his sword in his hand so improbably fast that I barely saw his hand move. "Tell Bastet that I am here and don't pretend you don't know who and what I am. Tell her *now*. You can do that as you are or with my sword through your heart. That choice I leave up to you. Are you listening to me, you misbegotten vulture? That glazed look of insipid boredom, believe it or not, is not inspiring me with reams of confidence. *Go.*"

She gave him a look that was anything but bored. It was seething with the metal-edge of rage and the red haze of hunger. Her kind was always hungry. It didn't stop for them. For a moment I thought she'd act on it, but she turned, and moved toward the stairs, suddenly all but drenched in disinterest. To the eye. I pulled in and sampled a deep breath of the adrenaline leaking out into the air before asking with casual curiosity, "How attached is your friend to the help? She a big fan of her pet peymakilir?"

"Of one such as this? Not likely. Rudeness to the clients wouldn't be tolerated if she knew about it." Sword still in hand, Robin deposited his woefully charitable wallet into a small trash can that looked to be made of gold. Idly, I wondered if it would fit under my jacket. "And, believe me, she'll know the very moment I see her."

The peymakilir was halfway up the stairs now, as slow as if every step was weighed down by chains. Slow and not worth a second glance, you would've thought. Yeah, and if you had that thought in our world, you wouldn't have many more of them.

Because here she came.

In a heartbeat the Hindu scavenger of war's battlefields had turned and leaped into fluid motion over the banister. She almost flew. Like a bird following a propeller of whirling steel, she soared toward us . . . nearly beautiful even knowing what she was. One who stripped the meat from the bones of the dying, consuming their flesh and life gleefully all in one. An inexplicably cruel part of nature. Yet, still impossibly beautiful—an angel of death with every sword a flash of quicksilver.

Then she was nothing more than meat. That tends to happen when I open a gate inside of someone rather than around them. In midair she disintegrated in an explosion of tarnished gray light, followed by the billowing stench of burned flesh, the spray of blood and long, cauterized limbs scattered everywhere. What was left of her fell, a tangle of parts, swords, and snuffed-out wildness.

Bambi's mom goes down. And stays down.

Not that Disney ever showed you that part.

I had ducked a tumbling sword that had flown overhead, nearly taking off my head. I should've thought more about the swords. Eh, water under the bridge. I took another swallow of Mountain Dew. The caffeine was just not kicking in. "You're right, Robin. She was one rude bitch." Most murderers, male or female, were. The foyer was now somewhat of a mess, but it had been a little uptown for me anyway.

Goodfellow let the tip of his sword hit the marble floor, which wasn't the way to treat your weapons. "What did you do?"

"I'm having an identity crisis." I shifted my shoulders without much concern. "And there's the fact that she was trying to kill us, then eat us. Hopefully in that order. I did what I do."

"It seems as if the now ex-doorman liked her job and didn't want to lose it over your complaints," Niko said. He wanted to say more and he would say more, but not until we were alone. He trusted Robin, we both did, but there were things he said only to me—the things that I hated about myself. The monster in me that would never let me be right or clean. The darkness that waited and not at all patiently for its turn.

All that wasn't true anymore.

Niko hadn't quite gotten it in the past months. I wasn't shamed by what I was. I didn't hate it, not any longer; I was confused, some, yes, but not ashamed. Or more likely, Nik being Nik, he did know and that made it all the more important that the coming conversation be private. He didn't want anyone else, even Robin, to realize the half Auphe wasn't half these days. No . . . I was farther along the road than that now. He trusted me, but he wasn't the only one in my world and not all of them would feel the same.

Instead when he commented, he was as studiously detached as only he could be. "So . . . you know what a peymakilir is. Studying behind my back?"

"Goodfellow has one painted on his guest bathroom wall behind the toilet. It's screwing a satyr and the whole thing is labeled in hellish detail in gold paint. Hard knowledge to avoid when you've got a full bladder."

Robin, meanwhile, hadn't caught on to the fact that the peymakilir disposal conversation was over. "You *blew* her up. You opened a gate inside her like you did with Suyolak." Suyolak, the antihealer who'd started the Black Death. Suyolak, the Plague of the World. Suyolak, the asshole who'd totally had it coming.

Goodfellow moved his shoe so the remnants of a peymakilir hand slid off that fine Corinthian leather. "But Suyolak was desperate measures."

"Then," I agreed.

"You're wasting gates on something you could've easily shot. Gates are for emergencies," he continued, mouth twisted in distaste. No one liked a gate or the way it looked, the way it tore apart the world and made it scream, the way seeing it twisted the brain and stomach. No one liked them—except Auphe. *"Emergencies,"* he emphasized.

"Then," I repeated with a dark grin. "And emergency is a relative term."

I wasn't a morning person, nope. I hadn't had more than two hours' sleep. I was fuzzy headed and irritable. I smelled like milk gone off and was sick of the taste of Mountain Dew. None of it was excuse enough. It wasn't an excuse at all. I'd done it because I wanted to—simple as that. She was far more of a killer than the men I'd sent away by the Ninth Circle, and she wasn't human. There was no thought needed on her before or after the fact.

Robin had been our friend since we'd met him six years ago at his car lot. He was the first we'd had, the first we'd trusted. But Nik had protected me from . . . hell, the entire world basically . . . for so damn long that he simply couldn't stop, whether I needed it or not. He hadn't mentioned anything to Robin and he wouldn't.

But I would. The puck deserved to know that things had changed. That *I* had changed over the past months and more radically than he'd no doubt already guessed. He knew I'd been more shadowed. He knew that in the past weeks I'd regained my gating ability, but he hadn't known to what extent. The way of the gun was all right—I still loved my babies, but the Auphe way was a new toy. And I wanted to play with that toy.

And now Robin did know.

Goodfellow was a trickster. He lied, but not to us. I wasn't going to lie to him.

"Goodfellow, what havoc have you wrought now?" A smooth voice came from the top of the stairs as jade green cat eyes blinked at the carnage decorating her foyer. "This reminds me of when you were mourning the fall of the Sacred Band of Thebes. You ravaged and eventually burned down my establishment in Greece."

"But every lady and gentleman on the premises fled the flames in a state of complete sexual satisfaction," Robin countered promptly.

Above the eyes was an elaborate arrangement of amber-fire hair . . . or a mane that would cover feline ears if she had them. Her face was smooth skinned and without fur, but there was a split in her lush upper lip and ivory fangs when she smiled. She was a cat, in some aspects at least, and who better to run a cathouse after all? She lifted a hand and beckoned. If she was furred in other areas, her green silk dress kept that a mystery. "You may as well come up. I don't care for peymakilirs, but they are excellent guardians. I assume you had good reason to kill her?"

"Don't I always have good reason for my kills?" he challenged, willing to take the heat for this one. Keeping the Auphe swept under the rug for the moment.

"These days, perhaps." An eyebrow arched. "You have mellowed. But you will have to pay the cleaning service's bill. I am most certainly not running a charity here. Now come along and introduce your friends. One of them smells absolutely delicious."

We spent the next hour in a room full of expensive furniture and more expensive cats, male and female. Our hostess—she preferred it to madam—was Bastet, the original Egyptian goddess of fertility and sexuality. After tiring of being worshipped she took her avocation, so to speak, on the road nearly four thousand years ago and now owned fourteen of the best houses of the most ill repute around the globe. She was a proud businesswoman and only incidentally a former lover of Goodfellow's. Of course, who over the age of two hundred and didn't mind pucks wasn't a former sexual partner of his? Only those with quick minds and quicker running skills.

Surrounded by silk cushions, he asked her about all the storm spirits and gods while stunning humanoid felines tried to feed Niko peeled grapes and tiny dead shrew from a golden bowl. He didn't seem pleased. I, who was having the milk thoroughly licked out of my hair by four of Bastet's purring employees, wasn't exactly weeping with sympathy for him. Robin had been right about the milk. They couldn't get enough of it. *Loved* it. Four rough tongues scratching my scalp and drenching every strand of hair I had in *paien* cat saliva, I, conversely, loved not at all.

Although the bare breasts were nice, even if covered in silky fur.

"I am sorry, my precious goatling," Bastet sighed as she lounged on a massive sofa with sapphire silk cushions large enough that each one was designed to substitute as a bed. She had a bare foot in Robin's lap and was using it to massage his crotch lightly. Ishiah wasn't going to care for that at all, no matter what he said about accepting the puck in all his ways. "No storm spirits have come our way and no rumors of them either."

"And what about Jack?" he asked grimly. "Have you heard any rumors of Jack?"

Her slit pupil eyes widened. There seemed to be only one Jack in the *paien* community and it wasn't Jack the Ripper. Bastet stared at us with the unblinking wariness of a cat cornered by a coyote before looking away. "Now is not a good time to be human in New York. Nor is it ever a good time to get in the way of Spring-heel himself." She removed her foot from its perch. "Go. I want no part of this. You know he prefers humans, but if he thinks one of us is carrying tales, he'll kill us just the same. More quickly, but we'll be dead nonetheless. Now go."

"He's here then. You're certain?" Niko asked, pushing away the bowl of grapes with its fur-covered garnishes.

This time Bastet bared an impressive brace of pointed teeth, survival instinct triumphing over fear, and pointed at the door. "*Go.*"

That was a yes if ever I heard one.

Goodfellow's face was more grim than his voice had been. He had his confirmation and he wasn't happy about it. Some things in life you'd rather not know. Not believe. Life didn't care about that though. Once you're stuck with something, especially when that something is known to be unstoppable, you're screwed. That was the truth of it. And it appeared as if we were stuck.

Whether we wanted to believe it or not.

6

Niko

Twelve Years Ago

I didn't want to believe it. Yet there it was. Black and white, a piece of someone's soul stapled to a telephone pole.

It was brutal and ugly and in no way matched the pure blue sky of a perfectly crisp autumn Saturday. The sun itself was cooperating, spreading a buttery glow on peeling siding, warped wood, weeds masquerading as grass and scrawny trees that had two or three poppy red leaves—gilding something tawdry into a place that for that hour looked as if it was a home you'd actually want. It was the same as that moment in *The Wizard of Oz* when it turned from black and white to every color in the spectrum. This wasn't a movie special effect; it was a natural one.

And it was ruined by the paper fluttering against the wood where it was pinned.

Cal saw it first, but then he had been watching for something like this. I hadn't. He didn't point it out. He stopped the skateboard that was all but useless on the cracked and broken sidewalk and squatted down to pretend to tie his sneaker. I noticed that it was already tied in an effective, if sloppy, Cal knot almost at the same moment I noticed the poster. It covered layers of Lost posters but it didn't say Lost. It said Missing in bold black letters. I always wondered about that—the difference between missing and lost. Whichever word was chosen for you, you were still gone all the same.

Whichever was chosen, you rarely came back.

"Kithser." I studied the face on the cheap photocopy. "David." I hadn't known his first name was David. I'd only known him as the seventeen-year-old drug dealer and probably thief three streets over who'd once tried to sell crack to Cal. It was the week we'd first moved in. Kithser was big for someone who did crack. Big boned, muscle-bound enough that if he wasn't doing crack, he was certainly juicing. Definitely well fed, I guessed, by the family who was now looking for him.

Did his family know how he was on the streets? That he was mean and nasty with the steroid psychosis lurking in the twitching beside his glassy eyes. Who knew? Either they were softhearted and hoped he'd change or they'd made him the way he was and missed that drug money.

When had I become this cynical? I reached out to fold a corner under and keep the paper from flapping in the wind. "It's an old picture," Cal noted, giving up on his sneaker. A finger plopped directly in the middle of David Kithser's face. "See? It doesn't show where you broke his nose."

Whether someone loved him or not, you didn't try to sell my little brother crack. Cal wouldn't have taken it, but the next step would've been Kithser trying to steal any money he had on him. That would've led to Cal bashing him in the balls . . . testicles. Damn it, whacking him in the *testicles* with his battered skateboard. From that point on, it was hard to say what would've happened. Cal had been armed. I didn't let him take a knife to school, but after school and on weekends, I wanted him able to protect himself. Against Grendels. Against Kithsers, against those even worse than the Kithsers. The only good neighborhoods we knew were the ones we rode through on buses.

Luckily I was two blocks down, saw it, and that was the end of Kithser bothering my brother. I could've taken him down without hurting him much. Steroid muscle is useless muscle for the most part. But with drug dealers, bullies, perverts, and what else oozed about, you needed to make an impression. A thoroughly broken nose did that and was essentially harmless in the long run. Kithser had never seen a drop of his own blood in his life until then, I could tell. Most bullies haven't.

And Cal helpfully kicking him in the b— testicles when he was down and rolling around screaming about his nose hadn't done much for his pride either. Kithser had paid attention to the lesson and he hadn't come back to our street. So I'd thought.

Or maybe someone had gone over to his street instead.

Expectant eyes slanted up at me in a rainwater gaze. Now I'd see the truth. No way to avoid it. Not even I could ignore this. "You know the killer got him. Right, Nik?" You're not an oblivious idiot anymore, are you? Because worrying about keeping you alive is getting to be a chore. I could see all those thoughts spinning under the dark hair.

I rested a hand on his shoulder and squeezed lightly. His bones were thin and light under my fingers. Fragile. Breakable. A spun glass version of a brother. I hoped for that growth spurt soon. A knife and some hand-me-down martial art moves from the dojo wouldn't always be enough.

"Maybe," I answered, noncommittal. "He leads a bad life. Lots of trouble." Missing a week now, the poster said. Not crashing at a friend's place then. "But . . . maybe."

Cal blew a random strand of hair out of his eyes and rolled up the too-long sleeves of his cast-off sweatshirt one more time. "Can we get pizza after?"

I'd already ripped the stapled poster free. I'd done it completely without thought and stared at it with a combination of dread and curiosity. What was I doing? "After what?" I asked, distracted.

Picking up his skateboard, Cal tucked it under his arm and nodded at the paper. "After you go around the neighborhood asking stupid questions about Kithser."

"How do you know that's what I'm going to do?" Bemused at his sudden psychic ability to know what even I hadn't known, I folded the missing poster in half.

"Because that's you. Good." He had an expression of patient resignation on his face that I knew was identical to the one I wore when I was cleaning up his SpaghettiOs and soda handprints in the kitchen. "Just . . . good. You can't help yourself. You don't want to get someone in trouble if they don't deserve it. You know, in case the weirdo next door is a butcher." There was a heavy load of sarcasm on the word butcher.

"Wouldn't you want the same benefit of the doubt?" I knocked lightly on top of his head. "Although all the trouble you get in you almost always deserve," I added with exasperated affection.

Cal was stubborn and getting him off topic wasn't easy at the best of times. This wasn't the best of times. "You're right, Nik. He *is* a butcher. But he butchers people, not cows." That's when the glow that hung in the air faded and the sun was only the sun again. The wizard behind the curtain was just a man, possibly one with an inhuman grin and huge, serrated knife dripping blood.

By then Cal was already walking toward our rental, done trying to convince me. There was work ahead and he wanted it over with as soon as possible. "Bible or crutches?"

We'd learned a few techniques from watching Sophia. She could work an entire block in twenty-five minutes lifting valuables to be fenced later and she had a routine that didn't fail often. It was difficult to get into a house to talk to and scam suspicious neighbors in our crumbling section of town. It helped to have one of two things.

"The Bible or the crutches?" Cal asked again. "And what about the pizza?"

"The crutches," I decided. The Bible worked less and less for Sophia. It seemed people were as upset by pushy Christians knocking on their door as much as they were the possibility of a home invasion. "Yes, pizza, but vegetarian. You need some vegetables. Otherwise you'll turn into a can of SpaghettiOs."

"Okay, but extra cheese." Which was remarkably agreeable for a kid who loved pepperoni and any other kind of questionable meat more than life itself. It made me wonder uneasily exactly how bad the smell was to him coming from next door. Was there meat in that basement and was it questionable in a very different way?

I planned to find out.

After retrieving the hard-used crutches, we started canvassing the neighborhood. I went from a fifteen-year-old who looked seventeen to a teenager with a hugely swollen foot and ankle, two pair of socks stuffed with more socks, a pathetic limp, and a solemn-eyed little brother holding a box of cookies he could only be selling for school. Granted it was an empty box, another prop and victim of Cal's appetite, but it would get the job done.

Crutch and drag. Crutch and drag. I looked down at Cal. "This is wrong, all right? We don't do things like this unless we're trying to find out if a killer lives next to us and I don't think that will ever come up again. We don't do it to steal. We're not Sophia."

"I know, Nik. You've said it like a thousand times. We're not. But sometimes I think things would be easier if we were." That was true. I wasn't so naïve I didn't know that, but that didn't mean it was the way it was going to be. Not for me and not for Cal. I'd remind him as often as I had to. If it had to be a thousand, then a thousand it would be. He was holding up the box, taking a whiff, and giving a small smile at the lingering aroma of cookies.

He caught me watching him from the corner of his eye and gave me a look of his own as he kicked a small chunk of concrete down the sidewalk. "You should slump more," he suggested. "You still look too tall and too . . . um . . . ninja-ish. Badass."

Right then I gave up on the language. His school was the educational version of *Pulp Fiction*. Mine was a teen version of a supermax prison, metal detectors, police, and all. If we made our way through with only foul mouths, we would be doing well. There also might be a serial killer and there *were* monsters. All that was enough to worry about. So I let it go and took his advice. I slouched more, aimed for a pained expression, and slowed my pace.

We talked to Mrs. Spoonmaker first, Cal remembering to cough once or twice for that flu I'd told her he had the day before. We didn't pull the cookie scam on her. I thanked her for calling our schools and casually asked if she knew David Kithser? If she'd seen him around lately. We went to school together and he owed me money for doing his homework. That she would believe. If I said I was his friend and she knew him, she wouldn't talk to me at all. He was a bad guy. In our world minding your own business about bad guys was good business for yourself.

Cal perched on her couch covered in faded orange and red roses. Covering him were her seven cats. Cats liked him, loved him really. The moment they smelled him they would swarm. Now wasn't any different. They draped over his shoulders, lap, and feet. If they happened to have a dead mouse tucked away, they'd present it at his feet like an offering. Cal didn't mind. Affection from anyone but me was rare. He knew when to appreciate it—even in the form of a dead rodent. He stroked the cats, surrounded by a cloud of purring and flying fur. Each one took a turn bracing on his chest to stare into his eyes. I didn't know what they were hoping to see, but they always seemed satisfied when their turn was over.

Mrs. Spoonmaker knew Kithser. "No better than he had to be," she'd said with pursed pink lips that matched the pink tint in her short curly white hair. She also said that she hadn't seen him in months and good riddance. We moved from house to house after that. Five houses down Cal stopped on the sidewalk, several feet away from the porch. "Dog," he warned. "Big dog."

I couldn't smell him like Cal could, but a second later I heard the barking. Loud, ferocious, and absolutely crazed. Big dog was right. Big and wild to attack. Unlike cats, dogs did not like Cal. Not some dogs, not most dogs. All dogs. They had two reactions: fight or flight. And when the reaction was fight, it was instinct that ran back to their prehistoric ancestors—to the death.

Dogs were good for howling their lungs out when the Grendels were around too. We didn't talk about that, Cal and I, but he knew. Dogs hated him because dogs hated Grendels. Man's best friend hated monsters and man's best friend hated Cal. There was nothing to be said about that because it didn't mean anything. It didn't.

"We'll take the next house," I said.

Cal stood silently behind me as the dog next door continued to bay the invisible moon down from the sky. This door, boiled cabbage green, opened to a hugely tousled mane of platinum blond hair with glossy black roots, long red fingernails with a rhinestone at each tip, and an impatient expression. "I'm running late. What the hell do you kids want? And what the hell is that damn dog barking at?" Beyond the yellow, crimson, fake diamond glint and irritability, there was a woman. She was dressed in a skintight miniskirt, thigh-high boots, and a glittering bikini top that, while extremely skimpy, NASA must've helped engineer to hold up an enormous cargo load. She was holding a shirt in her hand as well, but that didn't seem quite as important.

How did they stay up? Physics had never been so interesting or useful until now.

"Mrs. Breckinridge," Cal said, surprised, moving up

beside me. "Nik, she's a substitute teacher at school." I
cleared my throat. He was never going to be the male
equivalent of Miss Manners, but there were some re-
quirements I expected of him, behavior that helped us
blend into average society. "Um . . . sorry. Mrs. Breckinridge, this is my brother, Niko. He broke his ankle.
He's helpless and pathetic and won't rob you." He was
curious at her presence, but he was also a Leandros
when he had to be, there with the story. "Hey, I didn't
know you lived on my street."

"I'm never home long enough to really live anywhere. Too many bills to pay." Thick, fake eyelashes
blinked. "You're the kid with the weird name who always sits in the last row? Haliban. Caliban. Something
from Shakespeare, right?"

His teacher but obviously not a very good teacher.

Cal said flatly, "Cal. My name is Cal." Sophia had
told him long before school ever would about Caliban,
Shakespeare, and *The Tempest*. She wanted him to know
why she'd named him after the shambling monster-
child of a bitch sorceress. The only part she'd gotten
right was that about the bitch.

"Well, Cal"—she fished a five out of her pocket and
passed it to him—"my new favorite student. How
about you forget you ever saw me and what I do for a
second job. The principal is the stick-up-her-ass kind.
All sorts of morals—*her* morals, the judgmental old
witch. She'd fire me like that"—she snapped her
fingers—"if she knew I was stripping. Dancing, I mean.
Dancing. You think you can do that? Keep your mouth
shut?"

Cal gave her a "no skin off my nose" shrug, the five-dollar bill already a mere afterimage in the air, before grinning cheerfully. "You know me and rules, Mrs. B."

She grinned back under a thick layer of scarlet lipstick. She looked as if she'd broken more than a few rules in her life too. "You walk to the beat of a different drummer, there's that for sure. You spend more time talking to the principal than her own damn husband does, which he's probably happy as hell about. And, sugar, I'm forty. You might want to look me in the face, appreciate me for my brain because when this top comes off my brain is still in the same place but my tits will be four inches lower."

It took me a second to realize that last part was directed at me and I could feel my skin flush hot and mortified. I read about Buddha, Nietzsche, Sun-Tzu, Jung, poetry, physics, chemistry, advanced mathematics, and I trained to kill Grendels, to be ready if they came looking for a fight, but I couldn't do anything about the fact I still had normal teenage hormones.

"Hold it in," Cal whispered. "Virgins live. Horn-dogs die."

"*Horn*-dogs? You're *eleven*. Do you know how much trouble you are . . ." I swallowed the rest and asked Mrs. Breckinridge, while looking directly at her face this time, politely, "We were wondering if you knew about David Kithser." She worked at Cal's school. The cookie excuse wouldn't work on her. I might as well come out with what we actually wanted. If our neighbor was a murderer, I doubt I had to worry about her spending any time with him—droopy and pitiful as he appeared, and definitely not enough time for them to discuss our interest in Kithser.

"Cecily? Cee-cee? Who are you screwing around with now? Every time I turn my back, there you go." The man, once big and athletic, now just big and fat, appeared out of the gloom of the tiny house. Graying hair stuck up on end, small ferret eyes shied away from the light. He was shirtless and needed Mrs. Breckinridge's structurally improbable bikini top more than she did. He was in boxers, splitting at the seams, but still fighting the good fight. "Look at him. What is he? Sixteen? Seventeen? You're into jailbait now because a real man's too much for you? I oughta—"

"You oughta get out of my face, Virgil, or the next time you're sleeping off a drunk, I'm taking the shotgun out of the closet, loading for bear, and sticking the barrel up your fat—" The door slamming in our face cut off the last word, but I didn't think either of us had to guess at what it was.

Cal, again, checked the cookie box, hoping against hope a sympathetic universe had magically refilled it. "Mrs. Breckinridge is my favorite teacher," he announced with a more than slightly evil smirk. "She never gives homework. She knows everything about everything. And she tells us."

"I'll bet she does and she really shouldn't do that."

"And she said you shouldn't look at her tits but you did." His expression was pure and guileless as a baby on Santa's lap at Christmas.

"That is it. No TV next week. None. Maybe some

silence and a good book will bleach your brain of that filthy language." As I started for the next house, the complaining started and didn't stop as we trudged through the front door of our own house fifteen minutes later. I thought I saw the twitch of a curtain in one of Junior's windows, but he had no reason to be suspicious. We had the box of cookies. We actually took two orders for the nonexistent sale, and I didn't ask about Kithser at every house. I also had never seen Junior outside talking to anyone on the street. He didn't socialize with the neighbors. I'd say that was a bad sign, but except for Cal and me and the old ladies, none of the neighbors wanted to have anything to do with anyone else. It wasn't that kind of neighborhood. That was good. It meant that word shouldn't get back to him.

Not that we'd found word of anything suspicious. Either no one had seen Kithser in weeks or didn't know him at all. To me that meant there was no evidence of a connection between Kithser and Junior. To Cal it meant that Junior was still not killing where he lived but close enough for convenience. But his belief that Kithser's body was now in Junior's basement was nothing compared to the lack of television.

"Yes, I know it's not fair. You've said that twenty-two times now. But I'm trying to keep you from saying words that will incite any dates you have in the future to stab you in the eye with a nail file." I leaned the crutches on the wall and sat on the couch to peel off all the extra socks that had faked an impressive swollen ankle. I then picked up the notebook and looked at the list I'd started before we'd left the house that morning. There were two columns—the For and Against regarding serial killer evidence.

"Maybe I won't want to date. Girls might not like me. When do we go get the pizza? You promised pizza." He sprawled in the ugly plaid chair that had come with the house, his legs flopped over one arm and his head and arms over the other. His upside-down gaze was accusing when he mentioned the pizza.

"Why wouldn't they like you? Once I go to college and we get away from Sophia, we'll have a normal life," I said. "And if you stop cursing like a forty-year-old bouncer there's no reason girls wouldn't like you."

There also wouldn't be any reason that I couldn't let myself like some girls without our wonderful mother trying to steal their jewelry, wallet, or their hair to sell to a wig maker. That wasn't advice I wanted to give to anyone I brought home: please keep moving at all times or you'll wind up penniless and bald. Cal wasn't the only one that thought it at times. Life did suck. Buddha might not agree or he might agree in much more flowery language, but he had dealt with it much better than I was. I still had so much to learn.

For now I had other things to think about. Tapping the notebook with the pen, I reluctantly put Kithser's name under both the For and Against columns. They instantly canceled each other out, but I did it anyway. It was part of the plan after all.

"Nik, monsters follow us wherever we go, I'm half freak, and we live next to serial killers. It doesn't matter if I say bad words or not—we're never going to be normal."

Startled, I looked up from the paper at him. His hair was hanging in a dark waterfall toward the stained carpet, his hands were linked across his stomach, sneakers randomly knocking heels with boredom, and his face was as smooth and unaffected as if he'd said the earth revolves around the sun. It was what it was. It wasn't going to change and thinking differently was not only pointless, but incredibly naïve on your part.

"Cal, that's not true." He'd said two days ago that of course our neighbor was a murderer because that's the way things were, but I hadn't thought he'd meant that's the way things would always be. I didn't know he didn't believe that I could change that. Most of my life had been spent thinking of ways to fix it all. Get away from Sophia, be able to fight the Grendels if necessary, obtain an education, raise my brother to be the person I saw in him—strong and proud. To be normal. Something that Cal accepted wasn't going to happen, wasn't ever going to happen. Had accepted it a long time ago as offhand as the words had been.

I wasn't letting that go. He deserved a life. We both did and we were getting one. There was not a thing in this world I wouldn't do to give us that.

"Besides," I said firmly, "if our normal is dating only in the daytime to keep the Grendels from watching and moving away from any neighbors who kill spiders in their house much less people, then that normal is good enough for me." I pointed my pen at him and added, "And if you call yourself a freak again, the next TV you watch will be the one you have when you're old enough to get a job and buy one yourself."

That was a threat that hadn't failed me yet.

Cal's sneakers smacked together again, the expression on his face thoughtful. "Grendels aren't much uglier than Mrs. Breckinridge's husband. Maybe you're right. It might not be so bad—our own kinda weird normal."

Before I could say anything about the husband comment and judging people by their appearance, although there was some truth to it in this case—quite a bit of truth—there was a knock. Brightening, Cal vaulted out of the chair toward the front door. "It's the pizza genie. We won't have to walk four miles to get some after all. That's better than seven wishes."

"Cal . . ." I was about to remind him, but he was already peering through the blinds. We couldn't know who might be standing on our porch. Monsters, Sophia's exes (worse than monsters), Sophia's victims with baseball bats and vengeance on their mind, cops. Social workers—the list was long and not good. Not good in any way whatsoever.

"It's just a guy in a fancy suit with a cool car. A really cool car. He looks lost." Leaning closer to the window, he reconsidered. "Not lost, but he looks like he doesn't want to be here."

If he had a nice suit and an expensive car, chances were high that Cal was right. He didn't want to be here and wasn't here on purpose. I stayed on the couch, but kept my eye on my brother as he opened the door and my hand on the handle of a switchblade I hid under the well-worn cushion of the sofa. All that Cal knew about hiding knives, he'd learned from what I'd taught him and from watching me from a very young age. Monkey see, monkey do. Monkey do, monkey survives.

I couldn't see the man but I could hear his irritated voice in answer to Cal's less than polite and borderline hostile "We don't want religion. It gives us hives. Go away."

"I am not offering religion, you incredibly rude creature. I have a flat tire and a dead cell battery. I need to borrow your phone."

"We don't have a phone." Cal scratched the back of one calf with his foot, his tone implying that was the most stupid request he'd heard in all of his eleven years.

"Of course you have a phone. Don't be absurd. Everyone has a phone. Fetuses are issued one with a friends-and-family plan two months before they pop out of the womb. Are you after money? You are rude, but hustling me for money does make you a con man after my own heart. I'll pay you to use the phone." The irritation was now smoothed over by a mellow flow of amusement that made me think of a symphony's rich sweep, the velvet thrum of a satisfied cat's purr, the warmth of a fire in a huge hearth in an expensive house. All good things, all comforting things. The best con artists had voices like that. Our mother sounded like that—to everyone but us.

Cal had grown up listening to her voice pouring the richest of verbal chocolate, sex, and brandy over marks. He was immune to it. He switched feet and scratched his other calf, squinting in suspicion. "I'm eleven and you want to give me money? Are you a pervert?"

The amusement vanished as the unseen man squawked much like a startled rooster. I knew the sound as we'd once squatted at an abandoned farm for three months. "*No.* I am not a pervert." There was a pause. "Technically . . . no, that's only been with consenting adults, always has been, which is legal or should be. Therefore *not* a pervert."

With a very obviously unconvinced expression as he loved nothing more than poking people, mentally or physically, Cal crossed his arms and looked up and down at the man that I couldn't see. "Your clothes are kind of fancy, like a pimp in those old cop movies. You don't belong in this part of town and you're giving away money. Yeah," he announced his conclusion, "you're some kind of weird door-to-door pervert."

"Pimp?" There was an audible grinding of teeth. "Have some respect. This suit is *Versace*. I'm not a pimp and I'm not a pervert, you foulmouthed little . . . oh." The exclamation was ripe with surprise and what I thought sounded like eagerness. "I know you. I *know* you. Where's your brother? May I speak to him?"

"How do you know I have a brother?" Cal wasn't playing anymore. The suspicion was real and I was already moving, the switchblade hidden in my hand.

"You always do. Or a cousin or a best friend bonded by blood. Something of that dramatic overwrought nature. Someone who is virtually attached to you at the hip. Let me speak to him. He's invariably more reasonable."

"Nik, the pervert wants to talk to you."

"And I am *not* a pervert," the man declared. I was at Cal's side by that time to see him when he said it.

He had wavy brown hair, green eyes that every chicken saw right before red-furred jaws snapped their necks, a mobile face, and a wide grin that could've sold pornography to the Pope. A con man through and through, but from his clothes and car—a screaming red Jaguar—a much more successful one than Sophia. There were all kinds of con men. He could be a politician or a talk show host or a car salesman.

I rested a hand, the one without the hidden blade, on Cal's shoulder. "What do you mean you know him? I know everyone my brother knows and I don't know you." The threat was audible, just as I meant it to be.

He waved a hand that was holding a pair of sunglasses I thought cost more than the house we were living in. "Like him. I mean I know kids such as him. With attitudes like his . . . very . . . ah . . . lively, yes, precisely the word I was looking for . . . which means that they usually have someone who makes certain everyone shows appreciation in nonviolent ways for their smart-a— their challenging attitudes."

"You can say smart-ass. He knows what he is and, worse, he's proud of it."

The stranger was suddenly enthusiastic and friendly instead of demanding, but that didn't mean the man was harmless. He was too balanced on the balls of his feet, a nonstop mouth yet a stillness within and an awareness of everything around him from the periodic rapid flicker of his eyes to take in the street around him.

He reminded me of some of the older and more lethally skilled teachers I'd learned under over the years. I wasn't there yet. I hoped to be someday. No, this one was not harmless at all, but he didn't have any reason to be dangerous to us personally that I could see.

He looked down at Cal and the grin changed to a smile you'd have to be blind to see wasn't full of affection. "Proud. Why doesn't that surprise me?"

It should've made me tense and on edge. Cal had been toying with the guy in his best cat-and-mouse style, but in our world molesters were a real threat. You had to be careful and willing to cut off someone's balls in a heartbeat. Cal and I were good enough with the threat and the flash of a blade that we hadn't had to castrate anyone yet, but there was always a first time.

Past history should've made me wary, but I wasn't. I knew the monsters, otherworldly and human, when I saw them. There was nothing twisted in that smile and the affection was what you'd show a close friend or a family member. I knew because it was the same as Cal showed me. "You know kids like us?" I glanced at his car. Flat tire. He hadn't been lying.

"I had friends who had to be kids like you. I know because when they were adults, they were very much still like you." The smile faded somewhat, but he remained cheerful enough. "But friends go and they come." The smile faded further at that. "About the phone?"

Go and they come? That was an odd way of saying it and the opposite of the usual "they come and they go." "Sorry. Cal's right, mister. We don't have a phone."

Sophia had a cell phone, but she was elsewhere and there wasn't a landline in the house—not one that had been paid up and worked. I aimed another look at his woefully deflated tire. "Why don't you just change it?"

"Call me Robin . . . Rob Goodman, I mean, and hello?" He spread his arms, hands flicking inward then out to cover all of what I highly suspected he thought of as his glory and magnificence. He could be a televangelist. There was the same strong self-loving vibration coming off of him that I saw in quick flashes Sunday mornings as Cal channel surfed.

He repeated the "behold the splendor that is me" gesture, making sure I didn't miss it. "As I said, Versace. Oil, grease, and the essence of manual labor do not come out of Versace. Ah, idea." He fished out a wallet that was made of alligator, ostrich skin, velociraptor hide, who knew, I reflected bemused. The most exclusive of choices to be sure. "I'll pay you fifty dollars to change it for me. You look as if you could make use of fifty dollars." He was studying our clothing. The smile was gone now as he switched his gaze from us, stepping back on the porch to get a better look at the house that was held up by spit and the million husks of dead termites. I knew what he saw. I hadn't lived in better, you would think I'd be used to it—accustomed—think it normal, but I didn't. People didn't let you. People judged. People never failed to judge.

Poor. Worthless. Lacking.

Goodman's lips flattened and this time I couldn't read the emotion behind it. "You know, you're lucky. I'm in a hurry. Someplace I have to be. Important man, that's me. In constant demand. Busy, busy, busy. There would be hell to pay if I'm not . . . wherever. I'll pay you five hundred dollars to change the tire."

Charity.

I would rather he'd judged instead.

I had a thing about charity. Issues. We were clothed thanks to Goodwill and the Salvation Army. Our lunches at school were free thanks to the county. Half our furniture came off someone's curb or out of a Dumpster, but that didn't mean I liked it even when it was anonymous and to accept it from someone standing in front of me feeling pity for me, that I hated. The humiliation burned through me to curl down deep inside like an ill-tempered cat with claws slicing into my stomach.

I was about to refuse when Cal, who thought I was an idiot on the subject, intervened. Things were things, whether you scavenged them, bought them, or people were stupid enough to just give them to you. He had the same attitude about money. He snatched the five one-hundred-dollar bills out of Goodman's hand and elbowed me. "Nik, go on. Change the tire."

He elbowed me again when I didn't move and asked Goodman innocently, "What kind of watch is that? It's really cool. I don't have a watch. We're too poor." He drooped, a sad victim of a rapacious economy. His eyes had the bleak thousand-yard stare straight out of the pictures of children from Depression-era photos I'd seen in my history books. "I'm always late for school 'cause of it, the no watch. I miss so much class I can barely read. I'm shockingly illiterate. I'm afraid they'll

kick me out and I'll end up living in one of those cardboard boxes on the street." Finishing mournfully, he
added with the perfect touch of wistfulness, "I wish I
had a watch like that."

Goodman's smile was back and as amused as ever.
More so actually. It showed more brilliant white teeth
than a human being should have. With that in his arse-
nal, he'd leave Sophia in the dust when it came to swin-
dling a mark. "You're shockingly articulate to be so
shockingly illiterate. Nik? That's what your brother, Cal,
called you, correct? Nik, do you think you could change
my tire before your brother talks me out of my watch,
clothes, and future firstborn son?"

"It doesn't look like I have much choice." I didn't.
Pride had to bow before money that meant college and
that future I would make for us. "Naïve of you to assume he wouldn't get your car too though. And it's
Niko. Only Cal calls me Nik." I caught the keys he
tossed me and headed for the car.

There was a noncommittal hum that said Goodman
wasn't as worried or gullible as Cal believed. "Niko and
Cal. I don't suppose you want to tell me your last name."
Cal had shown his true colors when he'd opened the
door: suspicion personified in a pair of sneakers. I was
more subtle at showing it, but I was the same.

"What do you think?" I said mildly. They say what
people don't know won't hurt them. I said what people
don't know wouldn't hurt us. Cal's version was what
people don't know won't make him stab them in the
foot. Three different variations and all true.

Goodman wasn't offended by the answer. He wasn't

offended by Cal or me in any way and wasn't that peculiar? Particularly with what Cal was currently doing. "Fair enough," he replied as he moved his hand and wrist above Cal's head as small fingers had drifted with invisible stealth toward his watch. Almost invisible as Goodman saw the movement clearly.

Twenty minutes later the car was ready to go and so should've been Goodman, but he lingered several minutes talking about nothing whatsoever but making it somehow fascinating like con men do before he finally squared his shoulders as if he had an unpleasant task ahead of him. He was reluctant, I realized, to leave. He didn't want to go. Someone not wanting to leave us, there was a first.

That was definitely Cal talking, I thought with fond exasperation.

"Here's my card." He handed it to me. "If the two of you make it to the Big Apple in the next eight or so years and need a job, look me up. It's rare that I don't have some sort of business going. I'm an entrepreneurial soul. I can always use the help."

"You're not a car salesman?" I asked, surprised. With the Jaguar, the suit, and the whole Goodman experience, snake-oil mouth included, I'd finally mentally labeled him with that.

"Cars?" He gave an intrigued quirk of his lips. "I haven't done that yet. It's a thought."

I tucked the card in my pocket. "Eight years is a long time. You'll forget all about this."

He climbed behind the wheel of the Jaguar and flashed a wicked, knowing grin. "Eight years is nothing and I never forget anything I don't want to." He took a last look at our shack of a house and went solemn as quickly as if a switch had been flipped. "Life gives hard lessons to mold brave boys into great men." Eyes remaining grave, he gave one last smile. "Tell your brother to take good care of the watch."

Now I did smile. "It'll be pawned before your car makes it off the block."

He laughed. "Tell him to at least get three thousand for it. I paid ten." Then he was gone, the roar of the car's engine the only thing left. It hung in the air, a predator's lazy howl, even after the Jaguar disappeared from view. Strange guy. Nice enough, but . . . strange. Strange to be giving when I knew his kind were more into taking. Strange with the "I know you" and playing it off as if we reminded him of friends "gone but yet to come"? I knew an accidental truth when I heard it. He had thought he knew Cal and I'd seen and heard that same bloom of recognition with me. Strange that he'd want to help us years from now when most would forget us before they made it a mile down the road, because people generally weren't like that. People helped themselves and their own. Anything else would be as strange as Rob Goodman himself.

I pulled his card out of my pocket and bent the thick creamy stock between thumb and forefinger. It had been a strange experience altogether. It couldn't have been much stranger, if I thought about it.

"What a nut job," Cal proclaimed as he moved up beside me, holding up the watch to admire it in the afternoon sun.

"Maybe." I didn't necessarily agree, but as for Goodman's good-natured ways and his willingness to throw money around like beads at Mardi Gras: things that seemed too good to be true always were. Decision made, I let the card flutter from my hand into the garbage can at the curb.

If there was anything we didn't need more of in our lives, it was strange.

I picked up the lid Cal had left lying carelessly on the ground beside the can as always and wedged it in place. It was trash day Monday. That meant that I'd have to get up early, around three a.m. that morning, to make sure Junior didn't have Kithser's body stuffed in his own garbage can. Cal would insist.

The things you did for little brothers.

7

Cal

Present Day

The things you did for big brothers.

I gave a philosophical—a big word Nik had taught me—sigh as I tossed the man in the Dumpster face-first. Catching his kicking feet as he bellowed in rage, I snapped, "Stop dicking around. I'm trying to do a good thing here and that's not a big hobby of mine."

If anything, the flailing of the feet doubled. It wasn't as if I could hear what he had to say if he was choking on garbage anyway. I grabbed an ankle and yanked him back out to dump him on the cracked asphalt of the alley. Landing on his ass, he snarled and tried to scramble backward. "Hey, asshole, cut it out." I pulled my Desert Eagle from its holster under my jacket and pointed it at him. "That?" I nodded at the garbage container. "Wrong place. This?" I glanced at my watch. "Wrong time. Me?" My lips curled, then bared teeth in a wolfish grin. "Totally wrong fucking guy to mess with. Now stop moving and answer my damn questions."

This little interrogation was going down in broad daylight, but in this part of town, the fact I was holding a gun on a steroid-popping, greasy-haired semi-brain-dead shithead wasn't going to raise an eyebrow. If I got any reaction at all from a passerby, it'd probably be a thumbs-up and an offer to help dispose of the body for half the take. This guy had nowhere to go and nothing he could do.

Too bad he was too stupid to know that.

He propelled himself to his feet and charged me, fists swinging. They were big fists. He was a big man, but being big doesn't mean you can fight. You're only as good as the last ass you kicked. From the looks of him in motion that had been either a hundred-pound starved druggie or a five-pound ankle-biting pooch.

I could've ducked under his wild swing easy enough, but that meant his momentum would carry him toward the street. I'd have to chase him and while it would be a short chase as he was no better a runner than a fighter, I wasn't in the mood.

I'd been at this for hours, since the whorehouse pussycat had confirmed it was Jack peeling people like bananas. Nik had obtained a list of the victims from the Internet and split it between us. We didn't know if Jack thought all humans were wicked or there was an actual reason he was choosing particular victims. Nik was hoping for the latter. Catching a killer with a pattern would be a helluva lot easier than assuming every single human in NYC was fair game. We had skills, but bodyguarding millions of people nightly wasn't one of them.

That led me here to this particular piece of crap. There are some nuggets of info about the victims that news articles miss. You had to do it the old-fashioned way—talk to the friends and family. This was the first one I'd tracked down and I didn't know if his sister had been Jacko's definition of wicked, but her brother was covered head to toe in it. He was a bad, bad boy. I'd gone to the address Niko had traced from the victim's name, talked with the half-blind and wholly pissy grandma. She'd assumed I was a "customer" and told me Big Mike was at his regular spot. I'd been curious enough to ask how she'd known I wasn't a cop. Her cackled laughter had followed me down the three flights of tenement stairs.

When the half blind knew what you were and what you weren't, maybe it was time to stop calling it an identity crisis and just go with identity.

Big Mike was still coming for me with all the speed of a nearly dead, morbidly obese cow and I stepped to one side, extended my arm and clotheslined him. His neck hit my arm with a meaty thud and he was back down. I stood over him as he gasped for breath, his face turning faintly blue. I bent over and nudged him in the ribs with the silencer on my gun. "You know I train every day thanks to an anal-retentive brother? Nah, I know you don't, but I'm telling you. I could've broken your neck. I could've hit your nose and driven bone splinters up into what passes for your tiny brain. I could've kicked your testicles so far up into your body that you sneezed them out. But I didn't. I took you down with a move I saw on WWF, you pathetic sack of shit. Here's some advice: get a new job."

Big Mike's current job was drug dealer and occasional leg-breaker for anyone who needed that sort of thing. I glanced at my gun, snorted, and put it away. I'd planned on using it only for the fear factor, but I didn't even need it for that. I slapped the man's violet-colored cheek lightly. "This is how it's going to go, Mikey. When you can breathe again . . . *if* you can breathe again, you're going to tell me about your sister. What did she do before she was killed? What was she into? Was she like you or was she innocent?" After seeing Big Mike and his grandma, I was on the fence.

Nobody knew better than I did: sometimes genes do tell.

"Hooker," I said over the steaming plate of Chinese. "Sixteen and new to the trade. That's probably why it didn't make the news." Sixteen and a prostitute. I hadn't blamed her genes for that. I had blamed her brother though and thoroughly enough that the world's most dedicated plastic surgeon would pin up a picture of Frankenstein's monster to aim for as the best possible outcome.

I'd always known I was lucky when it came to brothers, but sometimes I forgot others didn't have that. It had been the one thing in my life I'd not once had to question and because of that might be my only true blind spot.

I stabbed at the orange chicken with my fork. I'd decided years ago that if you hadn't grown up with them in your hand, then chopsticks were for posers. The fact that I hadn't been able to learn to use them was coincidence. "Thanks," I added.

Niko, who could do that catch-a-fly-with-chopsticks thing and therefore not a poser, tipped his head slightly to one side. "For what?"

I shrugged as the loud chatter in the tiny restaurant ramped up another notch. There were cockroaches in the bathroom big enough to take a plunger to the toilet themselves if it stopped up, but nobody cared. The food, whether it had an antenna or two in it or not, was too good. "Just for doing the brother thing." And doing it in a way many brothers couldn't be bothered to. "What'd you find out?"

"Thief and rapist." He went for a square of tofu that shivered the same as a tiny cube of vomit-flavored Jell-O would. I grimaced and savored my chicken all the more. "I believe we have our pattern. Jack is targeting those with what some would consider to be wicked behavior and with no leniency for the unwilling, those who are actually victims."

I frowned, not completely convinced. "But that doesn't explain you. I mean, I get why Jack would want me if I were human. I'm a killer."

"And you think I'm not?" Niko raised his eyebrows.

I waved my fork, dismissing the words. "You're lethal as hell, I know, but you kill in self-defense or in defense of others. You drip nobility instead of sweat. You're Buddha, Jesus, Mother Teresa, and the Easter Bunny rolled into one. You shouldn't be on Jack's Naughty versus Nice list."

"You forget Cherish." His eyes were clear. He had killed Promise's daughter, but he didn't feel guilt over it. I would have known if he did. Damn good thing too. He had not a single reason to feel blame over her.

"She had the supernatural living version of a nuclear bomb and planned on using it. Hell, you saved the world, Nik. If that's not the definition of noble I don't know what is."

"She did, that's true, but that's not why I killed her. I killed her for revenge. For what I thought she'd done to you. For what she did do to me. And while she did fight, it wouldn't have mattered if she'd been unarmed. I would've killed her all the same." Matter-of-fact. He made no apologies.

I understood, and I was glad he did as well. Cherish hadn't been a person. She'd been a swirling void of sociopathic lies and murder. Whatever made a person or a *paien* what they were . . . their soul if souls existed in that way . . . she didn't have. She killed, manipulated, and then psychically brainwashed anyone who got in her way with visions so terrible they were capable of driving you mad. Niko hadn't killed her. He'd exterminated her. She'd had far less worth than one of those bathroom cockroaches and far less purpose on this earth.

Not to mention she was a serious bitch.

"Wish you'd let me come. Grabbed some popcorn and cheered from the sidelines. But whether you think that makes you a killer or not"—and it didn't—"Jack couldn't know about that. He just hit town. His victims now are obvious, right? He can see them spreading all that wicked far and wide. We haven't had a job in weeks. You haven't had to put anyone or anything down. There's nothing I can think of that would have him all over you. You should be innocent in his beady, psychotic eyes."

Niko passed me his fortune cookie—a tradition long-standing since the very first time we'd had Chinese food. "It makes no difference. In fact, if he continues to come after me, it would be convenient. Knowing his victims are on the shadier side of the law, moral and otherwise, doesn't make him much easier to locate. There are still too many. There are over ten thousand prostitutes alone in the city. There's certainly no way to shadow them all. And when you factor in thieves and rapists and murderers, whatever else Jack considers wicked, it's impossible. There simply is no way to track him down coming from that angle. But him coming to us, that is useful."

"Would be useful if we knew how to kill him or even touch the bastard. I can't do to Jack what I did to the peymakilir, not unless we're far, damn far away from him. The explosion would send those spikes of stone or crystal, whatever the fuck, that covers him flying. That's the kind of shrapnel you can't avoid or live through."

Suddenly the shadow of one righteously pissed off

brother was looming over me. He hadn't moved, the sun hadn't shifted its rays through the front window— how he managed to loom, I didn't know, but he did.

Unblinking eyes fixed on me and stayed. As far as Niko was concerned, the restaurant had disappeared. It was him and me and I was screwed. "Yes," he said softly and the word was worse for that unsettling softness. On Niko it was the pause and stillness the split second before a copperhead struck and pumped your veins with venom. Nik was my brother and he loved me, but that meant he'd do anything to keep me alive. Sometimes with me that took tough love—and a lot of it. "The peymakilir. I was saving this for home, but now that you've brought it up. There is absolutely no excuse for what you did to that creature, Cal, and you know it. I know you think you need to practice to face Grimm and you're most likely right, but that was not practice. That was reality."

The anger was gone as abruptly as it came. I expected that. Nik couldn't stay angry with me and, believe me, there were times he should have. Would've been better for the world if he did. So I wasn't surprised when it bled out of his face and eyes.

But what came in its wake was worse.

He reached across the table and looped his fingers around my wrist, holding my hand down against the table. The grip was immovable. "Do you feel that? The heaviness? It's the same in battle. You feel the consequences of killing in the weight of your gun, the heft of a blade. When you can kill with a thought, you put yourself beyond that." I wouldn't have thought it possible but the weight on my wrist and hand increased. "And beyond that, Cal, is the step you take to not fighting Grimm but being him."

Nik always said I never would become that. He wouldn't let me. I waited to hear that certainty again.

I didn't.

"When you were a child you would take some things on faith, even if you didn't understand why I asked you to do them." His set face softened, settling into lines of regret. I would've given a lot not to hear what he was saying, but he would've given anything at all not to have to say it. "You need to do the same now. What you're doing is . . . wrong." There was a brief hesitation but it was said firmly. With belief but not the kind of belief Niko had always had in me.

Wrong? Niko thought I was wrong?

"You've said if you became what you didn't want to be that I should stop you. Cal, look at me." I only realized as I heard it that I wasn't. I was looking past him, around him, anywhere but at him. Niko was my one true mirror and I didn't want to see myself there. Not now. "Cal." Reluctantly I moved my gaze back to his. I'd joked to myself about my identity crisis and now it was time to pay the piper.

And he didn't even know about the men by the Ninth Circle, the ones I'd thrown off the world before I'd kick-started my conscience into bringing them back.

His grip loosened and his thumb passed over the back of my hand; then his forefinger tapped it, the same as he'd done time and again when I'd been a child. "If your first instinct is to fight as an Auphe with gates and not as a human with guns and knives, you'll become too quick. I won't be able to stop you. But, Cal . . .

"You will be able to stop me," he ended.

There was no running. I didn't knock my chair over. I got up casually, if a little woodenly, and walked to the bathroom.

I didn't vomit in that bug-ridden restaurant bathroom either, but it was a near thing. Gagging and dry-heaving didn't count. Niko was doing what I'd asked him for years now. Watching me. Making sure I didn't become too much of a monster, because, face it, there was no escaping being somewhat of one. I didn't blame him for doing what I told him, for trying to save me before it came to that. I didn't blame him for anything. I blamed myself. For the first time in my life Niko thought I could hurt him. I'd known I could if the monster came. I'd known the monster would try. Cal would be gone and to the monster, to the Auphe in my place, Niko would only be meat in its way.

I'd known, but for the first time . . .

For the first time Niko accepted the truth. I'd told him he should, more times than I could remember, but I'd never meant it. I'd said it and I'd not once meant it, because I was a fucking coward.

His denial before had let me wallow in that same denial occasionally. Now that was gone. And denial. Jesus, denial is a fucking miracle of a thing. I had no idea how badly I'd miss it—need it like the air I breathed. I wanted it back. And I wanted Nik's blind faith in me back. The faith that while I could change and I could try to murder the entire world, that I would not do the same to my brother. I wanted to be able to see myself through his eyes and not see the constant potential of his blood on my hands.

But we all wanted something. I also wanted the old identity crisis back, because this new one was no goddamn fun. Life was like that. Hey, you over that whole tormented pity party about being a monster? You seeing the upside now? Feeling good about yourself? Yeah, that shit ain't happening on my watch. Now stand still while I rip out your guts and make you wish for the good old days when self-loathing was your favorite hobby. I have bigger plans for your fucked-up psyche now.

Fratricide—it's a big word, but say it with the class, Cal. There's a good boy.

I hung my head over the toilet and retched one more time. Then that luxury was over. Soon Nik would be kicking down the door and the manager would be calling the police.

He was giving me a moment, but it would pass. He'd think he'd broken me when it was the other way around. Okay, yeah, I had to give up a few patches of denial. Suck it up. Niko was giving up what he'd thought was the truth and having to live with a new one—his brother might not always be his brother.

That if that happened I could kill him with less thought than it took to make a gate.

Straightening, I grabbed a paper towel as cheap and rough as they came and dry-scrubbed my face hard enough to hurt. I wanted that tiny bit of pain. It distracted from the mass that roiled through me, a dirty whirlpool filled with the debris of doubt, fear, and the sharp and terrible thought that being a monster would be better. Easier. Painless.

That I'd process later. Actually, that wasn't me, not how I rolled. I would pack it away in one of those mental strongboxes and that would be good enough. Dealing was for heroes. I was no hero. For now I would do exactly as Nik told me. If that made Grimm the better Auphe, that was how it had to be. I would do anything, stop anyone who tried to hurt my brother and that included myself. I wasn't going to let it get to the point where Nik had to do it for me. I'd always asked him to be ready and it had not once been fair to put that weight on him. I was responsible. No one else. That he had to tell me was bad enough. How that felt for him, I couldn't imagine.

All I could do was make sure he didn't have to feel it again.

Tossing the wadded paper in the general direction of an overflowing garbage can, I reached for the door handle. Time to see if my brother needed gluing back together.

I underestimated him—mentally. I knew better than to underestimate him physically.

Rubbing my shoulder where it had impacted the wall instead of the mat, which was what I got for not paying attention, I grumbled, "Sneaky bastard."

Folding his arms, not a bead of sweat on him, he looked down at me with raised eyebrows. "Would you like to tell me what you did wrong with that particular move? Everything. Every single thing you did was utterly wrong."

"Isn't it usually?" I rolled from my side to my back, making no effort to get back to my feet. The sparring area of our converted garage apartment was generally the most humbling place around for me. Nik was right. If I stopped using the gates as first line of defense or offense—offensive on so many levels—that was me. If I did stop and then went sideways in the worst possible way, he could handle me—the same way he was handling himself now. With perfect ease.

Nik was good. Fine. Better than I'd begun to hope back at the restaurant.

I, conversely, wasn't doing such a bang-up job. Unless you counted the banging-into-the-wall part of the workout.

His eyes narrowed as he studied me. "You're thinking. When you should be thinking, you don't. When you shouldn't be, you do. Research puts you in a virtual coma. There have been times I'd have been tempted to check your pulse if I couldn't see your drool spreading over my antique books. And this"—his bare toe prodded the bottom of mine—"should be pure muscle memory by now, but your brain is bouncing so hard inside your skull that you ran into a wall simply because I stepped out of the way."

Flipping me over his shoulder—hell, nearly over his damn head—was not "stepping out of the way." But in our version of a sparring routine it was close enough to the truth that I let it slide.

Crouching next to me, he swatted the side of my

head. I'd been thinking all right and as usual Nik knew what about. "Do not be an idiot, little brother. You're still you. You told me you needed my help to keep you that way. I should've listened. I didn't, not like you needed me to. Now I know. I'm not humoring you any longer and that means I'll make damn certain you will stay Cal. Now and always." His lips quirked fondly as he gave me a light pat to the chest. "The once and future king of smart-ass."

Knowing the truth and feeling exactly the same about me, wasn't that better than denial? Hell, yes. It was the best. If you got that in your lifetime from anyone, you were damn lucky. Feeling an ugly knot of bristling barbed wire unwind itself in me, I grinned up at him. "You're getting your feelings all over me. It's disgusting."

"There are many times, uncountable really, that I've mentally replaced you in this scenario, Caliban. You can't imagine." Robin had drifted silently, as always, through our locked door to lean against the concrete wall and watch us.

"You're right. I can't imagine. Don't want to imagine. Your fantasies have to have been banned by the Geneva Conventions as psychological torture." I sat up. "And even you can't find being smacked and lectured a turn on."

The smirk was so rapacious I could see the neon XXX pop up over his head like in an old Acme cartoon . . . with an added huge dash of porn. "Do you think I've not been so naughty in my life that I didn't deserve some discipline?"

The images of Catholic uniforms, rulers, the principal's office—basically every porno cliché I'd seen in my life with the addition of Goodfellow and my brother shut down my brain instantly. For my own protection. Minutes later when it rebooted or whatever computers do when you turn them off and then back on after kicking them viciously, I was still sitting on the mat and Niko and Robin were talking about Jack.

"No," the puck was saying. "I've had no luck. The *paien* community wants nothing to do with him. They've a good track record of they leave him alone and he sticks to humans for the entire skinning and horrific deaths situation. If they knew anything, which they don't, they wouldn't help. They're quite big on survival instinct."

Niko had sat down on the couch to pull his socks back on. He made that simple action look deadly. Considering how many times he'd threatened to kill me with one of them, that wasn't surprising. "Cal and I did find out some further information on his victims. They were all involved in behavior that the strictly moral with no shades of gray could find objectionable. There is no centralized location from where he chose them however."

Goodfellow frowned. At least he wasn't looking at Nik's feet. A foot fetish might've finished me off right there. "That will make him impossible to hunt down. Over eight million people in the city and call me cynical, but you can take it to the bank at least four million are doing something morally objectionable in Jack's eyes. Even jaywalkers aren't safe. Some hipster might dine and dash and be skinned before he had a chance to digest that stolen appetizer. There isn't any possible way to anticipate where he might go and his next victim. There simply is no way to narrow it down." Then a smile flashed across his face. It was more lascivious than the one he'd given while watching the aftermath of our workout.

"I was wrong. There might be one place that would draw him in. I had my annual reminder in my e-mail this morning." The smile widened far enough that I didn't need to worry about Jack. My skin was ready to leap off my body and leave without me all on its own.

"Oh God," I said involuntarily.

"Keep that thought. You'll be saying it repeatedly over the next few hours. Get dressed." He frowned. "There will be a pat down involved. Weapons might be a problem. And, Niko, any coat like your dusters that resemble trench coats well loved by flashers will probably be frowned on."

"Oh God," I repeated. "Let Jack have New York. We'll move."

Goodfellow slapped my shoulder. "Be brave. We're going on a field trip."

The Javits Convention Center was hardly a field trip, but what was inside was a different world, I'd give the puck that. We'd come to the sane conclusion that we'd need our weapons if Jack did show up. That meant getting into the center via a fire door locked from the outside and avoiding security while getting the badges necessary to wander around without paying for them.

For a trickster that took less than ten minutes.

That there was a storm system brewing above looked promising on the Jack front, but what was inside was so much more promising I may have forgotten about Jack temporarily.

I moved through a not particularly busy crowd but a very enthusiastic one and did my best not to walk right over anyone who stopped in front of me because my attention was elsewhere. Too many elsewheres to keep track of.

"What did you say this was called again?" Niko asked Robin as they walked beside me. That's where it sounded like they were, best guess. I wasn't going to waste any of my vision on them to confirm it. My vision was all booked up, thank you very much.

"The Triple-Xpo. It's a yearly event that applauds quality in the adult film industry and the sexual lifestyle industry that goes with it," Goodfellow replied as smoothly as if he were president of it all. Hell, he probably was.

"Ah," Niko said at the same time I summed it up. "Porn stars." And they were everywhere. This was a thousand times better and easier than trying to stake out ten thousand prostitutes, most of them in Brooklyn.

There was no ducking the smack to the back of my head. I didn't even try. "You are to respect these women and their career choices," Nik told me firmly.

"I have nothing but gratitude in my heart for each and every one of them," I said truthfully. "Do you know how long it's been since I broke it off with Delilah?" If that's what you called threatening to shoot your sociopathic, murder-spree-bound werewolf friend-with-benefits—broke it off, gun to the head. To-mato, ta-mato. "These women have gotten me through a very difficult period in my life. God bless them, each and every one."

We were meandering through a maze of booths where actresses and models autographed pictures and nobody was naked, which was more than I could say about most of the people that I'd met through Goodfellow, especially in his premonogamous days when I'd make sure to call before I dropped by his place to prevent the awkwardness of walking in on an orgy. That had happened several times, more than it ever should to someone just wanting to hang out, watch a game, and have a beer.

There were also booths that sold "toys." Toys for adults and I left it at that. I had no interest in toys. Nature had given me all the toys I needed.

"This reminds me of a time when the three of us were in Greece for the bacchanalia," Robin mused with a lascivious grin, "and . . . ah, I meant when I was in Greece with some friends of mine. Fertility rites, drinking, festivals, plays. Of course this was before the modern miracle of silicone, but nonetheless, very good times." He lifted a hand in a casual wave. "Ah. Savannah, lovely as ever," Goodfellow addressed as we passed an autograph booth with a woman with dark hair, wry blue eyes, and a pixie smile.

"Robin!" She waved enthusiastically.

"Lisha," he called at the next booth. She lifted her head from the fantasy book with a dragon and a head on a pike decorating the cover that she was reading between autographs.

"Robin!" She said his name like a four-year-old would say "Santa Claus."

"Miranda Lee." That was the next booth. Blonde, freckles. The girl-next-door type who was about to eat her dinner. New York's biggest cheeseburger.

It went on like that for several minutes until it ended with a run of platinum blondes.

"Robin!"

"Amber."

"Robin!"

"Amber."

"Robin!"

"Amber!"

"Robin!"

"All right, enough." Niko took Goodfellow's collar and urged him at a faster speed while I marveled at how many Ambers there were in the business. "Yes, we're very impressed. You know every woman—"

"And man. Don't be sexist," Robin interrupted.

"Fine. And man in the business," Niko went on, "but we are here to find Jack. He wouldn't attack someone in the middle of this exhibition hall. It would be beyond noticeable. We need to find a secluded spot where those he judges so harshly might pass while alone and unseen." I heard the faint clank of metal in Niko's coat as he moved. Whether he'd be mistaken for a flasher or not, he had to have the coat to cover his katana and cover up the various other blades on him.

"Very well." Robin pulled free and straightened his

suit jacket. "Although it wouldn't hurt you to learn to enjoy yourself while on the job. Shop for a gift for Promise. She's hundreds of years old and has gone through five elderly husbands in the past fifteen of them. Do you think she might not want something to tuck away in the nightstand drawer for nights when you're not there or for nights when you *are*—"

Nik snared the handful of suit collar again and this time dragged the puck along. "This looks familiar," I drawled. "Oh yeah, you're usually doing that to me."

"I have two hands. Do not test me." He moved faster yet and I had to pick up the pace as he and Goodfellow began to leave me behind. In minutes we'd left the color, noise, and milling people behind us and were down a hall Robin knew had an available bathroom only those familiar with the convention center would know of.

"The guest stars are here every year. They've sussed out the nooks and crannies and where best to go and not be bothered by a persistent mouth-breather. There are occasionally those who aren't as respectful as they should be. This is the most remote of those locations." There'd been three such remote locations but with two hastily improvised OUT OF ORDER signs, we'd whittled it down to one. Goodfellow was keeping his distance from Nik while staring morosely at the wrinkles in his jacket.

Leaning against the wall by a very sad plastic potted tree, I asked, "We're staking out a bathroom for a monster? I read *Dracula* and I remember Van Helsing doing some impressive shit, but that wasn't one of them," I snorted. Niko lifted an eyebrow at the statement and I revised it. "Okay, I *watched Dracula*, the old one with that guy from *The Matrix*, and I don't remember anyone in that looming outside a bathroom either."

"I despair of you. I honestly do. I didn't make you read *Dracula*, a classic, while homeschooling you because you said it made you uncomfortable. That it reminded you of the Auphe."

I grinned. "Lying to get out of homework. I feel bad, Cyrano. No teenager would do that. What was I thinking?"

"Eighteen was far too soon to let you graduate. I don't know what I was doing all those years ago. I should still be assigning you research papers on a weekly basis and hiding your guns until you complete them." He leaned against the wall with arms crossed, but feet planted and spread slightly for balance. Always ready—on bathroom duty or not. After all these years it still didn't fail to impress. I was wondering when a copy of *Dracula* would appear on my pillow when I had a chance to be impressed further.

There was a scream, a banging of the door at the end of the hall, and a woman with long brown hair came running past us, her face gray with terror. She was blind with it. She didn't see the three of us as she ran between us. The only thing that registered was escape, the end of the hall, the people she'd left behind for a quiet moment to herself. Whatever was after her was horrifying enough that three people would be no help to her. She needed the three thousand in the exhibition hall.

"Jack," I said, pulling my Glock with a silencer in deference to the crowd several hallways away.

Jack it was. He came boiling through the door, ripping it free, buckling the metal and tossing it across the hall to bounce off the wall and then slam onto the floor. The hall wasn't as well lit as the rest of the place, but it became less so as half the lights fried from the electrical discharge that simmered in the air around the storm that was Jack.

"Where flees the adulteress?" His voice was all that I remembered it being—disgusting and spine-chilling for a reason I couldn't put my finger on. "Where goes the wicked one?"

"That was Mandy," Goodfellow said as he unsheathed his sword from his own long coat that hung over his suit Nik had traumatized him by creasing. "She is married, but her husband is in the business, and is it adultery if it involves your occupation and the party of the first and the party of the second both consent to said parameters of the relationship?"

"Be grateful he doesn't know Shakespeare," Niko grunted, his own katana already in hand. " 'First kill all the lawyers.' "

"Every trickster, pucks or others, has a law degree. It's the perfect con." Robin was trying for cheerful, but seeing Jack for the first time and having heard our story of failure of all our weapons against him, the cheer was strained.

Jack filled the back of the hall entirely. The destroyed lights and his own inherent darkness made him the same form impossible to pin down. Mist, fog, shadows, sparks that circled like a whirlwind within him and two oval-shaped eyes that were the last color you'd see if you were an unlucky bastard standing outside when a bolt of lightning struck you from an overcast sky. He was everything and he was nothing, all in one, and that was a problem. You can't fight everything and you can't fight nothing.

"What the fuck." I just shot him seven times. Shooting him hadn't worked when he'd attacked me in my room, but I liked to think two of my best qualities were persistence and the ability to hold on to resentment to my dying day. And I did resent Jack for showing up at one of the least convenient times in my life—especially when I'd been ready to give him a pass and ignore his existence.

The bullets disappeared into the tempest and Jack didn't react, same as before. Niko was on him then, katana moving in an arc of sheer quicksilver beauty. It struck Jack and the force of whatever it hit threw Nik back several feet. He managed to land on his feet, growled, and attacked again.

"This is not your time. This is not your turn," Jack said thickly . . . so thickly it sounded as if he had a mouthful of shit, blood . . . or the skin he was so fond of taking. That's what bothered me. A storm spirit should sound like the wind or the rushing train of an incoming tornado, not as if he had a mouthful of fresh, blood-soaked flesh.

"I am coming for you, but now the wickedness of the adulteress." The rest of the lights exploded but there was enough drifting in from the entrance of the hall to see that Jack hadn't gone. His electric-chair eyes were bright and hovering in the blackness.

"You were right. He is quite annoying." Goodfellow was at Niko's side now, both swinging blades at Jack.

"Go right and get down," I shouted. Over the strike of metal against God knew what and the rising sound of wind and the sizzle of electricity, it was getting loud. We wouldn't be alone here much longer. As Niko and Robin went flat on the floor, I raised my other gun. I had the explosive rounds custom-made by naughty people for the Desert Eagle. Time to see if they worked any better on Jack than normal rounds did. I fired high and to the left. I waited for the explosion—when it came to explosive rounds you didn't worry about a silencer. You shot and you ran like hell before the cops showed up.

I knew the round had hit Jack and I waited, but I heard nothing. Not a muffled thud, positively no explosion. I fired again, and again nothing. I'd have heard more if I'd chugged a marshmallow at him.

Then it was Jack's turn. He turned the hall into . . . hell. I was struck by something. I didn't know if it was Jack himself or the force of a hurricane, but I was slammed from wall to wall, up to the ceiling, then back down to the floor. It hurt, distantly, because what I was thinking over all that was that I couldn't breathe. All of the oxygen, all of the air itself was sucked out of the hall and my lungs did more than burn. I felt them almost collapse from the negative pressure. It couldn't have been a complete negative pressure or they would have, but it was close enough to leave me sprawled on the floor, half believing I was dying and wholeheartedly wishing I would. It would be less painful.

After moments or minutes, I couldn't tell, my lungs were slowly beginning to cooperate again. Bit by bit. It was a long time before I was breathing anything close to normal and it would've been longer before I remotely thought about trying to get up, but Goodfellow was slapping my face hard and yanking at my arm. "Humans," he muttered. "You depend far too much on breathing as often as you do. Cal, up. We need to go before Mandy brings back every man, woman, and security guard who swings a mean dildo."

Niko appeared on the other side of me, took that arm, and between them, they had me on my feet. "All right, little brother?"

I wasn't going to get into it with Nik over how meditation taught him control over his breathing and therefore he could recover faster than I could. I'd let him have this one, no argument. "Anyone . . . else . . . hit . . . the . . . ceiling?" I gasped as they hurried me along down a different set of halls toward yet another exit only Robin knew about.

"Yes, that was unpleasant," Niko replied, tucking my Eagle back into my holster as he and Goodfellow slung one of my arms over each of their shoulders in order to move more quickly.

"Rather like I imagine clothing would feel in a dryer—if I were poverty stricken and didn't have everything I own including my Armani socks dry cleaned." Robin gave me a concerned glance as we exited into the night. "Did you get that, Cal? I'm incredibly wealthy and snobbish to boot. Aren't you going to comment?"

It was nice when people cared enough to rub your nose in their high-and-mighty lifestyle in an effort to provoke you and determine you're not brain damaged from hitting the ceiling. "Fuck you," I mumbled, my legs working better now that my breathing kept improving.

His lips curved upward in relief. "There's the ass we know and barely tolerate. Of course there's no need to believe a mere ceiling would make an impression on your brother, Achilles reborn."

"Jack will have moved on," Niko said. "We've spoiled his one opportunity to take someone unseen. There is much light and too many people currently rushing about looking for a mysterious attacker for him to be able to accomplish anything further here. This hunting ground is ruined for him. We may as well go home and try again tomorrow."

"Great." I tried standing while Goodfellow hailed a cab. "Maybe we should get some oxygen tanks."

Or, as I'd thought before, move the hell out of New York.

The next afternoon I felt surprisingly not too bad. Niko and I both had plenty of bruises, but nothing broken. That was the good news. The bad news was Goodfellow was back and we were having the same conversation we'd had yesterday before the cluster-fuck with Jack. Considering where we'd been while having it, clusterfuck could have several meanings, but I wasn't about to say that aloud and have Niko threaten to spar political correctness in me if it took him and my aching muscles the rest of both our lives.

"That was the last day of the convention," Robin sighed, playing with one of Niko's knives in the workout area. He was uncannily talented in hitting the crotch on the silhouette printed on the paper targets. "There is nothing else in the city like that right now. Nothing I could think of large enough that it would be guaranteed to draw in Mr. Judgmental."

"He does seem to have some unknown problem with us or me now that Cal is off his menu," Niko reminded. "And he did say my turn—or our turn, as Cal has annoyed him greatly and he'll kill him for that alone—was yet to come. But we can't depend on that to have him show up anytime soon. He could commit unlimited more murders before he decides to pay another visit. We can't wait."

I was sprawled on the couch and reaching for the TV remote when I had a tickle in the base of my brain—the lizard hindbrain where violence and fun are one and the same. "I have an idea."

Niko blanched, visibly as he hadn't done at Goodfellow's plan. To be fair, he'd heard and gone along with more of my ideas over the years. His recovery, as they say, was ongoing. "I'd prefer you didn't."

"Have some faith." This could be good. "He doesn't like the ethically challenged or the morally conflicted, right?" It was a shame he didn't want me as I had all of that with a cherry bomb on top. "Fine. Since we can't narrow down crime, let's go *make* some crime. A big one, one he can't possibly ignore."

"Please do not tell me what you have in mind." Nik pinched the bridge of his nose. "I am not a begging man, but, Cal, please."

My grin was so wicked I was almost disappointed Jack didn't appear and promptly skin it right off my face. "Let's burn some shit down. A whole lot of shit."

I didn't often come up with the plans, too lazy, but when I did, they were frigging spectacular. When it came to devastation and destruction . . .

I was a genius.

8

Niko

Twelve Years Ago

"I've got an idea," Cal announced.

"No. We are not searching that man's basement for dead bodies. No. Now do your homework."

"You don't know I was going to say that." He carefully folded one page of his English textbook into half of a paper airplane. "But if I was going to say that, it's totally genius." He then folded the opposite page the same way for one complete bound and grounded paper aircraft. Where were Orville and Wilbur Wright when you needed them?

There was no doubt he was a genius.

Genius at avoiding homework. Genius at taking a bite of an idea, clamping down his jaws, and never letting go. Genius at making me want to bang my forehead repeatedly against the kitchen table where we sat.

I glared at him. It wasn't a painless or guilt-free effort, not after checking the bottle-inflicted bruise on his chest fifteen minutes ago, but I did it. "I do know that's what you were going to say. I know how your ball bounces. I also know that is not how we treat books. Are you trying to be difficult?"

He shook his head, shaggy hair flying, the grin shameless. "Nope. Not trying. Don't have to. It's really pretty easy."

I pushed the sandwich on the plate toward him. Two pieces of bologna, three of cheese, sweet-and-sour pickles, mayonnaise, ketchup, and mustard, it was his current favorite. Mystery meat and lard, but we'd gone to the grocery to spend some of the money the rich guy had given me for changing his tire. That deserved a celebration, for at least a few days, of whatever we wanted. We'd already had two pizzas instead of the usual one and now Cal was making his way through whatever the janitors swept off the slaughterhouse floor.

It was a good day—when I managed not to see bruises blotting the pages of my own textbooks when my attention wandered. Closing my eyes momentarily, then watching Cal work his way through his first sandwich with the manners of a starving pig tended to make the black-and-purple blotches disappear. Lack of table manners and Cal were linked to reassuring and normal in my brain. That let me say, yes, today was mostly a good day. Sunday, our last day before we had to be back at school, and I would've liked it serial killer free. But with Cal and his bulldog teeth firmly embedded in his theory, that wasn't going to happen.

I did trust Cal's instincts on the majority of things, but he was eleven. He'd seen monsters, the genuine horror movie article. He'd seen people behave in ways most average adults couldn't comprehend, knew things most adults saw only on the news or on after-school specials. That was our life. We were a walking, talking PSA filmed by Wes Craven. Through it all, though, he'd stayed a triumph of sanity over endless shit.

Sometimes life did deserve a curse word or two.

But . . . the bottom line remained, he was eleven. Paranoid and cynical and with every right to be, yet still eleven. Once in a while eleven-year-olds jumped to wild conclusions. I'd talked to Junior. I didn't automatically think he was innocent. It'd been years since I'd made that assumption about anyone from a casual hey-how-are-you? He might be innocent, he might not. He might be innocent of murder, but less innocent of other things. He certainly didn't seem very bright. Calling the police on him because Cal thought his house smelled bad? It didn't seem right.

And I did want to do what was right. Right thinking. Right action. Right speaking. Just as many of the sensei and masters of the dojos and gyms taught. It wouldn't be right to tarnish the reputation of an innocent man and it was hard to do what was right in our world. If I didn't try, every day, then one day it would become too hard to do right and very easy to do wrong. What kind of role model would I be then to Cal?

With Sophia the lines of wrong had already blurred

drastically. I wanted, needed to hang on to keeping all
the right I could in my life to balance that out. Even the
smallest of good acts helped, each from a pebble to a
massive stone that built the wall that kept me clean
from the world we lived in now. Our world, Cal's and
mine, was not clean. We both were dealing the best we
could. He bounced back, no matter what, and I built
walls.

Then there was the police. If our neighbor was guilty
of something lesser such as drugs or having three
wives who didn't leave the house, because I couldn't
buy uncatchable serial killer in the muddy dimness of
his eyes, the police would come. It wouldn't matter
that the call was anonymous—they'd knock on all the
doors, question everyone. I didn't like to lie, Cal didn't
care either way, but through sheer osmosis from sharing the deceit-heavy air she breathed we'd both learned
to do it well from Sophia.

But cops were all different. Some were indifferent,
some polite and easy to fool, but some were razor sharp
and they'd slice though the paper tower of lies we lived
in. There would be a ruin of confetti the color of ashes
at our feet before we knew it if we ran into one of those.
They were rare, but there were cops who could take
one look at the two of us or worse, if Sophia was
around, the three of us and know at first glance how
dysfunctional our "family" was. They would know we
were left alone for weeks at a time no matter how clean
we were and well behaved Cal pretended to be. They'd
seen it before a thousand times, and maybe, like Cal,
they could actually *smell* it on us. Taste the unbreakable

codependency in the air—the kind that happened when it was only the two of you against everything else including your own mother.

There were teachers like that too and four years ago one had a social worker on the way to Cal's school on his first day in the new town. She'd been moving across the parking lot toward him at the same time I'd showed up to walk him home.

I'd grabbed Cal's hand, yanked him into motion and we ran. The teacher was sharp, the social worker was sharp, but neither were nearly as experienced as we were at running. Sophia was as eager to go. She had the same amount of desire to spend time in jail for neglect as Cal and I wanted to spend separated in foster homes. None.

I didn't know what Junior was doing in his house. I doubted anything—he barely had the brainpower to tie his bathrobe, but even if he was up to something, the police were a last resort. Only if our backs were to a metaphorical bloodstained wall. It was too risky. We were good runners and disappearing came as second nature to us now, but it takes only one time. One mistake. One trip over your own feet. If that happened, I might not see Cal again, no matter how long I looked, how hard I tried.

Grendels . . . monsters outside our window, that I could handle. They only watched so far. The police—the state—the government, there was nothing I'd learned in a dojo that would make the fear of them any less.

"Nik, it's a good idea. It is. We can wait until he's gone, break in through one of the windows, drag a body out on the front sidewalk and let someone else call the cops on him. Genius."

I sighed and reached across the table to wipe the mayonnaise/mustard mustache off his upper lip. "Cops . . . policemen, I mean . . . aren't good." I back-tracked. "They are good, but . . ."

Cal gave me the look again. I'd gotten it so often in the past few days I was going to start assuming anything that came out of my mouth was so utterly ignorant that it made Cal's very brain cells melt under the vast stupidity of it all. And what I'd been about to say was stupid. He knew as much as I did how badly things could go if the police looked too closely at us.

I held up both hands. "Sorry. I underestimated your enormous brain. You can have an extra cookie for dessert."

Mollified, Cal started wiping mustard off his plate, licking it off his finger, and rocking back and forth on the back two legs of his chair. Multitalented, that was my brother. "We should move. Now. You have that nut job's money. Sophia can find us when she comes back." He shrugged. "Or not."

I wished "or not," but she'd already made it clear to us both if I left with Cal she would find us and she would involve social services, do jail time, whatever it took. Cal was an investment. If I wanted him, I was going to have to pay for him. Cal knew, he remembered, but memories were the twilight of lost hopes. In the bright of the day, they could be banished . . . for a while.

"How about this: we'll go to the library"—because

we weren't going to have a computer of our own unless we stole it—"and research the victims. We'll see if there's a pattern to where they've been taken." There. That had to satisfy him. It made it clear I wasn't dismissing him and it kept him from breaking into our neighbor's house. This was all Kithser's fault. If he hadn't disappeared, Cal would've stayed on his live and let live as long as the serial killer's not killing you personally policy. But Kithser was too close. If he had only run off with his drug dealing loser friends, I'd be tempted to kill him myself for putting me in this situation.

"Boring." His chair finally tipped too far and began to topple backward. I'd been waiting for it. I hooked an ankle around one wooden leg and caught it. After fifty plus times it was pure instinct now. Cal, who knew I wouldn't let him fall, had never let him fall, kept talking, unfazed. "Let's follow him."

"Research," I contradicted firmly. I'd disproved a hundred things in papers for school over the years with it. I could disprove a serial killer too.

"Following him would tell us for sure. You said we need to be sure."

"I know what I said and I know what I'm saying now." I settled his chair upright. "Research, grasshopper. Absolutely no following."

"How did this happen?" I hissed out loud as my hands white-knuckled on the steering wheel. If I'd kept the question mental, I thought the stress and humiliation of being outthought by an eleven-year-old might trigger some sort of psychotic split. I'd read some advanced psychology books. They hadn't said that could happen, but it was an imperfect science at best. They didn't know everything.

"I lied to Mrs. Spoonmaker about your age and you offered to get her oil changed. You were right there, Nik." Cal was digging in the ancient glove compartment looking for candy bars or cookies in what was a habit so ingrained I didn't remember when it started. Dogs humped legs. Cal sought sugar. Two universal laws. "How do you get straight As? You can't remember anything.

"Cool!" He popped up with a petrified package of Ho Hos. "Besides, your research sucked. We didn't find out anything except people at the public library are doing things in the bathroom they should do at home."

"I told you to wait for me on the bathroom trips," I said—a little more loudly than it needed to be said, but that good day I'd been savoring this morning was gone. Cal had driven a stake through its bright and sunny heart.

"You were glued to the computer, like, literally, superglue between your eyeballs and the screen and I had to go. So I went to the women's just in case. Women can be perverts too. Who knew?"

That was a discussion for . . . not now. My knuckles turned whiter, if possible, under my darker skin as I tried to tail Junior's beat-up pickup truck with a grimly dark camper, the serial killer–mobile as Cal was calling it, without being made in a giant metallic green Cadillac born long before I was. "And the research did not fail. It showed the people are disappearing from an area approximately fifteen miles in radius and no bodies have been found."

"Yeah, you showed me the map with all the colors and miles and stuff. It was a big blob. On TV they're a perfect circle, like a bull's-eye, and the killer's house is right in the center." I heard a distinct crunch as he bit into a Ho Ho, the kind of crunch icing and cake aren't supposed to make.

"Now you see why I tell you to stop watching so much TV." I sighed and wove around a BMW. I'd learned to drive when I was twelve. It was a useful skill for picking up passed-out mothers at bars before the police came sniffing around. "But"—as much as I hated to admit it and I honestly did—"Junior's house is inside 'the blob.' The outer part of it, but it's there." But so were a lot of very bad people, cheap and unsafe, how we always lived. "Which is why I let you talk me into following him." And at night, making this area more risky if possible.

Along the rooftops of the cinder block–style apartment buildings I saw a Grendel racing along, our pale shadow. I wondered if it was curious. I wondered for the thousandth time why they watched. And I thought, with the denial of all that is wrong in the world, that it might be better not knowing.

I looked away and back at the street. "Now finish cracking your teeth on what used to be food and let me concentrate." Then because I felt bad about letting Cal lie to Mrs. Spoonmaker, I muttered under my breath, "I think I'll get her car washed too."

Cal knew the signs of my guilt. In knowing me there wasn't much Cal didn't pick up on instantly. "Isn't lying to borrow her car better than letting a murderer kill somebody?"

He wasn't wrong. Cal had grasped the gray shades of morality before he grasped potty training. I was different. But I was learning. Too late and too slow, but I'd get there.

"Look! He stopped." Cal bounced in the seat as if we were two rogue cops about to make a bust. I was throwing out the TV when we got home. In the trash. I rolled, yes, *rolled* down the window for a better look. The car's windows were permanently cloudy from age. Cal followed my action because when it came to things not involving work that's what Cal and most little brothers did. "He's picking up a whore."

I reached over and flicked his ear lightly. "Not a good word." But I was also watching Junior talking out the window to a woman selling it for what looked like a harsh drug habit. Even in the night and where only one out of three streetlights worked, that was easy to see. She had a long black Goth wig, short leather dress with fishnet hose and skin yellow with hepatitis.

"Ow. Hooker?"

I flicked again.

"Prostitute?"

"Better. Not too great for her, but better vocabulary wise."

I saw movement out of the corner of my eye and a gun was in my face as a snarling twist of a mouth and mad dog eyes demanded my money. Beside me Cal sounded as if he were choking on his Ho Ho. "This," I told him, "is not funny."

The man, boy, whatever he was—that far into the downward slide into drugs it was hard to tell—shoved the gun closer. He hadn't even bothered to get a pellet gun and paint the orange tip. He'd gone for painting a *water gun*. I was embarrassed for him. But not so embarrassed that I didn't break his wrist and shove the gun in his mouth, grip first. Less room and more of a lesson learned that way.

There was another one coming from the opposite side . . . toward Cal. From the way he moved, belligerent but uncertain, he was unarmed. Good practice then. "Cal, time for school." He accepted the knife I handed him. It wasn't his kitchen knife, which I'm sure was on him somewhere. This was a K-BAR combat knife with a happy smile of serrated edges. I'd be passing it down to Cal when he was big enough to carry it and it not be instantly obvious under his clothes.

"Finally. Some fun homework." Cal already had the knife in the practiced grip I'd taught him, parallel to his body with the edge toward the throat that presented itself.

"You little shit. Tell the bastard driving to hand over his money or I'll tear you . . ." It took the kid, about sixteen and skinnier than the first, that long to realize he could feel the faint trickle of blood down his throat and metal resting against his skin.

"I'm hungry and Ho Hos aren't enough," Cal said cheerfully. "How about you give me all your money so I can get a Big Mac and I won't cut your throat?"

"Cal," I said reprovingly, but the kid was already gone, his partner with him and unfortunately Junior's truck as well as we'd sat at the curb looking like easy prey. "We don't mug or steal and we don't hurt people unless it's absolutely necessary."

"I know." He bounced again. "But his *face*." He laughed and handed the knife back to me, not pretending he didn't covet it. "People can be so stupid. I betcha when he tells his friends how it happened I'll be seven feet tall and so full of muscles I almost couldn't fit in the car."

"Rambo in the most cunning disguise." I started back down the street searching for Junior's truck. I didn't spot it again until we were at home. There it sat in his driveway. I groaned. "Hookers . . . I mean, prostitutes disappear every day for different reasons. I'll check the papers for the next few days, but even then, we won't know."

"You won't know." A hand patted my arm as we crossed the street. "You're smart, Nik, but sometimes I don't think you'd know the house was on fire 'cause you were waiting for the oven timer to beep. You think too hard about the little things and not about the big things."

Cal smiled happily and it wasn't a good kind of happy, not for me. I'd seen this particular brand before. I tensed myself for what was coming. It would be painful and it would make my brain hurt, but there was no getting around it. Cal's mouth could not be stopped.

"Hey, you know what? We could burn down his house."

9

Cal

Present Day

I liked fire.

Not in a sick arsonist burning down a nunnery full of kittens way. But if something had to be burned down or up or sideways, I didn't mind being involved. It was better than fireworks and no annoying noise . . . or not until the fire trucks arrived.

"It's an abandoned bridge. Yeah, they were going to fix it up but of course they haven't gotten around to it." I waved a hand at the Google Earth pictures Niko had printed off . . . never mind, we all knew what High Bridge over the Harlem River looked like already. "It's stone and metal. Can't burn that. But we can get a garbage truck, soak the garbage in diesel fuel for more smoke and a longer burning time, push our way through the concrete barriers off Amsterdam Avenue with the truck, drive onto the bridge, dump the garbage, light her up with my flamethrower, and torch the fucker. Or at least half of it. We need the other half to fight on. If Jack Sprat doesn't notice that then we'll get him a Seeing Eye dog and forget worrying about his homicidal and *blind* ass."

This was perfect and going right at the top of my resume.

"You cannot have come up with that on the spur of the moment," Niko protested with what sounded a good deal like suspicion and hope mixed into one. I tried to get a fix on whether he was proud or appalled. I was hoping for both. I did love to mess with Nik.

"Sometimes I get bored. When I get bored, bam, mental mass destruction is my hobby. I've had this one on file for a while now." Did I say that smugly? A little. I asked Goodfellow as Niko appeared too scarred for words, "It's a gift, yeah?"

"It is that. I could not be more proud if you were a trickster yourself. I wish you'd been around for the whole Trojan horse event." Something wistful and somewhat secretive shifted behind his expression but he kept that gleeful grin on his face. "Somehow there would've been at least a thousand pounds of flaming horse manure involved. Homer would've loved penning that part of the tale." He took out his cell. "Garbage truck. Give me three minutes."

"You can locate a full garbage truck for us in three minutes?" Niko sounded curious despite his automatic caution. After a few years the combination of Robin and me was beginning to send him into Stockholm Syndrome I thought. About time. It would be better for his mental health if he closed his eyes and enjoyed the roller-coaster ride.

Robin smirked. "In five minutes I could find you a tanker truck of boysenberry-flavored self-warming body oil and six men and women willing to apply it. Care to put it to the test?"

While he made his call, I was digging out the fruits of one of my own from under my bed. I'd made the call last night after our encounter with Jack to my weapons supplier, Rapture. She'd recently added delivery service—you got your weapons in an hour or ten percent off . . . and as always a free cupcake from the bakery that served as a front to the best weapons dump in the tri-state area. That was what I loved about NYC. You could get anything delivered.

I'd decided to up the ante, weapons-wise. Since explosive rounds didn't work and I couldn't open a gate and turn Jack into an explosion himself, the bastard, for fear of turning us or innocent bystanders into the annoying potential of hamburger-textured collateral damage, I went with a nice piece I'd been going to hit up Nik for Christmas. An MP7A1 Heckler and Koch submachine gun with suppressor. Compact, not quite twice the size of my Desert Eagle and with the added bonus of forty armor-piercing rounds. If that didn't make a dent in Jack, I didn't know what would. He was too damn fast to depend on the leftover grenades I'd also shoved under my bed.

Oh yeah. I made another grab. We needed the flame-thrower. This was shaping up to be a party.

"I have the garbage truck and the location to pick it up." Robin disconnected his cell and checked his watch. "Two minutes forty-five seconds."

Niko gave Robin and me both a curdled expression: Goodfellow with his smugness and me with an armful of weapons meant to make people go dead in the night. "I know the two of you want me to praise your excellence in thievery and your preparation to kill anything that might escape *Jurassic Park*." I did love that movie. "But any encouragement on my part would only push you to greater heights and the eventual destruction of Western civilization. I'm going to get dressed. Cal, unless you want to fight in a T-shirt that says '*With a good spotter, snipers can find the G-spot every time*' and a pair of sweatpants, you might want to as well."

I decided that wasn't a bad idea, more as I didn't want Goodfellow volunteering for the spotter position. I went with the usual black shirt and dark jeans for night-fighting, but didn't take my leather jacket as usual. The MP7 hung from a shoulder strap and I dug a knee-length black coat out of the winter-wear pile of clothes on my floor. Nik and Goodfellow went with the long dusters to cover their swords but the last thing I needed was to get snagged climbing over some fifteen-feet-tall chain-link fence and hanging there like an idiot—locked and loaded and nowhere to go. The flamethrower I stuffed into a large duffel bag and hoisted it on my shoulder.

Back out in the living room, I gave the most evil fucking grin I had in me. "Is this gonna be fun or what?"

* * *

It was not fun.

I plowed the garbage truck through four Jersey barriers, destroying the top half of the walls on either side of the bridge with the garbage truck—I'd remembered the bridge being wider last time I was in the neighborhood, but what the hell? They were planning to renovate anyway. Braking at the middle of the bridge, we dumped the diesel fuel, obtained from Goodfellow's car lot, into the garbage, then covered the last half of the bridge with it. Backing away, I lit it up with the flamethrower. All-you-can-eat arson—come and get it. If Jack couldn't see that . . . if Russian cosmonauts couldn't see that from space . . . then I didn't know how to do my job. And while there were a whole shitload of things I didn't know how to do, my job wasn't one of them.

It was a good plan and all we needed was Jack to show up and he had. It had looked like it was our turn now. An enormous cloud of billowing black, as dark as the smoke rising from the flames of the burning diesel fuel, had appeared, blocking our way off the bridge. That was fine. We weren't looking to run off. We were looking for a fight. There had been the spark of those electric blue eyes, the crackle of what I thought might be lightning in the cloud and then it was gone. Jack had vanished—but he'd left some friends. And he did his little trick a few more times. He was a low-flying ace strafing us with bombs of the undead.

I hadn't seen anything on World War II week on the History Channel that had been anything like this.

This was where the entertainment element plummeted.

"Zombies!" I shouted as they rushed us. It was a slow rush, I'll give you that, but they were serious and there were a shitload of them. We'd have to get rid of them before we could get Jack back out to play. I kicked one over the side of the bridge that wasn't currently on fire. "Real zombies! You"—and by you I meant Niko, Goodfellow, and anyone I'd met in the *paien* community—"said they didn't exist. Not real. Just legends. Now I'm in the middle of every fucking crappy horror cliché known to man!" I hated zombie movies. If you couldn't speed walk, then you were too fragile a flower for this world anyway and the apocalypse had always been in your future. I used the flamethrower on the next one before kicking him over. Not that it was necessary or useful as it continued to drag its burning torch of itself along, but it made me feel better. But if it was no use, other than improving my mood, there was no sense in carrying the extra weight and I shrugged the pack off.

"We've faced mullo before," Nik started as he first sheathed his katana in one gaping eye socket to puncture the withered brain, then separated one's head from its neck. Guess what? It kept coming. That's why I was throwing them over the side where they could be the problem of the fish, assuming there were any fish alive in the Harlem River that weren't somewhat zombified themselves.

"Mullo were not real zombies. You said so. Just corpse flesh reanimated by a pissed-off antihealer."

There'd been no bones. No lingering brain stem harboring the chow-down instinct. Basically remote controlled undead Jell-O. "*This* is not the same." Considering what we'd fought in the past—gods, we'd fought *gods*—this was just humiliating. Humiliating, time-consuming, and not at all entertaining. "Why can't they at least be the kind that can run? That would be something. This is like shooting fish in a barrel. Dead fish. Dead putrid fish that are stinking up a five-mile radius." I felt grasping hands at my back and flipped yet another one to the river about a hundred and forty feet below. It was brown and stiff with arms like twigs and wearing a wedding dress. That would've been sad if I hadn't been her first bite of "wedding cake." "Shit." There was the dull pain/teeth grinding pressure that only came from the bite of blunt human teeth at the base of my neck. "One of them bit me. I'm not only part murderous monster from the beginning of time, but now I'll be an undead one. A stinking slaughterer running amok, even more unkillable as I'll already be dead. And I thought it was bad before. Everyone happy now?"

"If your tongue would rot with the rest of you I'd be ecstatic." Niko gave up on the tried-but-not-true putting metal, bullet, or sword through their brain and did the same as me, booted their undead asses over the crumbling wall down to the water below. One, fresh and gooey, was wearing a horrific red, blue, yellow, orange, and green Hawaiian shirt. He'd been *buried* in that thing, apparently going with the theme song of "life was just a party and parties weren't meant to last."

"And I highly doubt they're infectious," Niko added, "or we'd have seen this sort of thing a long time ago. You watch too many horror movies." He swung his katana again and impaled one moving toward me and flung it through the air over the rail, its frozen limbs windmilling like dead winter tree branches.

"Watch? I live horror movies! Watching a horror movie is a frigging comedy treat for me, okay?" More of the undead were shuffling out from the end of the bridge where we'd rammed our way through with the truck.

Goodfellow had muscled his way through the pack to fight beside me as I threw the latest zombie-wannabe. This one had gone to his heavenly reward wearing the worst toupee in all of history constructed out of possum ass-hair, over the edge. "What's up, buttercup?" I said, tossing another one. "I'd thought you'd be more pissed over the chunks of rotting flesh on your Armani."

The puck looked worried and, for once, not about his clothes. "He raised the dead. I don't know of any storm spirits that can raise the dead. Yet, he has."

"Yeah," I said impatiently, although thankfully only about twenty or so and we'd handled most of them so far. "So did Suyolak." Suyolak, the pissed-off antihealer.

"Suyolak animated their flesh, not the entire body. It's different."

I lived in a world where there were different types of mobile putrid undead flesh. That wasn't disturbing at all, was it?

I gave a one-shouldered shrug, using my other arm

to send the last one flying at Niko, who vaulted him over the edge and zombie playtime was over. The smell, however, was going to linger with me for a while. "Suyolak's were much harder to deal with. They were fast as hell." Mounds of amoebalike flesh that moved so quickly you couldn't avoid them no matter how badly you wanted. Considering how they smelled, much worse than these, that was damn badly. I did wonder where Jack had gotten them though. I couldn't think of a cemetery near this area. But with him appearing and disappearing, a new development I didn't care for, he could've brought them in from Jersey for all I knew.

"True." But he didn't sound entirely convinced. "The mullo were more formidable. More power had to be involved. Perhaps. But it's still not the behavior of your average storm spirit and he's annoying enough without a new power. He could be a new species of storm *paien*." He peered at the back of my neck. "And no worries. That's barely a hickey. I doubt a zombie lifestyle is in your future. Although with your fashion sense and ability to sleep twenty hours a day, I know Niko might disagree with me on that."

"It would be a step up in his ability to function," Niko said dryly as the sirens wailed in the distance. "We don't have long. We've taken care of Jack's miniature and slow-moving mob. It wasn't even worth the time and had no amusement value at all. Now where is Jack himself?"

"Jack is here, betrayer of the Flock. I will take your skin but I will not save you."

He was above us by nearly twenty feet, a cloud with shadow tendrils stretching out, a hundred—no, a thousand small storms. I already had the MP7 out and pointed up. "Hear that, Nik? Your skin isn't worth saving now. No Niko-shaped square in his quilt. Maybe you should loofah more? Is that what they call it? A loofah? You know, one of those scrubbing things?"

I'd already pulled the middle part of the trigger to disarm the safety and now eased the trigger down. No single shots for me. I had a forty-round magazine and I didn't plan on taking a single round home with me.

Robin and Niko had already spread out. Jack was too far for a sword and they'd proved ineffective anyway, but Niko had scooped up the flamethrower, our third use now since we'd bought it. It was nice to get the bang for your buck. He sprayed an astounding plume of flames, the finger of a fiery god, at Jack. That, combined with my armor-piercing rounds had Jack spinning, a small agitated tornado. The rounds seemed to be pushing him back. He might be made of rock or crystal or God knew what but it wasn't much stronger than armor because he felt it. I could see it in the shudder as I aimed the blast higher toward the glow of his eyes.

Jack decided that was enough. Robin had gone away from the fire and Nik toward it to cover as much of the bridge as possible. Jack, who apparently disliked the armor piercing rounds more than flames, fell on me with the force of a demolished building. Knocking both of my arms outward, the MP7 almost skittered out of my hand, almost being key. My breath exploded from my lungs from the force of his landing. I thought I felt a rib or two crack as well. It wasn't a good feeling and unfortunately I was familiar with it. The weight of him was the same as the night in my bedroom, not crushingly heavy but immovable. I started to gate, this time hoping to take something important of his with me—something he couldn't live without, but then hesitated. Niko had said that wasn't the way. Fight like an Auphe, become an Auphe, kill my brother like an Auphe. I didn't want to die, but I didn't want to be that Auphe even more.

"You are not mine to save, but, if I wish, you can be mine to kill. I protect the Flock from wolves and vermin such as you." He was skinning humans, but I was the wolf at the door in this scenario. That hurt my feelings. Okay, maybe not so much. He was a dick all the same though.

His breath was cold against my face, the frigid cold of altitudes so high oxygen clung there precariously. Not that I could see his mouth behind the shaded mist. Not that I wanted to. There were probably teeth there, the kind that would make a great white suck his fin and cry for his mommy. That tended to be the kind of teeth that I usually found less than an inch from my face.

"Cal, gate! Gate now!"

That was Nik. Nik was telling me to gate. If Nik said it was okay, I was going with that.

And go I did.

I tried to take half of Jack with me through the gate I built around myself in the span of a thought. It should've worked. It would've worked . . . if he didn't disappear in the very same instant as I did. I saw it as I went. He was there. He was gone. I reappeared near Robin as he was the least armed of us. Too old school for our new toys. I wrapped an arm around my ribs and scanned the bridge, the part not burning. He had gated, the son of a bitch had gated. Well, not gated, but he'd done *something*.

I spotted his form in the air in less than a blink. Literally. I was looking at Nik and there was only flames behind him; I blinked and Jack was behind him, silhouetted against Sodom and Gomorrah or the *Towering Inferno*, whichever catastrophe-type media you were into.

"Nik! Behind you!" I shouted and gated again.

I shouldn't have bothered with the warning. Niko had already been turning when I traveled. He could've felt the change in temperature—Jack ran ice-cold. But against the flames of the bridge behind him that might not be so. It could be Nik knew because Nik knew these things since he was . . . shit . . . fifteen. Nik knew things humans couldn't know although he was one. He knew things *paien* couldn't know although they thought him a sheep. I didn't care how he knew as long as he did. He needed to watch his back long enough for me to get there and do it for him.

I gated above Jack's whirlpool form of smoke and racing electricity, but not too far above him. This wasn't an action movie, which meant when I appeared in mid-air, I immediately fell, no hovering, no momentary suspension of gravity or shit like that, convenient though it might be. I simply fucking fell. With Jack, I wanted to fall the least amount I could. I did not want to skewer myself on whatever glassine spears that hid in that dirty dark haze.

Landing on top of him and feeling the skin of my legs split open—not good. I jammed the MP7 into the mass below me and fired at least ten more rounds before he vanished again and I fell to the concrete beneath me. That didn't do my ribs any good at all. Instantly I saw Jack appear again, this time by Robin. It hit me, a memory close to as fucking freaky as Jack himself.

We had a neighbor once, we had lots of neighbors that we used for, you know . . . reasons. Good reasons. Getting us medicine if we needed it. Calling us in sick to school. Signing flu shot forms—all things Sophia couldn't be bothered with or was sober to do. Most of them were nice old ladies and one of those nice old ladies had given me a toy when I was five—the same year I'd found out about the Auphe and how I was half one. She meant well. The people who screw up in the most interesting ways mostly do.

She gave me a jack-in-the-box. I'd never seen one before. There I was, an unsuspecting kid, because monsters were lurking outside the window, not in an innocent box a nice lady gave me. I cranked and cranked, the music screeched and played as best as its rusted innards let it and then . . . pop goes the weasel!

A clown came exploding into my face. And this clown, he'd been around a long, long time. His once white teeth were brown, dirt you'd say, but I knew better—it was dried blood. The blue eyes faded to a blind white . . . but the blind that could still inexplicably *see* you. The carved hands curled into talons from the damp. That's what Niko had said, the damp. I wanted to believe him, but, shit, I knew better. Five years old and I knew better.

Jack-in-the-boxes were evil. Beginning, middle, and end.

This Jack was no different.

I staggered up with Niko's hand on my elbow, careful and slow. He could tell by the way I was breathing, shallow and panting, that I'd messed up my ribs. With most people that would've bugged me, knowing that much about me with one sweeping observation. With Niko I expected it and I didn't mind. Again, that's what Niko did. What he'd always done.

Jack was drifting closer to Goodfellow and I could hear the music in my head. Hear it plain as day. *Round the mulberry bush, the monkey chased the weasel . . .*

Robin had his sword between him and Jack, but would that be enough?

I watched as Jack grew, a storm cloud no one wanted to chase.

Probably not enough.

The monkey thought 'twas all in fun . . .

"Let go, Nik," I said urgently. He hesitated, then let go of my arm. Robin was one of us. He knew that the same as I did.

I was gone and then back again, right between Jack and Goodfellow and firing the MP7 at nothing. That was how quickly he flickered in and out. He was something and then he was nothing and then . . .

Pop goes the weasel!

He was on me again, grinding me down into the

rough surface beneath me. This time the MP7 did fly from my hand. "A wolf who hides among the Flock. I am not surprised," he said as thickly cloying as the first time I'd heard his voice. "That is why the Flock needs saving."

At this point my vision was wavering between bizarre *paien* serial killer and a jack-in-the-box clown from hell. To be fair, weren't all jack-in-the-boxes and clowns both from hell? I didn't wait to sort it out. I gated again.

I was back with Nik, who'd moved closer to the action and who was still scanning the sky with the flame-thrower ready as Jack had disappeared at the same time I had. Beside Nik, the gate around me fading, it took me a second to get my balance with both arms wrapped around my ribs. Cracked definitely, the first time. They might be broken now. I let my head hang for a second and concentrated on shallow breaths to ease the stabbing pain. "I lost my gun. I fucking never lose my gun," I panted.

Niko and I both knew now wasn't the place for an impromptu physical, and he knew just by the way I was standing I had either cracked or broken ribs. The medical advice would have to wait. But he wasn't waiting on another type of advice. "Cal, you idiot. I didn't mean die instead of gating. I meant if there's another way then use it. If not then at least weigh the mental cost to you later, *after* the fight, but don't let yourself be killed if it can save you." His arm hooked lightly around my neck, his breath a human warmth and not Jack's frostbite cold exhaled against my jaw. "Can you fight? If we can get your gun back?"

I gave a nod. "Yeah, I'm good. You know how much that gun cost?" Ruptured spleen? Lacerated liver? Screw that. I laughed at internal bleeding. I truly loved that gun.

"Then let's see if we can save Goodfellow's ass as Ishiah treasures it so much. And, Cal, do not die," he ordered. "Or I'll have this Jack raise you from the dead so that I might kill you all over again."

"You're a marshmallow inside, Nik. I've always known it." I grinned as best as I was able with a distinct lack of breath and gated again, scooped up my gun, and gated one more time to end up beside Robin, a bruise of a light—purple, gray, and black—still swirling around the outline of my body. "Hey, Jack, we can both come and go. That makes this game more interesting, doesn't it?"

It did. Besides Auphe and half Auphe, I'd not seen anyone who could do what Jack and I could. Although I was ripping holes in reality. Sometimes I tore them open and stepped through them, sometimes I opened them in monsters that deserved it and they exploded/imploded—a little of both—sometimes I built them around myself and it almost looked as if I were teleporting, but I wasn't.

Jack wasn't building gates. As far as I could tell, Jack *was* teleporting. He was here. Then he was gone and he was quicker than I was as I hadn't managed to take any of him with me when I went. Now he was almost on top of Robin again who was fighting him off with his lighter version of a broadsword. He was having slightly better luck than I'd had with my combat knife on Jack's first visit, but he also had hundreds of thousands of years of fighting experience with weapons. Millions with a pointy stick and a hefty rock. His blows were so fast they were a blur.

"Enough banter with the psychopath," Robin spat. "Shoot the *malaka* and be done with it!"

The sirens were seconds away, lights were getting brighter and closer, I could hear the people collecting down in the park by the river. We were out of time, but we weren't winning this battle. That left the war and for that we needed Jack's attention on us and only us. "Got your attention with the bonfire, didn't we, Jack? We're bad, bad boys. If you don't take care of us we'll do the same tomorrow night and the next and the next. None of us are the Flock. We're the pack and we'll eat what you want before you ever have a chance to save it in whatever special Serial-Killers-R-Us trophy case you got from IKEA."

The eyes transmuted from pale electric blue to nuclear white. "Fire is for the pure. Fire is for the punishment. None of you are worthy to use it." While Jack waxed poetic on fire safety or whatever the hell he was talking about, I emptied the rest of the magazine. Lightning roiled in him and for a second in the mist I thought I saw something glittering. A vein of the purest white diamonds, the curve of a wing, but it must've been a trick of the dark cloud, the lightning, and the fact that Jack was gone. The same as if he'd not been there at all.

I could hear the voices of the police and firemen making their way through the smashed barriers and unless we thought we could survive a hundred-forty-foot jump to the water, which I didn't, and wanted to swim the Harlem River, really didn't, then there was only one way home. Niko was already running toward us, but still too far. I threw up a gate directly in front of him that swallowed him—*a hole in the world*—then grabbed Robin's arm and took us through one of our own.

Then we were home and we didn't know a thing more about how to take down Jack than when we started. Hell, we knew less if anything.

What a waste of a good fire.

10

Niko

Twelve Years Ago

"Give me the matches, Cal. I am not playing here."

He handed them over, muttering under his breath, but I knew enough to know when he was playing at teasing the big brother. He wasn't a budding pyromaniac. One fire didn't an arsonist make. And that one had been an emergency. I couldn't hold that one against him.

I was sure enough that he wouldn't burn down Junior's house, but while I more than still had doubts about Junior's basement of dead bodies, it was true that people were going missing. It would be safer if Cal weren't home alone after school while I worked, whether it was light outside or not.

"Why don't you stay after school today and play a few games of baseball, football—whatever your gym teacher has planned? Then I can come by after work and we can go home together." The students at Cal's school had many parents with odd schedules who weren't home in time for the bus to drop off their children. The principal had decided an after-school sports session was a good idea for those parents who needed two or three hours to come by and get the kids who couldn't take the bus to be home alone. I'd met Coach VanBuren. He wasn't especially bright and I didn't think he'd volunteered for the job, but he did it. He might not be a patient man or a man who loved his job, but being there until the parents could be—that made him a good man.

"I don't like sports anymore and they won't let me play," Cal finished without showing much concern. He hadn't been a fan of team sports since he knew there were team sports. Except football. He liked football. He loved tackling. I was hoping when his growth spurt came it would be enough that he could play on the team of whichever school we were in at the time. Or I had hoped, but now . . . what was this?

"Since when don't you like sports, and what do you mean they won't let you play?" I frowned. Cal was small but he could outrun anyone his age. "Why not?"

"Since this year." He started to scoop all his papers off the kitchen table and wad them into one big mass. "I got tired of faking it. I like to win. When you play games you're supposed to win. That's the whole point. If you're not trying your hardest to win, then you're not playing it right." He began shoving books and wads of what I hoped was doodles but knew, *knew* was his homework in his backpack. "If you're following 'rules'"—he pulled a face at the word—"then you're not trying your hardest. Games shouldn't have rules, not if you want to win. They're . . . um . . ."

"Mutually exclusive?" I provided.

He zipped up the backpack. "Exactly. If I'm going to play a game where I'm supposed to win, then I'm going to win. Coach VanBuren doesn't understand. He says I have 'poor impulse control issues,' 'the attention span of a frigging gnat,' and I'm a 'little psycho asshole.'" The three quotes, I could hear them as if that potbellied, balding, worthless excuse for a human being was standing beside me. I felt a flush of anger, but Cal was indifferent. He was snorting at the man's idiocy. "For a coach he doesn't know anything about winning."

I supposed he didn't. He'd also been demoted from good man to jackass in my book. "No, he doesn't. You know what my teachers tell me in the dojos?" I hadn't thought it was time for that yet, but I'd been wrong.

Stuffing a candy bar in the zippered pocket of his backpack, he slung it on, finally ready for the morning in his worn Batman T-shirt, faded jeans, and scuffed sneakers. "What?" he asked curiously.

"That in there are rules and honor, but outside in the real world, rules and honor only get you . . . mugged or worse." I'd been about to say killed, but we had enough of that word for the past few days. "You don't have poor impulse control and you're not a psycho. You know how to protect yourself, to come out on top, and that's something your coach doesn't know himself." I gave him a nudge for the front door. I could hear his bus wheezing down the street outside. "Come home straight from school, lock the doors, and don't let anyone in. All right?"

"And jack-off Junior next door?"

"Language." I'd told myself that battle was lost, but the reaction was knee jerk. I gave him a carefully light swat to the back of his head. "Behave." As for Junior, that sad miserable lump of a neighbor was making my life a living nightmare and he had genuine monsters to compete with in that area. "I'll think of something at school today. Now go. Catch your bus."

He was gone and climbing onto the creaking yellow whale. Looking through the windows he gave me a half wave. When you had one person in the world, just one, who gave you affection, you were slow to outgrow that. I waved back. I hoped he didn't for a long time, because it was true of us both. We each only had one person.

Inside the bus a kid nearly half a foot taller than Cal stood up and said something insulting from the sneer on his face. Behind the smoky glass I saw Cal look up at him and bare his teeth. It wasn't a smile or a grin. What had he said the other day? "I like lions. They're cool." Cal showed the would-be bully the teeth of a lion and the kid sat back down hurriedly, letting Cal walk on to find his seat. By now the bus was halfway down the street and I was thinking that hateful idiot VanBuren could be right this one time.

Cal probably shouldn't play sports anymore.

Lions didn't play to win. Lions didn't play at all.

Lions survived.

There was nothing in the newspaper or on the Internet in the high school library about a missing prostitute. But it had been only last night. That sort of information would take days, maybe weeks to pop up considering her occupation. Considering if she went with Junior at all. She could have the worst drug habit in the world, but one look at the sweaty, watery-eyed, generally leaky blob that was Junior could change anyone's mind and put them on the straight and narrow. It could be that Junior had been asking for directions or decided that a prostitute the hepatitis yellow of old chicken fat was one disease risk too many. He did work in a hospital, cafeteria or not. He had to know some people were deathly ill by looking at them no matter how dim he was.

The hospital. Lawrence Memorial, had to be, it was basically the only hospital to speak of in New London. I could tell Cal we were checking to see if Junior did work there or if he'd lied. If he was behind plastic, slowly scooping up burned squares of lasagna with a blank expression, wearing a hairnet and plastic gloves, looking as harmless as he had in his bathrobe only more so, Cal could be persuaded no one like that could be a serial killer so clever that the police wasn't aware he existed. I could convince myself as well. After last night, I was not having doubts, but . . . questions. Junior wasn't a killer, but you didn't have to be a killer to be a predator. It was best to cover all the bases.

"Hey, Leandros." There was a hot and heavy breath hitting the skin of my neck not covered by my ponytail. "My uncle lives on your block. He says your mom's a whore." There was the laugh of an excited monkey, screeching and aggressive. " 'S'at true?"

I turned off the library computer and swiveled in my chair to see buzzed brown hair and gunmetal eyes. Rex. That wasn't his real name. That wasn't a dog's real name these days, but it was all I could be bothered to remember. Rex. Bully. Brothers who were already in prison and waiting for him to join them. Completely not worth my time. "She is," I said agreeably, standing a little too close in his personal space. He automatically stepped back and my lip curled. Bullies, so predictable. "But she charges extra for pathetic fumbling virgins like you. You might want to save up." I walked around him and went out the door.

Cal was a lion, but he wasn't the only one.

Cal shifted from foot to foot in the autumn brown grass. He was nervous. Cal didn't get nervous or he hadn't much past the age of seven. "It's a good plan," I repeated. "We go in, find the cafeteria, check that Junior actually works there. We might even be able to talk to some people there." Or I would. Cal was not especially adept at being casual if there was nothing physical to be gained. "Ask what kind of place it is to work. Are the people nice. Are there any weirdos because I've worked with them before and I don't want to again. It's simple and it'll work." I wouldn't use the word weirdos if it weren't a con, if only a little one. When I went to college, I'd fit in. My vocabulary would be correct, my behavior perfect, my grades exemplary, and that would save Cal and me.

Being perfect.

Ducking his head, Cal stared at the strip of grass we stood on along with its one spindly tree that would explode with cherry blossoms in the spring. For now it was bare and vulnerable and Cal was doing a flawless imitation of the same. "It's a good plan," he echoed me with an uneasy mutter. He looked up at the ER entrance, the place that had the most people coming and going. Blending in would be easier there than the front. I'd taken a look there first. The moment you stepped in you were facing an information desk with sharp-eyed elderly volunteers who wanted to know where, why, who, when . . . trying to be helpful. They would've been more helpful without the security office six feet away.

"Then what's the problem?" I said impatiently. I shouldn't be that way, but this was mostly for him. It was getting old, all of this and I was losing my patience. I had more important things to do than to keep trying to drag the ridiculous and stubborn delusion of a killer out of my brother's head.

He wrapped his arms around himself. Normally he would've snagged a hand on my sleeve if something was bothering him, but I was annoyed and I had let him hear it. "It smells." He swallowed. "Even from here. It smells like blood and death and cancer. Cancer smells like blood frying in a burned skillet, did you know? It does. But it smells like that mouse that died in the wall that one time and rotted until we found it. It smells like that too. And pus—it's sweet but sick at the same time. How can it smell like both? They put alcohol over it all but that only makes it worse because it's all still there. It's like a graveyard but no one knows they're dead yet. No one knows. . . ."

I squatted down and pulled his face into my chest. His arms went from wrapping around himself to me and he held on tight, shaking—but minutely, because this was Cal. He was proud and he wasn't afraid of anything. He couldn't let himself be. "I'm sorry," I said quietly, trying not to sound guilty, trying not to make it worse to him, that his difference stopped him from doing something that anyone else could do without thinking about it. I rested my chin on top of his head. Sorry, sorry—I was sorry, more than. Worse I was an idiot. The sheets from the Salvation Army that made him sick to be near and I wanted to drag him into a hospital? I didn't ask myself what I was thinking. It was clear I wasn't thinking at all. "It's my fault, Cal. I was stupid and I'm sorry."

"I don't think I can go in, Nik." He straightened and turned his back on the hospital. He had to smell it, but he didn't have to see it. "You shouldn't go either. If he's killing people, you shouldn't be by yourself."

"It's an entire building full of people." I stood. "If Junior was Jack the Ripper himself he couldn't do anything there." I pointed at a bench across the entrance for the ambulances. It was close to fifty feet away but security was patrolling hospital grounds. It was safe enough. "Think it'll be better over there? The smell?

You could wait until I come back. I won't be longer than a half hour." This was it. I was done with Junior. I was done with his messing with Cal's head and turning me into an ass to my little brother by sabotaging my self-control. Today I proved he was nothing, no worse than that jack-in-the-box that had scared Cal when he was five. That had been a toy. Junior was less than that.

He took in the bench with a quick glance and nodded. "It'll be okay." This time his hand did snag my shirt. "Be careful."

I smiled and thumped him gently on the top of his head. "Isn't that what I always tell you?"

"Yeah, but I never . . . um . . . just be careful." He was dashing for the bench before I could take a swipe at his shirt. Never listened—this time I had a real reason to be annoyed and I couldn't do it. I waited until he was on the bench and headed with grim determination toward the ER entrance.

Junior, each word resounded darkly in my thoughts with every step, you have truly become an unbelievable pain in my neck.

Junior did work in the cafeteria, which was in the basement. He was exactly as I imagined: slow, mumbling shyly to the employees and visitors, and a hairnet far larger than what little hair he had required. After getting a glimpse of him, I moved back to a corner of the cafeteria behind a pillar out of his sight. I took the last empty table and waited for an impatient short man in scrubs to give me the look. It was a universal look for hardworking people with short lunch breaks: why are you taking up a table if you're not eating? I waved a hand at him and started to stand up. "Oh, sorry, I'm leaving."

He swooped in as fast as a hawk on a field mouse. I waited until he had a mouth of mashed potatoes while eyeing me suspiciously in case I tried to snatch the table back. "My dad's upstairs," I offered. "Getting some sort of stomach scan. I'm just waiting until it's done." I could've added that he was all I had and did this guy know where the chapel was so I could pray and maybe I should think about getting a job in case my dad couldn't go back to work right away. It's what Sophia would've said, which is why I wouldn't. I went straight for the "get a job" lie as it tasted the least like chalk and tin in my mouth. "What are the people like who work here now? Are they nice?"

It turned out he was a cardiopulmonary surgeon and he certainly did not know the personalities and/or characteristics of the common cafeteria worker. In other words, in this hospital he was a god and the rest ants beneath his sanctified feet.

The next person was a proctologist. She had no problem talking about the cafeteria workers, their probable bowel habits considering the food they served and told me stories about the odder things she'd removed from people's anuses including a set of Russian nesting dolls. They kept coming out and coming out and coming out. I couldn't help but laugh while simultaneously wondering if I was going to have to give the red-faced doctor choking on her own hilarity the Heimlich maneuver and promising myself to never repeat the stories to Cal. I might leave them to him in my will, but he wouldn't hear them while I was still alive. The moral of the story being if I decided to go into medicine and I wanted good-humored colleagues, proctology was the field to aim for . . . so to speak.

As for Junior, my new friend Dr. Linda Wilner said he was a nice enough guy, gave big portions and rarely sneezed on the food, was religious as he'd seen him praying over his own lunch, and with what he ate could use some roughage to help out with regularity. I decided I likely didn't want to be a proctologist after all.

I thanked her and was leaving the cafeteria when I saw Junior not concentrating on the stewed cabbage as I'd planned, but gone and a security guard at the entrance to the cafeteria staring at me. It was a toss-up whether Junior had spotted me and called security or the first doctor I'd talked to had. I was betting the doctor. If Junior saw me, he'd assume I was here looking for a job as I'd told him I'd planned to. The doctor—he could not like unescorted minors taking up tables that Heaven itself had set aside for him or not believed I had a parent here at all. Hospitals are great places for thieves. Everyone's worried about their sick or dying family member, no one's watching their purse or wallet. It was a pickpocket's dream. Our second week in New London, Sophia had gone to Lawrence Memorial with the intention of being a one-woman crime spree. Unfortunately for her, it had already been picked clean several times over in the past months by thieves who had the same idea as Sophia. After that kind of pattern, it made sense they'd be on alert. I should've thought about that.

I thought about it when the security guard started walking, then running, my way. I thought about it more than once as I ran through halls, up and down stairs, went up to the roof and memorably all the way down to the morgue. In a cold metal drawer lying on my side next to a gray and blue man with a missing leg below the knee and a stench I didn't have to be Cal to smell, I wondered irritably what made this security guard this dogged? He was in his forties. How much were they paying him to be this devoted to his job? Where did he get all that energy?

Not getting laid by his wife, Cal whispered in my mind. *But at least that'll keep him safe from the serial killer.*

If he were here, that was what he'd say—how could an eleven-year-old get a foul mouth so quickly without my noticing it was on the horizon? But he and his smart mouth weren't here. He was waiting for me outside and I was now an hour overdue. If he stayed on the bench, it would be all right. He would know better than to come to try to find me. I was the oldest. This was my job. I would get out of here and he would stay where I'd told him. He'd listen, he'd obey, he wouldn't come in this place. I'd get out of this damn morgue and I'd see for myself. Cal knew better than to try to save me, not here.

Of course "here" was where I found him.

He'd made it as far as the automatic sliding glass doors of the ER before collapsing. I could see the people running toward him as he convulsed and vomited on the cheap tile floor. The cavalry had come to rescue me and I meant that without an ounce of sarcasm. He'd risked his life over this and he knew it. Cal, who looked all human on the outside, but we had no idea what he looked like on the inside and I couldn't take a chance.

I'd lost the security guard, but I didn't make any new friends when I hit a doctor with one shoulder knocking him flat, and then did the same to a nurse on the other side. Scooping Cal up, I kept running through the still open doors. It was dark outside now and none of the ER staff were the runners the security guard had been. Even carrying Cal, I lost them after several blocks of twists and turns.

I had him up with his head over my shoulder. I didn't enjoy the warmth of his vomit spilling down my back, but that was much better than him choking on it. The convulsing turned to squirming, and then he was gasping in my ear, "Nik, get away from me. Nik, get away!" That might not have halted my running, but his fists pounding as hard as they could against my back did. I stopped in an alley between a long out-of-business store and a church and gently put him on his feet. He fell instantly, scrambling backward on all fours, horrified eyes on me.

"Cal?" Confusion and a flash of panic wrapped dual hands around my lungs and gripped tightly. I took a step toward him.

"No." He moved farther away, then lunged to his feet and toward the nearest garbage can, digging through it until he found a can of Coke that was not

quite empty. He poured what was left over his hand, then covered up his nose and mouth.

That's when I got it. For an hour and a half I'd been in the hospital soaking up the stench of illness and dying that had had Cal on the floor flailing in his own sick. Worse, I'd been in a drawer with a corpse, who from the whiff I'd gotten, had died of gangrene. I was making Cal as sick as the hospital could. I backed away. "Tell me when I'm far enough," I asked as if it were an ordinary question. Right now we both needed to believe things were ordinary if we had to lie to ourselves to do it.

After several more steps he nodded, still keeping his mouth and nose covered. I'd have to write a thank-you note to the Coca-Cola company, I thought with only a slight edge of relieved hysteria.

"Where'd you go?" he asked, accusing words muffled by his hand. "You said a half hour. You were gone an hour and a half. You were gone forever. I thought he got you."

"I know. I'm sorry, Cal. I am. A security guard chased me through the entire place. I had to hide. . . ." He didn't need to know where I had to hide. "We forgot Sophia said that place had been picked clean. They're still watching for anyone who looks suspicious." A wandering teenager alone in a place that had been repeatedly robbed would look suspicious.

He was only half listening to my answer. The rest of his attention was taken with jerking his gaze from my feet up to my face, back down, and then over again. "You don't smell like you. You smell like that mouse in the wall. You smell like you're rotting. I can't smell you at all. You're not you." He took a sliding step back, the unsteadiness better but not gone.

Cal was the same as any ordinary person in having only five senses, but he was different in that one of them was incredibly heightened. With my normal nose I could detect the nauseating taint of gangrene that clung to me. For Cal it covered everything else, including the way that I had always smelled to him. I hadn't known until this moment the extent it factored into how he perceived people. For him to not be able to smell the usual me at all would be the same as if I'd suddenly gone blind and couldn't see him. I'd be able to hear him and touch him, but a huge part of what made him Cal to me would be gone.

"But it is me," I assured. "Same hair." I tugged at the short ponytail. "Same voice, same willingness to not yell at you although I'm half covered in your vomit. It's me, Cal, and as soon as we get home and I wash, I'll smell the same as always." The clothes, I'd have to throw away. No, burn.

"It's you?" His other foot was hovering in the air about to take him yet another step away. He looked at me searchingly up and down one last time and let his shoulders slump and his foot drop. "I'm stupid. I know it's you. You're just not . . ." He shook his head.

"Just not all of me. Not that you can smell. I know. Let's go home and I'll fix it, all right?"

He nodded, hand firmly in place between me and my new smell. "Okay. But could you walk ahead of me? Really far ahead of me?"

"Behind you," I amended, to watch for the same type that had tried to rob us the night before. "But far behind. I'll wash out back with the hose and soap." That would keep the smell out of the house. "You can go tell Mrs. Spoonmaker since you already lied about me being seventeen. She might get a thrill."

That made him smile. I could see the dimple beside his covering hand. "It's cold. The water's going to be colder." He held up his free hand, the index finger and thumb about half an inch apart. "That's not going to impress anybody. She goes to mass though. She might pray for you."

"You know more than you should for your age and way too much than is good for me at any age." I shook my head in mock despair. "Home. Move it. Even I don't like the way I smell right now. Your puke isn't like rose petals and baking apple pie either."

We started walking. Home would be good. I could get clean and not think about how if I hadn't had to hide in the morgue, the plan would've worked in a different way than I'd thought. If I'd walked out of the hospital smelling like death after only being in the cafeteria that would let Junior off the hook. It took only one goal-oriented security guard and one dead man who'd liked sugar more than his leg and life to throw that all out the window.

"Walk slower," Cal said from in front of me as he plodded, steps tired and occasionally wobbly. "I can still smell you."

By the time we were home, Cal had recovered and took a quick shower before coming out back. I kept as far away as our tiny backyard would allow as he threw me the soap. He uncurled the hose while I stripped and dumped my clothes in the garbage can for later burning. For once I was thankful we couldn't afford to live in a neighborhood that had streetlights. If any of our neighbors saw me as anything other than a smear paler than the night, then they were trying too much. Cal would be happy to go paint a giant P for pervert on their doors if they did.

"Ready?" he asked. But he didn't wait for my answer. How would that be fun for him? A stream of ice-cold water hit me in the face. I grimaced but began soaping up as Cal hosed me down like an elephant on a hot day at the zoo.

I scrubbed every inch thoroughly before waving my arms. "Cal, all right, stop. I think I'm fine now." Except that I expected my skin had turned blue and I was freezing. Cal was right. Mrs. Spoonmaker would have to pray for me.

Cal took an experimental sniff, then shook his head. Part of the decision, I thought, was driven by how much he was enjoying himself. Little brothers and water hoses are deadly combinations. "One more time. To make sure it doesn't get in the house. You really, really stank."

I couldn't disagree with that.

11

Cal

Present Day

I absolutely stank.

Being attacked by the dead will do that. A few years ago I would've been yakking my guts up over it, but you can, as they say, get used to anything. We'd fought enough things that while weren't dead, they did smell that way or worse. It turned out the real thing wasn't quite as bad as some of those. It wasn't enjoyable, hell no, but at least I could fight now without taking a time-out to puke on the feet of whatever I was shooting or carving up at the time.

We did keep an all-but-industrial-strength soap on hand for these occasions though, as Niko's hippy-churned natural crap wasn't going to do the job—

unless the job was making me smell like a bowl of zombie cereal with a healthy serving of goat milk over the top.

The cuts on my legs weren't as bad as I expected. Whatever type of mist hid Jack's inner jagged self, it had been enough of a barrier to keep me from impaling myself when I'd gated on top of him. It wasn't as if I hadn't thought about it, but a little impaling—the kind you survived, if not walked away from—was worth it to take out Jack. I'd have happily crawled away from the scene of the deed if it meant putting down that son of a bitch. But, as it was, the cuts were superficial. Some antibiotic ointment and I was good to go, no bandages required. I did have at least one cracked rib though, maybe two from where Jack had fallen on me as shockingly as if the moon had fallen from the sky. But I'd had cracked ribs before—and I'd have them again if we could get Jack out of the picture. Move carefully, don't breathe too deeply, eat pain pills like M&M's, and I'd be fine.

Bending my head down to scrub my wet hair with a towel, I stepped into the main room in time to hear Promise say, "But there are no such creatures as zombies."

"You're ruining a lot of fantasies by saying that," I pointed out as I straightened and dropped the towel on the floor. "Don't get between a geek and a good apocalypse. They'll probably kill you quicker than Jack would."

Promise turned her head from where she sat on the couch and gave me a glance as opaque as they came. It didn't help her. I knew what she was thinking. I was wearing sweatpants but was shirtless. That made it easy to see that I had more than my share of scars, some of them uglier than others. I also had a line of stitches across my stomach and a dark garden of bruises blooming up like black roses over my ribs. I thought Promise could make her peace with scars, more specifically Niko's. He had fewer than I did; he was the better fighter, but he still had a few. But when a job ended in spilled blood, and as she was a vampire I knew she could smell mine, and cracked ribs—that was new, wasn't it? Not old scar tissue you could write off to "he was younger then. He's better now. Undefeatable, human or not."

If a half Auphe like me was this mortal, what did that say about the true mortal?

I knew what Promise was thinking and who she was thinking it about because I thought the same thing. Nik, oblivious to his mortality while others brooded over it, glared at my discarded towel. "If it weren't for your ribs, I would rub your nose in that."

"You wouldn't do that to a puppy." I grinned. There was something wrong in enjoying injury as a license to bad behavior, but I'd never claimed there was anything particularly right with me.

"A puppy is capable of learning. A puppy doesn't devote his life to seeing how far he can push me before I break mentally. A puppy does not order pizza and expect me to pay for it because he's out of money." Promise laughed at his seething outrage and rested her shoulder against his on the couch.

"Children can be such a blessing," she said with mocking good humor as she continued to braid his wet hair, the bastard having beat me to the shower.

"Hardly," Niko retorted. "I have done that tour of duty and have the post-traumatic stress disorder to prove it. The sex talk alone . . ." He gave a minute shudder.

The memory hit me and I rubbed my ribs with an absent, cautious touch. "Oh yeah. Isn't that when I asked you what doggy style meant and did we need to borrow our neighbor's poodle for a demonstration?" My grin transmuted into a smirk. "I think you foamed at the mouth a little. Good times, huh?"

"I don't care about your ribs any longer," he said. "I don't care if they are broken and shards of bone are slicing your lungs to shreds. Pick. Up. The. Towel."

Playing my "get out of brotherly violence" injury card, I ignored him and sat down very slowly in our beat-up recliner. Once in a comfortable position, I relaxed and waited for the warm wave of codeine to wash over me. "It is funny . . . not funny like the poodle thing . . . but funny weird how Goodfellow and Promise both insist there aren't any such things as zombies, but they were there. If Robin hasn't seen any and he's literally old as dirt, the dirt T. rexes walked around on, then what the hell?"

Promise finished Niko's braid and curled the end around one slender finger, her heather-shadowed eyes thoughtful. "I cannot think of an explanation. From Niko's description of his appearance, Jack does sound like a typical storm spirit, but storm spirits, that I know of, don't use skinning as a manner of killing."

"And he is all about the skinning." I yawned. "He was still going on about that at the bridge: wanting to save people's skin. He's like the world's most homicidal stamp collector—he has to murder to do it and he just freaking won't stop talking about it. I miss the monsters that just try to kill you, not tell you about their hobbies."

"How are the legs?" Niko had leaned down to snag the towel and was folding it in his tragically OCD way.

"Not bad at all. That cloud he floats around in, it acted like a buffer. I've a few scrapes. Nothing major."

"The pain pills working yet for your ribs?" He was a good brother: asking about my health, picking up my towel. I could probably get him to order that pizza for me if I looked pathetic enough.

"Feeling no pain," I answered honestly.

"Good." I was promptly hit in the face with my wet towel.

Of course, good brothers know tough love inside and out.

That night Promise stayed. Normally Niko and I would've switched off on watch, but Promise had no problem staying awake all night to wait for Jack to appear. Somehow I still managed to pull a two-hour watch. I say somehow because as much as Niko didn't want to remember giving me the sex talk when I was a kid, I didn't want to think about him and Promise doing the things I'd asked about back then.

Really didn't want to think about it.

When I was a kid, I used to love giving Niko shit

about sex. It drove him nuts. It was better than cable. But not now. If Niko hadn't raised me in addition to being my brother, it could be different. I'd have bumped fists, blown it up, slapped his back, whatever the hell the wild and crazy kids did when their brother got laid. I didn't know. Between the spine-shivering sensation other people had at the thought of their parents having sex and knowing my best friend was doing it with my boss, probably on the same bar where I served drinks, I was surrounded by a whole shitload of "I don't wanna know."

I spent those two hours simultaneously watching for Jack and telling myself that Niko and Promise were either practicing the lost, deadly art of flower arranging, or sharpening their already incredibly sharp blades. I hung grimly to those images, then slammed into my bedroom faster than I should have with my ribs when Promise appeared out of the darkened hallway with her elaborate coil of soft brown hair loose and spilling around her hips. Her feet were also bare, but bare feet were essential for flower arranging and sword care and no one could tell me differently.

The fact that she whispered as I passed her, "Who's your daddy?" made her a stone-cold bitch and had me popping an extra pain pill. If Jack killed me in my sleep, I couldn't say I'd be that sorry to go.

In the morning, if five thirty a.m. could be called morning, when Nik and I were walking through East River Park, I hadn't stopped twitching at random moments. We were headed for the river itself. Goodfellow had said that if Bastet hadn't known anything about

Jack no one would, but Bastet had been afraid. She'd said it herself; Jack left the *paien* alone unless they pissed him off. She wasn't willing to risk it. Neither had the Kin, they'd made that clear.

That didn't mean I was ready to give up asking around. Bastet was afraid, the Kin were cautious, but there were some that were too stupid to be either of those. Jack had started off with a mad on for Niko and me for whatever unknown reason, so it wasn't as if we could back off. He wanted Nik and I'd gotten in the way enough that he wanted me dead—Flock-worthy or not.

That meant we hit up our last informational option because off the top of my head I couldn't think of anything else to burn down that wouldn't kill people in the process. Once we would've gone to our top informant, Boggle, but we'd accidentally gotten two of her children killed by Grimm and it'd be a long time before she was over that. If ever. Boggle would kill anything and everything that moved, but she loved her litter of man-eaters.

But there was a *vyodanoi* that lived in the East River. I'd never used him . . . her . . . it—I had no idea about their reproduction or genders and I didn't want to—but he came around the Ninth Circle on a weekly basis and was a helluva lot more chatty than his fellow *vyodanoi*. He seemed to have a rubbery leechlike extension on the pulse of the *paien* world in NYC. He knew things that would no doubt get him killed someday, but for now, he talked. And the more he drank, the more he talked, which was why I was carrying a jumbo-sized plastic bottle of vodka in each hand. Niko had commented the family-sized vodka was a truly classy five a.m. purchase. I told him they were out of grape-flavored condoms and beef jerky or I'd have thrown them in just to see the look on the clerk's face at how I wined and dined my dates. Niko's reply that that was actually a step up was uncalled for.

The bastard.

There was a reason the vodka was the cheap stuff. I doubted any *vyodanoi* I saw at the bar had ever seen Mother Russia because I hadn't once seen one of them drinking the top-shelf vodka.

"You're unusually tolerable this morning," Niko observed as we walked through trampled grass and mud under a sky that was clinging tightly to the darkness of night, stubbornly refusing the dawn.

"I don't want to talk about it. Promise is the devil," I added darkly. "But other than that, I don't want to talk about it." Life was much easier when he was spending nights at her place. Thanks to Grimm and now Jack, I foresaw a good deal more twitching in my future.

"I'd say I feel sorry for you, but I'd be lying. After what you put me through when you were a kid on that subject, turnabout is fair play." We'd reached the shore and I slid garbage—the seashells of NYC—out of the way while Niko spread two large garbage bags for us to sit on. We were likely to be here a good while. Boris, I didn't know his real name . . . I didn't know if *vyodanoi* had names . . . so I went with Boris. The *vyodanoi* species originated in Russia, so Boris was good enough, which made Niko and me Bullwinkle and Rocky. Joy. Regardless, Boris had his traditions.

He'd talk and he'd talk for free—the vodka didn't count. Seven ninety-nine was practically free. What Boris did demand is you keep him company. He didn't like to drink alone. When it came to passing along information, that wasn't a preference. It was a rule. It was some Russian tradition, Goodfellow once mentioned when I brought it up. In Russia, if you were comfortable enough to get shit-faced with someone, that made you family.

I didn't want to be Boris's family, but sometimes you had to take one for the team.

"I am not at all fond of this plan," Niko commented, sitting on the plastic he'd laid out. He assumed a lotus position that made my knees hurt just seeing it.

"It's not my favorite either, but it's how it works with Boris." I sat on my own plastic and felt the mud beneath it give and slide in a wholly disgusting way. I slapped the water twice. Hey, it'd always worked on Flipper. "Boris. Hey, Boris, I have a present for you. Wake up and come play."

I liked to think Boris was asleep and not finishing up gnoshing down on the leg of someone he'd dragged into his underwater larder. I'd like to think that but I'd likely be fooling myself. I waited a few more minutes and slapped the water again. "Come on, Boris. We don't have all day. Keep us waiting and we'll drink all the vodka ourselves." I wasn't too worried. There was nothing Boris liked more than company and vodka. He could be a few miles up or down the river. *Vyodanoi* were incredibly fast in the water. He surfaced in front of us in the next moment proving my point . . . about speed or love of vodka. Take your pick.

"Boris, buddy. The Ninth Circle is starting Two for Tuesday shots. You should stop by. Bring a date or a spore or whatever you've got going on in your social life." I nudged Nik, who went ahead and dipped into his coat pockets for two shot glasses and a large glass tumbler for Boris. A *vyodanoi*'s tolerance for vodka was unbelievable.

Boris raised up to settle on what would be knees if he had bones. A *vyodanoi* looked like nothing more than a giant six- to seven-foot leech in humanoid form, a very blurry, caricature of a humanoid form. It had arms, but no hands or fingers. They tended to be brownish-gray with a sloping mudslide of a head, a sucker for a mouth, and a coloration sketched on its face in black lines to mimic a human's nose, eyes, and brow. For a second in the dark or the shadows you might mistake them for human—only for a second, but with *vyodanoi* a second was all it took.

"*Sobaka.*" The sound of Boris's voice wasn't easy on the ears. It was a peculiar whistle, the sound of a drowned man whistling a dirge from underwater.

I opened the first, let's be honest, vat of vodka as Niko murmured, "*Sobaka*? Russian for dog?"

"It's short for *beshenaya sobaka*. Mad dog." Goodfellow had also filled me in on that as he liked delivering bad news as well as random cultural facts. "It's my nickname from that time Hob hired a ton of them."

And I hadn't played so nice with them then. "Of all the things I've been called I can live with that one."

Boris wrapped rubbery flesh around his glass and tossed the entire thing back in one swallow. "You've come to talk. So be not rude." That was Niko and my cue to toss our own shot back. I didn't drink much and Niko didn't drink at all. It wasn't a good idea when your mom had been an alcoholic or in our business when you had to stay sharp always. It didn't make a difference how much I drank though or if I'd had a liver the size of Kansas: what we were drinking would still have tasted like a shot of turpentine. I should've sprung for the good stuff, if for Niko and my sake. The hell with Boris and his lack of taste buds.

"We want to know about Jack," I said, filling up our glasses again. The faster my tongue went numb, the better. "He's in town skinning people like the good old days in Jolly Old England. God Save the Queen and all that good crap. What do you know about that?"

"Jack *mayashnik*. Jack the Butcher. I know of him. Little, but I know of him." The water sloshed around him. It smelled like cold metal. Boris smelled cold, period. The water washed away the blood he lived on and only left the cold.

He drank again and waited until we did the same. "I should've let you come alone. I'll have to do a juice cleansing for a month to repair this damage," Nik said.

"It might loosen you up," I needled. "Turn you into Goodfellow or anyone who doesn't think trimming bonsai trees is a wild and crazy Friday night."

"If I did loosen up, I might start swatting the back of your head and not stop until your skull and what little contents it contains is crushed to a fine paste." He turned his attention to Boris. We did need to wrap this up before morning light and the people that came with it. *Vyodanoi* were shy in the daylight. They'd eat a human—snack of choice—but they were shy outside the river even with coats and hats to help them blend in. "Boris, where is Jack in the city? How can we find him?"

"How can you find a single drop of rain in a storm?" Boris didn't have shoulders to shrug with, but the tilting back and forth of his glass had the same effect.

"Hey, if I wanted a bad fortune cookie cliché, I'd take my vodka to a Chinese restaurant. Niko has more than glasses tucked away in his coat. He has a gallon jug full of salt. Happy fucking birthday to you, Boris. So talk sense or we take you out like a garden slug." You serve the wrong drink to the wrong customer at work, in this case a margarita with salt, and you find out new and interesting ways to kill certain species. That unfortunate *vyodanoi* had ended up a river of ooze down the unisex/species bathroom drain at the Ninth Circle. I had no problem doing the same to Boris if I thought he was holding shit back.

Niko tried a less homicidal approach. "We know you like to talk, Boris. So simply talk. That's all we want."

"No one knows where Jack hides." He drank and waited until we followed suit. "The revenants in the sewers have not seen him. The Kin in their warehouses

have not seen him. Boggle in her forest has not seen him.
Vampires with their love of high places and fancy pent-
houses have not seen him. We *vyodanoi* in the rivers have
not seen him. We see the bodies he leaves but we do not
see him. Jack is *paien* but he refutes his own kind. Never
have I heard of him associating with any of us."

"Great. Even *paien* serial killers have to be the stereo-
typical loner. He's probably a white male between his
late twenties and early thirties too with a dislike of government authority," I groused. All three of us drank
this time. "Do you at least know what type of *paien* he
is? Goodfellow, you know Goodfellow. He's the puck
who stole your wallet two weeks ago. He said Jack fits
the description of a storm spirit."

"But all well-known and strong storm spirits are ac-
counted for elsewhere," Niko said. "And Jack would
have to be strong from what we've seen."

"And experienced," I added glumly.

Boris waited until more vodka had been poured and
consumed. I'd lost count how many shots we were
on . . . five . . . six maybe . . . all in less than twenty or
so minutes. I was starting to feel like Boris was a good
guy. He might not know shit and he ate people, but
were any of us perfect? I shouldn't have threatened to
salt him. That was rude. Funny, too, the way the other
one had melted like the witch in *The Wizard of Oz*,
which I've never seen and did not have a horrific fear
of flying monkeys until I was ten no matter what Nik
said.

Now . . . what were we talking about again?

I was either leaning heavily against Nik or he was

leaning heavily against me. I didn't drink a lot, but I did drink some. With Niko's body-temple philosophy his tolerance would be zero. I was surprised he wasn't facedown in the mud. Mind over matter. Mind over alcohol. Figured.

"The river has been turbulent. They do that when storm spirits are around. It is possible, but I cannot say for certain." Boris's whistle was getting sluggish, and as he bathed in vodka I knew it wasn't from overdoing in the drinking department. "The morning is here. Time for me to sleep at the river bottom. Wrapped in the mud. Peaceful. Would you like to see?" The line drawing of a human face was inches from mine, the large sucker mouthing hungrily at the air. It was so abrupt and fast that with half my blood replaced by vodka it was practically a 3-D special effect out of a slasher movie—aimed to surprise and terrify.

Which was what Boris was shooting for: terrifying. I fell over backward to get space between me and that round mass of pulsing blood-hungry flesh. Leeches . . . I wasn't terrified as Boris had hoped, but I was disgusted to the power of ten. "Why do all our informants try to kill us? Is it my breath? I was liking you, too, Boris. I really was. You're a good customer. Great tipper. Still a homicidal fiend though," I slurred. "Salt the son of a bitch, Nik."

Whatever his tolerance, he made with the salt like Paula Deen in her prediabetic days. Seconds later I was wearing what was left of Boris with no convenient bathroom drain for this *vyodanoi* to slime his way down this time.

"Come on," I groaned. "Zombie funk and now this?" I lifted both arms and Boris in the form of a half-gelatinous, half-liquid form cascaded off me onto the ground. "Seriously, Nik, if it's my breath, that's something I'd want to know." I closed my eyes and the world began spinning in a way I'd been unfortunately familiar with a time or two in the past. "I'd puke but I already *am* puke. Salty puke."

"It's not your breath." Nik stood, unsteady but only if you knew to look for it. He reached down and pulled me up. "You use that idiotic kid's toothpaste. Your breath smells like mint-chocolate . . . and onion chili-cheese dogs with mustard . . . and Mountain Dew. All right, it might be your breath. But more likely it's that we have tended to kill their friends or relatives—and perhaps neighbors, pets, babysitters in the past."

"They hold grudges . . . like bitchy little girls." I swayed but managed to stay upright.

"They hold grudges like murderous creatures who would eat us on the best of days." Niko raised a hand as if he was going to try to wipe away some of the goo that covered me, but then pulled his hand back. "You are a lost cause." Then he slid behind me, put a boot in my ass, and shoved me headfirst into the river.

Sputtering, I climbed back out of the water. "I don't like you drunk. You do hurtful things you can't take back. PSA from me to you." I was clean of slime, but not necessarily smelling much better. The East River wasn't a mountain spring, although the mob—the human mob—had stopped dumping bodies there years ago.

"I would've done that sober," Nik said placidly.

"True. You suck." I shook water off in the tried-and-true dog method and managed to splatter him in the process.

"So you have told me many times. Many, many, many . . . enough that I am considering buying duct tape for your mouth . . . times."

"You would be the one person, Nik, who doesn't change at all when drunk." I snorted and flung off more water. "I was hoping you'd loosen up and do some crazy shit. Crazy for you anyway—like try to trim Ishiah's wings into those creepy topiary shapes from *The Shining* if he was around. Or whip up some soy piña coladas—but, you know, *manly* piña coladas, then sit on me and force me to watch a *Kung Fu* marathon. But, nope. You're the same."

"And you excel at pointing out the obvious. Let's go. We learned nothing we didn't already know, that he might be a storm spirit, but no one knows for certain. I'm annoyed. Plus I imagine I'm going to have a hangover. I'd rather have it in my bed than facedown on the grass."

That I agreed with. It wouldn't do to leave the vodka bottles for whoever wanted to risk the *vyodanoi* slime for them. The homeless wouldn't be a problem. Some overly curious biologist who'd never seen slime of that particular consistency and color before so let's get that puppy under a microscope would be. I picked up a bottle in each hand and we turned to start slogging home through the park. The sky was now the color of snow melting into a sewer drain. It didn't bode well for blue skies and a sunny day. That was good. Sunny days were hell on a hangover.

Minutes later Niko took my arm. "Stop."

I knew that tone even in this state. I dropped the vodka and had a hand inside my jacket and resting on the butt of my Desert Eagle almost before the bottles hit the ground. There was a time I wouldn't have carried something in both hands; I always kept a hand free. When I was a little more human, a little less Auphe, and a lot less arrogant.

Maybe a little less drunk too.

My eyes narrowed. Not against the sun, which was practically nonexistent, but against two pieces of knowledge. The first being the uneasy fact I was going to have to come clean with Nik about what had happened at the Ninth Circle. The second being that I might have fucked up. It wasn't guaranteed, but it was enough to cut through the haze of alcohol blurring my vision with a spike of adrenaline. What were the odds of a *paien* obsessed with punishing the wicked and a bunch of humans talking about prayer and Heaven with knives in their hands and death in their hearts?

I'd sent eight of them out of this world three nights ago, if only temporarily, and now here were ten more to replace them. That made me question that "temporarily" issue with the others. They were the same as the others. Once-white hoodies, the smell of homelessness but not the smell of drugs or alcohol, fairly young, and each one with a knife that glittered as brightly as the judgment in their eyes.

They stood between us and the edge of the park and

how did they know that's where we'd be? A storm spirit that could appear and disappear at will would be good at following its targets, high enough not to be seen or smelled. *Shit*. I had fucked up. No way around it. But why would Jack have a human posse at his heels when a human was only another wicked scrap of flesh to be squirreled away and drooled over later? If there was logic in that, I wasn't seeing it.

One of the men, this one with dirty brown dreads, stepped closer. "Have you prayed? Have you prayed to Heaven to be lifted up?" He was staring at Niko, who had set his feet and looked much steadier than he had moments ago—definitely mind over matter. The man's question as earnest as it could be when framed by psychotic eyes and a knife.

Luckily there was no one in this part of the park this early—barely dawn. "What about me?" I drawled. "Isn't Heaven concerned about me?" . . . anymore.

That brought the attention of ten pair of eyes to me. The leader of this *Eat, Pray, Kill* club answered. "Heaven cannot hear your prayers, Godless creature. You are a blot on the earth."

Apparently once Jack had found out about the Auphe in me he had spread the good word. Heaven didn't want me, loathed my very existence, and I'd thought it had sucked to be picked last at dodgeball.

They were connected all right. Yep, I'd fucked up. Fucked up bad.

Now they were moving toward us. It seemed they'd happily stab Niko and sing a hymn or two as his soul was lifted up unto Heaven, but they'd also just as happily kill me and where my soul went, they didn't give a crap. As I wasn't sure I had a soul or that souls existed at all, I didn't much give a crap myself, but I would like to stay alive—screw the philosophical debate.

I pulled the Eagle and aimed it at the one in front. My hand wasn't as steady as I'd like, but at least I didn't have double vision. "Okay, Nik, time for a little guidance. They're killers, but they could be insane so technically it might not be their fault. This is one of those gray areas where someone with a better handle on morality should call the shots. My decision might be extreme." I'd already proven that once before. "Do we kill them or not?"

I personally thought that if they were crazy, it wasn't a kind of crazy you could fix. It was a kind of crazy they had chosen. They'd picked up knives instead of pamphlets. If they had chosen Jack on top of the rest of it, hell, there was no pill for that. Also, I didn't like being stabbed. It was one of my least favorite injuries. Avoiding that would be good.

"No killing." Niko had his sword out. "Even impaired, you're more than good enough to take them down without necessarily killing all of them."

It wasn't what I wanted to hear, but it was what I expected. Unless one of them got very lucky there was still more than enough distance to do as Nik wanted. The same hadn't necessarily been true at the Ninth Circle, but, then again, whose fault had that been?

"You will not touch us. We are sanctified, soon to be apprentices. You took once, but you will not be allowed to take again," said the one still striding toward us.

Yeah . . . that sounded good. But he was wrong. The crazies usually are. I liked that dependable quality in them.

I started firing. I was a good shot. I practiced daily and had since I was sixteen. That made a thigh shot easy enough and hopefully shatter the bone. They might walk after that, but they wouldn't ever run again, with or without a knife. If I hadn't been trading shots of vodka with Boris, I would've done that. But it was too risky now. If a single shot went astray, went past one of them, someone two blocks away could die while talking on their cell phone. Not good. I aimed for the good old center mass as they taught you first day on the gun range. The first three fell before the others realized what was happening and dissolved into a small charging mob. They had guts, crazy or not, and if Niko had thought they were more of a threat their guts would've been on the grass. As it was, he had ample time to flank them and hamstring four of them. That left one turning on him and two still coming at me. I shot them both in the stomach. Depending on the speed of the ambulances and the skill of the surgeons, some of them could survive. I'd made the effort. It was the best I could do.

Niko had grabbed the hair of one he'd put down either about to ask what cult he belonged to or to give him tips on how to better grip his knife while attacking, but the scream of approaching sirens put an end to that. I grabbed one of the bottles of vodka and tossed it to him and carried the last myself as we ran. I'd never been fingerprinted. Nothing would show up, but neither did I want my fingerprints on file as unknown assailant in a homeless Hibachi practice gone horribly wrong.

We were halfway home when Niko finally said what I wasn't jumping to volunteer. "I don't think that was any sort of coincidence, do you?"

I thought about opening the vodka, thought long and hard never mind my head was already aching, before admitting, "I think it's the second noncoincidence to happen to me this week."

12

Niko

Twelve Years Ago

Coincidence, I wasn't a big believer . . . philosophically or practically.

The books I'd started reading on men and women throughout history and their thoughts on the universe, the ones I was drawn to the most told me coincidence was my mind glimpsing a truth I didn't understand.

There were more coincidences around Junior than I cared for.

But a serial killer next door—it would be ridiculous overkill on the universe's part with all the rest we had in our lives. How could someone believe that? What I meant, of course, was how could I believe that?

I decided what I found in the library at the end of the

day would make up my mind for me. If I found something about a missing prostitute, unlikely, Cal and I would leave. If I found nothing, I'd tell Cal he was wrong, to stay out of Junior's backyard, and we'd get on with our lives—as weird and strange as those lives were.

The decision should've made me feel better, but the back of my neck itched as I continued with the test on my desk. Miss Holcomb, the psychology teacher, hovered over my shoulder watching for a few minutes although I always scored As and never needed help. Some teachers took their jobs very seriously and sometimes . . . I sighed and finished up.

With each period and through lunch the itch grew worse until finally it was sixth period and time for study hall and the library. I liked school. I always had. I liked any and all subjects. I liked reading ahead as the classes were too slow. That didn't change when I skipped a grade. But while I liked schools I was obsessed with libraries. I could spend an entire day in a real library. I'd not been to a school with what I considered a genuine library yet, but some towns we lived in were college towns and college libraries were amazing enough that I thought living in one would be better than any place else I could imagine. Cal thought I was crazy. He, naturally, wanted to live in the volcano lair of a supervillain. He considered superheroes too mopey and whiny with highly substandard costumes. He was so heated on the subject that when I pictured myself in college in a few years and Cal living with me, the mental image was always in a volcano with black capes everywhere and thousands of bookshelves, before the image morphed into your average student apartment.

Considering once Cal made up his mind, thus it was written and so it would be, I should give serious thought to either making certain the college of my choice was far from a volcano or finding lava-proof shelves.

This school, the Hermann T. Jeffries High School, didn't have the worst library I'd seen, but it didn't have the best either. Normally that would've bothered me as I spent study hour there, but today all I was interested in was the computer. The one single, solitary, slow enough ancient Egyptians could've carved the information I wanted in hieroglyphs into a pyramid inner chamber wall before it booted up computer.

"Niko, are you waiting for . . . Oh my God. I'm so sorry. I'm just checking my e-mail. I know you probably want to really work. You're completely smart. I get that. You need it more than I do." The girl stood up and spilled the contents of her backpack on the floor. "Oh my God," she repeated. "Oh my God. Shit. Oh my God. I know you don't say things like that. At least I never hear you. I'm sorry. Are you religious? Did I offend you?"

That was Avery. She wasn't in any of my classes, but she spent sixth period in the library too, more because she didn't have anything better to do than a love for books. She didn't wear makeup and was neither pretty nor plain, although she had autumn-gold eyes and dark brown hair that was thick and hung in long natural waves. She wasn't smart and she wasn't stupid; she was a nice average girl who didn't realize that average can sometimes be the best thing to be. There was nothing wrong with walking the middle path, being neither the high nor the low. I liked being smart, but I knew it was an accident of birth, a genetic gift. It wasn't encouragement on the home front. I enjoyed the escape that books and tailoring my future that intelligence let me have. The downside of being smart was realizing how hard it would be to get that future and the truly desperate need for escape I had.

I saw too much.

Cal was smart and Cal saw the things I did, but he reacted differently and saw what I saw in a way unlike mine. My intelligence had me clawing at anything and everything to get us free. Jobs, education, plan after plan. Cal's intelligence had him seeing the only way out as patience. He was like a wild panther in the zoo, still as a stone, eyes unblinking, never sleeping, waiting for the one day someone got sloppy with that cage door and then it would all be over.

I didn't know which way was the best, the least painful, but I did know at times I wished I was average, normal . . . even if that meant only I was somewhat less smart. I didn't like seeing too much, as necessary as it was.

Bending down, I helped a self-conscious, bright red Avery gather up her books, papers, a handful of discarded costume jewelry. "No, I'm not religious. My little brother curses worse than you. Don't worry about it."

"Good. Great!" She took everything from my hands and stuffed it, Cal-style, back in her backpack. "The last thing I'd want to do is embarrass myself in front of you. You're"—her blush intensified and she swallowed—"you know."

Avery also liked me. I thought it was another reason she spent her study period in the library. I liked her too. I wasn't the kind of snob that thought I was too smart for certain people. With my life, I appreciated, *wanted* normal. Average and nice was better than brilliant and beautiful in my mind.

But I also remembered what Cal had said, that we couldn't have a normal life. That meant we couldn't have normal people around us . . . any people when it came down to it. He'd been right for now. I hoped I was right when I said the future would be better, that then we could have a normal life—normal for us at least.

Now though . . . now I couldn't do anything about Avery liking me. When she finished zipping up her bag, I gave her the smile—it was a practiced one. It said you're a nice person but you're not for me. Friends? You could read a lot into that smile. He has a girlfriend at another school, he's gay, he actually is screwing Miss Holcomb. It usually worked and as Avery gave me a wobbly but not a terribly upset smile back, I hoped it had worked again.

When she was gone, I sat down at the computer, the itch now claws digging into my neck, and started searching the online news for New London. I wouldn't find anything. There was no chance, I told the claws clamping tight. If Junior had taken that hooker and that was very unlikely, it wouldn't be in the paper yet. Prostitutes disappeared all the time. Often they never make the news, vanished or not.

Unless you happened to be the daughter of a cop. Doctor, lawyer, cop—it didn't matter how high your parents were, drugs could take you to the lowest of places. Marcia Dawn Liese had known that. It was hard to recognize her with blond hair, a cheerleader uniform, and pom-poms from a two-year-old picture compared to the Goth wig and little else she'd been wearing when Junior had pulled up in his truck, but it was her. I remembered that distinctive mole at the corner of her mouth. Marcia had been missing at least twenty-four hours if not longer and that put her disappearance close enough to her interaction with Junior that I could've set my watch. The claws left my neck and now were ripping their way through my stomach.

Our neighbor is a serial killer.

He smells like blood.

Like roadkill.

The basement is full of bodies.

Cal had told me and I hadn't believed him . . . because I hadn't wanted to believe him. My life was an abusive mother and a little brother who wasn't completely human and the monsters who watched him. I didn't know what to do. Every day I straightened things, I kept schedules, I made rules, and it was all to cover up to Cal and to myself that I didn't know what to *do*.

I had known I couldn't handle anything more. A serial killer? That was insane and I wouldn't have cared what Cal had said; it absolutely was not an option. I couldn't believe it, as I couldn't deal with it.

That was the joke—because now it was dealing with me and that was much worse than anything I could've imagined. Junior right next door. Cal's school getting out a half hour before mine. I was already running for the door. It would be all right. Junior didn't know. He hadn't seen us follow him. He hadn't seen me in the hospital. He was a killer—I tasted vomit in my mouth—but he wasn't smart. I'd looked into his eyes. He was dull and slow. He didn't have any idea we suspected him . . . Cal had suspected him.

I'd go home, get Cal, and we'd leave. Like we should've done from the start . . . but hadn't as I was too much of a coward to believe my little brother.

Smells like blood.

Home and then out of this town. It would be all right. Junior wouldn't even suspect why we left. It would be all right. It would.

I kept running.

And my mind kept telling me no matter how true it was, I would always be stained a coward and a liar from this day on.

By the time I ran the ten miles home I was drenched in sweat, my lungs raw, and my legs cramping from a speed I'd not pushed them to before. I jammed the key with a fatigued shaking hand into the lock and threw open the door.

"Cal?" I slammed the door behind me and locked it. "Start packing. Hurry! We're going. Now."

I heard the sound of a comic book being thrown against the wall and fluttering to the floor from our bedroom. "We don't have time for this! Don't pretend like you're upset. You've been saying we should go for days." Cal rarely threw temper tantrums or showed physical anger of any kind. Not since he'd found out he was half-Grendel. He was afraid what might happen if he did, that he'd start and not be able to stop.

Grendels didn't have the teeth they did only to play peekaboo through the windows.

"Did something happen? Next door? Cal, seriously, we have to go. I looked up that prostitute. . . ." I stepped into the bedroom and two prongs hit me in the side of the neck. I fell, convulsing. Every muscle locked, the pain hot and unrelenting through every nerve I had.

"Something did happen next door, neighbor." Junior grinned down at me with dull yellow teeth. "And a fuck's sight more is going to."

I hadn't expected him to be in our house. It didn't cross my mind. It should've. Every instructor I'd had told me the people who go down in attacks, the people who sometimes die, they weren't watching. You watch every second and you don't stop that, not for any reason.

The prongs and wire retracted into the boxy shape in Junior's hand. "Your kid brother didn't much like this either. He's pretty small. I thought for a minute I'd killed him and that would've been a damn shame. I have big plans for him and for you, so don't you feel left out." A hand covered my mouth with a folded cloth as I tried to get up, but I couldn't do more than twitch.

"It's chloroform, but it's homemade. I'm afraid it'll give you one helluva headache when you wake up or if I mixed it wrong you might not wake up at all. You'd probably prefer that, but I wouldn't. Keep your fingers crossed for me."

Yellow and black pools of hazardous waste began to puddle across my vision. It was almost dark outside. He had to wait fifteen or twenty minutes; then he'd be able to drag me over to his house and no one would see. I used all the energy I could gather to reach up a hand and claw at the rag across my face.

"Now, Niko, that's the name your brother screamed when I was waiting for him like I waited for you. That must make you Niko. Don't be that way, Nicky. Don't you want to see your little brother again? Whole anyway? It's harder to make them out once they're in pieces, the bodies. You have to blur your eyes, you know, like at those crazy posters with the hidden spaceships."

The hand across my face was unmovable. I thought Junior was fat and sloppy, but there was hard muscle under it. It was one more thing I hadn't seen. I'd thought he was dim and slow. I hadn't seen the cunning predator in his eyes or heard the lie in his words. And now . . . now I couldn't see anything. I could still hear the mumble of his voice, dribbling on, but that too faded. I faded with it with five words echoing over and over in my mind.

Your little brother.

In pieces.

13

Cal

Present Day

Pieces of eight.

I'd wanted to be a pirate when I was a kid—after cowboy and before race car driver. I would rather have told a story about that kind of pieces of eight than the one I did have to tell. Eight men—eight pieces in a game—eight possible pawns.

I told Niko about the other men by the Ninth Circle, members of the same prayer circle as the ones in East River Park, and I told him exactly what I'd done with them—how I'd sent them away, how I'd brought them back. I was honest though—about how near a thing it had been to leaving them gone for good. All he had to say was we'd had this discussion and while unfortunately it had been after the fact, he wasn't going to insult me by repeating the lecture. He also said that while I had done it, I'd also fixed it. I should give myself credit for that. I'd overcome a bad impulse when it would've been easier not to. He was proud.

Back in the recliner resting my ribs and my growing hangover, I thought about replying that he always enjoyed both insulting me and lecturing me, but I didn't. I didn't want to turn that pride into a smack to the back of my head. And he could be right. At the park I had asked Nik what the right thing to do was. I was trying. That I was trying less for my sake or the world's sake and more for my brother's sake, that didn't matter. I was trying and the reason I chose to try was Niko. That counted. To me.

Considering Niko brought me a Mountain Dew to keep me from getting it myself and forcing me into another swipe at the codeine, which he would promptly confiscate as it didn't mix well with alcohol, made me think it counted to him too. My boss, Ishiah—they didn't come too much holier-than-thou than him—had once told me Niko was a good man, among the best of men, but his fatal flaw was that he'd burn down the world to save me.

That he was the sole reason that I wouldn't burn down the world said something . . . we were the flip side of a coin. That kind of balance was something the Buddha-loving badass that was my brother could understand. It didn't matter what you'd rather have or that things would be easier another way—the world was about balance. I didn't give a crap about Buddha and yet I knew that.

Nik disappeared down the hall and returned without his coat. He shrugged out of the harness that held his katana and placed it on the kitchen counter. Normally he would've left it in the bedroom with his duster, but with Jack popping in and out, he'd want his preferred blade close. He had more than enough practice and nonpractice blades in the gym area, but your favorite was your favorite. If you were going to be prepared, you may as well be prepared with the best.

"Goodfellow should be here by now," I grumped, "with my pizza." We'd called him to come talk about this new development, if it was one. I knew coincidences were rare, but I wasn't looking forward to admitting I'd been jumped by a bunch of homeless men in white who wanted me to pray to Heaven while they killed me and I'd casually chalked it up to that Cuckoo for Cocoa Puffs New York experience every tourist campaign told you didn't exist.

I would have stuck to coincidence, too, if it hadn't been for the second attack. Jack working with his prey didn't make sense and I wasn't sure I believed that's what was happening here. Didn't believe one hundred percent, which was important. I wasn't a gambling man. It was ridiculous to pin a theory on Niko's estimated eighty-nine percent. He was throwing numbers around and if I had to hear one more time how he scored first in his college statistics class . . .

"I have arrived." The door was wide, soundlessly

picked and opened as always. "Where are the flower petals beneath my feet? Where are the virgins to feed me honey and grapes? At the very least where is my theme song? Some Barry White would be astoundingly appropriate." The puck was grinning cheerfully, haloed by the weak sunlight. Ten hours away from Jack had either done him good or . . . shit, he'd gotten laid too.

Goddamn it, I remembered those days. I had to get back out there. Unfortunately the Auphe weren't popular with *paien* just for a chat. Screwing was almost always a no go. Humans were completely out of the question. I couldn't risk getting someone pregnant. I couldn't risk making another Auphe mix-breed like me.

"Where's my pizza?" I demanded flatly.

"I brought you pancakes the other morning. Once a year is my limit for taking pity on the celibate." He clapped his hands together and kicked the door shut behind him. "What's the lead on Jack? The sooner we put him down like a pack of plague-ridden squirrels, wretched rodents, the sooner I can stop babysitting you two and get back to the debauchery that is my life."

"Monogamous debauchery?" I tapped fingers on the arm of the recliner. "Is that possible? And what about Ish stealing all your cards from the bad old days of whoring, whoring, and a little more whoring?"

"He made that all better. Kissed it better, isn't that the saying?" The grin was all debauchery now, monogamous or not. "Would you like to know where he kissed it?"

"Nik," I said desperately, "how about you fill him in

on my massive fuckup." Forget the hundred percent bar. I would own that fuckup, propose to that fuckup, and marry that fuckup if it would stop Goodfellow.

Niko, whose face was more impassive than usual, meaning his hangover was epic, was leaning against the wall while Goodfellow sprawled on the couch. I didn't blame him. The wall looked safer. "We already told you about Jack's victims being what he could consider wicked."

"Not that that explains why Jack first went after Niko and kept on him once he dumped me like bad chicken salad," I interjected.

"You have much in common with bad chicken salad. I'd not thought of that. Nausea inducing, occasionally deadly. A smell that is decidedly off . . ."

"Hey!" I protested. "I shower every day. Ask Nik. He keeps trying to charge me for that Amish soap of his I steal."

Robin waved it off, having accomplished his goal of pissing me off for the day. "Back to Jack. It is still true about Niko. He shouldn't be wicked in Jack's eyes," Robin mused. "Wholesome and noble as a nun knitting socks for orphans, that is your brother. He is a warrior but not a murderer."

"Then there is the fact we have now run into two groups of humans. They're obviously homeless, but they dress in white sweatshirts, don't drink or do drugs, but they are very insistent that we pray to Heaven and God and they have large knives to force the issue," Niko went on. "It seems unlikely Jack who is concerned with the wicked and these humans who are concerned with sending souls to Heaven would appear at the same time and not in some way be connected."

"And once again, they don't give a damn about me, just Niko," I said. "How would they know I wasn't human unless Jack told them? They called me a Godless creature, which I'm guessing means *paien* and especially Auphe aren't welcome into their Heaven."

They had been concerned about my soul at first and were now concerned about Niko's. They wanted to save his soul for Heaven—just like Jack wanted to save the skin of the wicked. But Niko wasn't wicked, not immoral, not . . .

Sinful.

"Shit," I said. "A s*inner*. That son of a bitch Jack thinks he's *saving* sinners. He kept saying saving and I thought he meant it as in saving the skin of the wicked as trophies. He didn't. He meant save as in save us from our sins. Save our . . . what? Souls?"

Did it matter? There were a thousand types of crazy. Religious crazy was one pretzel in a jumbo-sized bag of them. How or why it got Jack's rocks off was irrelevant to the fact that it did and what he would do to make it happen.

"It would explain why he kills by skinning," Robin said with an uneasy edge. There was something peculiar in his voice, swimming in the depths. Something more than what we were now guessing. "'And the priest who offers any man's burnt offering, that priest shall have for himself the skin of the burnt offering which he has offered.' Leviticus 7:7–9."

I wasn't surprised the puck knew his Bible. If there was a commandment he hadn't broken, he'd take it as a personal challenge. As he'd once said, Christians love to take the sin out of "sinsational."

"Jack bases his pathology in religion—many do. He even has followers who want to be his apprentices. It's not that uncommon for religious cult figures. You led your own religion in the past not to forget," Niko pointed out to Goodfellow, "but that doesn't explain why he has zeroed in on us to begin with."

Nik was right—why Jack had fixed on us was still up in the air. The big question. How had we come on his radar?

"I'm bringing Ishiah in on this. He might be able to contribute . . . something." Robin had his phone out and was sending a text, the uneasy air about him thickening with every moment that passed. "And truly you are the unluckiest bastards I've ever come to know. First the Auphe race and what they did to you, the fact your career has you testicles deep in the worst predators in the city on a near daily basis, and then comes the serial killers. This is your second now in your mayfly-short human lives. That should be unheard of."

"What's Ish going to know? And actually this is the third," I corrected without much thinking about it. I should have. I should have thought about it with extreme and excruciating care.

Niko turned the color of mud under his dark skin and I gave my tongue a savage punishing bite. We didn't talk about it. I wouldn't put him through that again, not in word or thought. I knew better.

However, I didn't get the reaction I expected. His hands were suddenly on my shoulders, shaking me hard in the recliner, harder than he ever would have with my cracked ribs, control of his own strength abruptly gone. "In Connecticut, in New London, what was his real name? His last name? I never knew. I didn't find out afterward. I didn't try. I didn't want to know. Cal, what was it?"

At eleven there wouldn't be much reason I would've known. Kids aren't interested in things like that and after all of it, as Nik said, after all that happened I didn't want to know. But I had also been an eleven-year-old period. Niko had idealized me, as good big brothers do, in a way that blurred certain memories now and certain knowledge then.

At eleven, I stole shit like a motherfucker.

He never knew. It was only little things. Candy, loose change, skateboards, and just once a porno magazine from our serial-killing next-door neighbor. I'd taken it from his mailbox, scanned it, and trashed it far from home one day before Niko had gotten back from work. This was before I guessed about the killings, but I remembered his name from the address label on the cover—after what had happened, after the basement, the bodies, the attic . . . Jesus Christ, after the attic, as much as I wanted to, tried to, how could I forget?

"Hammersmith," I said, throat oddly dry from such a blood-soaked past. "James Hammersmith." Junior. Junior Hammersmith.

Junior who liked to kill drug dealers, thieves, and prostitutes the same as Jack.

Both with no tolerance for wickedness or sinners in any form.

Robin was staring at us, paused in midtext. "Spring-heeled Jack murdered several in Hammersmith, England. It was one of his favorite hunting grounds. What happened? Who is this James H—"

Niko cut him off with a fierce ruthlessness I could feel in the grip that remained on my shoulders, his fingers biting down to press on bone. I don't think he was seeing me anymore. "His worshipper. His murdering bastard of an *apprentice*." Like the men in the park who were waiting to become just that. "Junior who said his master liked to watch from above when lightning was in the sky. Junior who liked to *sign* his work just like Jack."

He was right. It was the only explanation. That's why Jack wanted us—for what we'd done to his apprentice. And while Nik had never told me twelve years ago that slice on my chest was Junior's start to "signing" me with a J for Junior or for his Jack, I had noticed the similarity in the slashes from Jack's first attack on me in my bedroom. But in our lives a slash is a slash and very easy to come by. The only reason I'd noticed is that they were both especially neat and straight, but out of as many as I'd had, nothing to get excited about. There wouldn't have been reason then for Nik to make the connection, not with that single clue, particularly not when we'd both done our best together and separately to bury those memories of Junior.

Jack drifted from town to town, city to city, country

to country. When he came to New York, we were just lucky enough he hadn't forgotten Junior or us. Ain't it the fucking way?

Peeling his fingers off of me, Niko took one breath, another, and then was in the gym destroying everything in his path. Weapons were thrown with savage force to shatter at the wall. The mat was being cut to ribbons.

I scrambled out of the chair, fuck the ribs, and pushed Goodfellow back when he would've followed. I'd seen Nik lose his shit only one other time. That had been bad. There weren't words for the level of bad that had been. But that had been internal with his lethal control intact on the outside to leave him somewhat functional—to leave the world itself somewhat functional. This . . . this was not functional. Not for Nik.

This was not Nik at all—not the Nik of now.

"What is wrong with him? He's gone mad. But Niko isn't mad. Niko is, *malaka*, the sanest of us all." Goodfellow sounded shocked. He'd seen only Niko's meticulously controlled outer shell. He didn't know what was under it. No one knew: not the puck, not Promise. No one but me and having lived through it with him, I wished neither of us had to know.

It could be a flashback, a genuine one. It could be finally dealing with what he hadn't let himself process then. I didn't know which, but it didn't matter. Getting Niko back from this was the important thing. I'd swear to anyone I hadn't read a psychology book in my life, but I had. I'd read a fuck ton of them as a teenager when I'd finally comprehended Nik's unforgiving life in a way that I couldn't at eleven. Even a few years older I couldn't protect him like he protected me, but at least I could understand him and what he was doing to himself for me. I read Nik's books when he was at work or school, when he couldn't see me. I'd read them for precisely this. I didn't know it would come, but I didn't know that it wouldn't either.

Now I knew.

No matter how deep you bury things, they always dig their way to the surface, more malignant and rotten than when you'd shoved them under in the beginning. No one would guess it and I wished I could deny it, but on the inside, Niko was every bit as fractured and fucked-up as I was. The leash on his issues was sturdier than mine, but eventually every leash breaks.

Sooner or later in this world, everything breaks.

Every*one* breaks.

"Do you know how old Niko was when he first killed for me?" I hissed in the puck's ear as I shoved him farther back out of range as a sharp sai flew over our heads. "Fifteen. He was *fifteen* when he killed Jack's homicidal buddy. Why do you think he is the way he is? All Zen and so fucking bottled up? It's because he's a time bomb. He killed a man to save my life when he was fifteen, lived through dragging my ass back to sanity after two years in Auphe Hell, ran with me to escape the sons of bitches, and lost me again. And then again and fucking *again*. You don't know what's inside him and what he's had to do to stay sane." To watch out for me, but not lose it so much that everyone he sees is a threat? To know that it's not necessary to bury his katana in everyone who walks within a block of me although that's exactly what his instincts and our history told him he should do?

Of all of it, what had happened when he was fifteen with Junior, it had been the worst. Over the Auphe stealing me away, it had been the worst, because I'd warned Nik about Junior and he hadn't believed me. He wouldn't forgive himself for that and I couldn't get him over it as we didn't talk about that time. We both thought we had our reasons.

I would simply have to make sure mine didn't come to light, but Niko's . . . it was time for them to see the light of day. No more hiding for him. It had turned cancerous, poisonous, and it had to be cut away before he could heal.

Because this? What was happening now? This was as far from recovery as you could get.

Nik was now chopping viciously at the pummel horse with a sword. I couldn't remember the god-awful jokes Robin had told when he'd first seen that piece of equipment, not with the raw snarl on Niko's face. I knew what he was seeing and it wasn't a piece of gym equipment. It was Junior. Given the opportunity Nik would kill Junior a hundred more times and it would still not be enough.

He'd left a part of himself in that attic he had not gotten back and now he was back there, losing more of himself. That was not fucking acceptable.

"Stay here." I shoved Robin down on the floor between the couch and the table. "I don't think he'll know who you are." He would know who I was. I didn't question that, not as I sprang up from my crouch, ran across the floor, and tackled him from the side as he sliced a blade into a punching bag. I knew he saw me coming. I knew he was armed. I knew he was out of his mind.

And I knew he wouldn't hurt me.

This brutality was aimed at himself, along with a stark self-blame that had his control so abruptly shattered. He held on to the sword like it was his only lifeline as we lay on our sides where I'd taken us down on the mat. "It's me, Nik. It's Cal. It's Cal, big brother. Junior's gone. He's been gone a long time. It's just us." For a second, I thought I was wrong. I thought he didn't know me, but then he turned his head back toward me and I saw the recognition, the blood from twelve years ago spilling behind his eyes. With the blood came sanity, although I couldn't be certain he was happy to have it back. He dropped the sword and rolled over to wrap his arms around me, hurting too much to know how tightly he was holding on. He had to hold on, because he was lost. Nik, my brother—the man I'd thought of just days ago as fixed and unmoving as the North Star, was lost. He rested his forehead against mine and whispered one word for me alone. "Sorry."

Fifteen. He'd been fifteen damn years old. A kid. As if any of it could've been his fault.

I lifted my hand to grasp his trailing braid and gave it a hard tug, that reassuring weight he was used to. He was sorry and I didn't know that there was much that I could say that would change his mind about anything. I said something else instead. "We're the reason Junior's dead. You're right, that's Jack's problem with our asses." I said it, because Nik needed it. The problem spelled out for him. That's how he managed to survive, to be able to take step after step, pretty much our entire lives, by fixing problems.

Goodfellow's voice was strained behind us. "Now that we know Jack's issue with you, we need to discuss something else." I lifted my head to see him standing now, only several feet from us with Ishiah behind him. Ishiah's wings were wrapped around Robin. To protect. To comfort. Both maybe? From their expression something bad was coming.

Could there possibly be worse than this?

"We need to talk about angels," Ishiah said.

Jack the storm spirit with wings who saved sinners, knew his Bible, raised the dead, had worshippers, and called humans his Flock. Goodfellow had been gathering the information and it had hit critical mass with "sinners," hoodie-clad praying followers, and the sacrificial skins. Enter Ishiah stage right. I shouldn't have been at all surprised by what my boss and Robin told us.

It didn't change the fact that I was.

"Let me get this straight: for six or seven *years* now you both, and everyone who works in the bar, have been lying to Nik and me about angels not existing. Is that right?" Hearing the words, I was still having trouble believing it.

I sat on the mat beside Niko, leaning against him. My ribs were screaming from the exertion, but they weren't my concern at the moment. I'd white-knuckled my way through worse. Nik needed me there and visibly alive rather than stumbling around the kitchen looking for pain pills. I could've tried to pull him with me, but from the set to his shoulders, moving wasn't part of his plan. Breathing was barely part of it. I wasn't the only one white-knuckling it, but while I'd gone through worse than cracked ribs, Niko hadn't gone through worse than this. Out of the corner of my eye I could almost see a short blond ponytail instead of a long braid, see a smaller frame, see eyes and a face that hadn't yet mastered the art of hiding emotion that could be used against him.

Niko looked much younger than twenty-seven right now. Younger and older and the misery and recriminations of twelve years ago so plain on his face that I glared at Goodfellow and Ishiah each time they started to glance at him. This was private and they had to be here, but they didn't have to see this. He'd recover . . . and he *would* recover . . . at his own pace. He didn't need them watching him like a lab experiment while he did it. Sympathy would make him feel only . . . lesser. Niko had stood firmly on his own two feet mentally before he could do it physically. He wouldn't be grateful to know someone saw him stumble.

"That whole 'peris are the seed behind the myth that became angels,' that was all bullshit?" I went on. I'd thought Robin lied as tricksters do, but that he'd never lied to us, nothing big at any rate. Well, he had and it was huge.

"It's only half a lie really." Robin was back on the

couch with Ishiah. "Peris aren't angels . . . anymore. Peris are retired angels with most of their heavenly powers stripped away. They're expatriates if you will. They've gone native. Earth is their home, not Heaven. So when you asked me if that first peri you saw was an angel I wasn't technically lying."

"You're a trickster. Jesus, take credit for it already, gloat, and go on. I'm used to watching your other victims be mortified. Why should I be any different?" And the other *paien* hadn't told me there were angels in addition to peris or where peris came from because I'd never asked. They assumed I knew. They knew, everyone knew. Why would they think anything else when it came to me?

"It's not like that," Robin protested, leaning forward to rest his elbows on his knees. "Although six years is a good record, and the fact you didn't even try to find out from anyone else because you found me that trustworthy while *knowing* I'm a trickster, that is rather priceless—" An elbow, and a sharp one if his wince was anything to go by, hit him in the ribs. "But that's neither here nor there. I didn't lie to simply amuse myself. Think, Cal. Think how young you were when you came to New York, the kid who thought he was a monster, the worst one in the world next to the Auphe. Your self-loathing was epic. Your angst astronomical. The whole emo-thing . . . well, it was a cultural trend and I won't go there. But if I'd told you that angels did exist, then you would've wanted to know about Heaven and then you would've asked about Hell. I knew precisely what you would think after that."

He was on the money, no doubt. Six years ago I'd have known there was a Hell. I'd have also known I was destined for it—no way out. "You're right." I leaned harder against Nik who hadn't said a word about any of this. I was beginning to worry. Shit, I was already worried. "I'd have thought I was on the Hell-express for sure."

"And now?" he asked, the curiosity plain in the inquisitive tilt of his head.

I gave him a black smile. "Hell? Let them lock the doors. They couldn't fucking survive my ass."

"Out of curiosity, where do *paien* go as apparently you're here to tell us Jack is an angel gone rogue and he cares nothing about *paien* souls?" It was Nik and better yet it was Nik with a pertinent Nik-style question and an instinctual leap that would be spooky if true. What the hell was I thinking: sinners, Bible, wicked, whores and thieves, raising the dead, judgmental ass—Jack was an angel all right.

"There are hundreds of *paien* heavens, fewer hells though—we're not quite so condemning. For every *paien* race there is at least one heaven if not ten or twelve. Anything you can imagine is out there."

I didn't ask Goodfellow about Auphe Heaven and Hell. I imagined they were one and the same. If all you know is murder and torture, then you can't comprehend wrong and if you can't imagine wrong, you can't conceive of a punishment for it. That didn't mean I wanted to go to wherever dead Auphe went. Whatever they considered Heaven, I knew I'd consider Hell five times over. For the time being I let that go and waited on the Jack-the-angel question.

Ishiah's wings had disappeared once he'd sat down, but now, as they always did when he was annoyed, pissed, unsettled, conflicted—you name it— they'd reappeared. "Once Robin found out from you about the human followers mentioning praying and Heaven and put that together with Jack teleporting and raising the dead, he knew it had to be an angel, a particular angel. Pyriel. He's one of the angels responsible for examining the souls for purity in Heaven. He's also one of the very few angels and the only one missing that is entrusted with the power to raise the dead."

"That fits Jack. Judging all over the place and a fan of zombies, but what do you mean missing? Doesn't someone keep track of that? Like, I don't know, God?" I asked with caustic disbelief. Was heavenly bureaucracy truly that bad? Angels disappeared in the paperwork of it all?

"Pyriel has been missing almost five hundred years," Ishiah said. "The other angels are aware and have searched for him." Now the wings spread and I wondered how I'd ever doubted warriors of Heaven walked among us. "God is always present but does not interfere."

"Does not interfere? What do you mean doesn't interfere? You've got a psycho angel frigging skinning people for at least two hundred years. I think the time for interfering has long since come and gone and circled back to do a victory lap. What the hell?"

"God . . . does . . . not . . . interfere," Ishiah said in a tone as frozen as his eyes.

Goodfellow leaned back again, this time with feathers draping over his hair. "Let it go. It's a story for another time, one when peris aren't around."

"Don't you mean angels?" Niko substituted.

"No. There are no angels in New York City. They were banned over fifty years ago when a fight between them and some demons managed to get way out of control. Humans were running about screaming about Armageddon. It was a disaster. From that time on *paiens* have banned angels and demons from New York. If you come from Above or Below and show your face here, we *paiens* will work as one to rip it off of you. Only peris are allowed as they gave up their powers and transferred their allegiance to Earth not Heaven."

"Except for this Pyriel. Except for Jack." Niko didn't sound interested, but he didn't sound lost either. That was an improvement. Something this bizarre had to take his mind off the past—although Jack had in some part been involved with our past. I didn't think he'd been there the night Junior died. Junior said his master liked to watch. I remembered that through a chloroform haze, but I didn't think Jack had been watching or we might not be sitting here worrying about his angelic ass now.

"That's right. If Jack is this Pyriel and *paiens* stomp trespassing angels like cockroaches, why is he here? Why do none of you even know he's an angel?"

Robin shook his head, got to his feet, and brought me back a Mountain Dew to replace the one that spilled when Niko had grabbed me in the recliner. "Caffeine for your failing brain cells. You saw him. Did he look like an angel? Not that angels look like Ishiah, not all of the time—only when interacting with humans. But regardless, they don't look anything like Jack. Whatever he was, Pyriel isn't an angel any longer. Something has twisted him, mutated him. We keep thinking Jack is a storm spirit from the mist and the electrical activity. My best guess is that Pyriel was injured long ago and a storm spirit latched on to him when he was incapable of fighting it off. Some storm spirits aren't very bright, but they can be powerful parasites. Pyriel is now Jack and Jack is both less and more than an angel. Angels actually aren't that difficult to kill if you're quick with a shotgun."

"Is that information you felt necessary to share?" Ishiah demanded.

"Cal has already used a submachine gun on Jack. A shotgun is but a tinker toy to him," Robin retorted. "It's rather pointless anyway. As I said, we've tried that route on Jack. It was useless. The storm spirit, if it is one, surrounding him could stop the bullets from penetrating with wind, ice, who knows what else. What customarily works against angels isn't going to work with Jack, it seems."

Nik took my Mountain Dew and swallowed several times from the can. I think he had been fifteen the last time he'd had caffeine. He'd always been serious about martial arts thanks to the Grend—the Auphe outside our windows, but Junior had been the tipping point to devoting every aspect of his life to being the best fighter he could and that included nutrition. It was a good thing that rice was cheap. It was a long time before he could afford a variety of health food. Without rice he might have starved himself to death back then, the stubborn bastard.

I snatched my Mountain Dew back and said under my breath, "Okay, Nik, you're really beginning to freak me out."

He ran a less than reassuring hand over my hair. It wasn't the lightly stinging swat-and-tangle I usually received. It was the smoothing and affectionate motion you used on a child, that he'd used on an eleven-year-old me. He couldn't pull himself out of the past and if I wanted to kill Jack for anything, it was for that.

"Can the parasite be killed," Nik asked, "leaving Pyriel behind to be dealt with using one of Cal's guns?"

"If the storm spirit can be killed, we might be able to save Pyriel." Ishiah put his wings away again. It was like a Vegas magician's trick that never got old.

"Yeah, saving Pyriel isn't at the top of my list of priorities," I said. "It doesn't even make the cut for second callback." I drank the rest of the Mountain Dew, if only to save Niko from himself.

"He could be an innocent in this, a victim." Ishiah folded his arms, but I don't think he believed Pyriel could be brought back to what he was. I know he didn't believe I gave a shit one way or the other. If he did, his skills at reading facial expressions were sorely lacking. I couldn't see my own face, but if there was compassion and hope on it, I wasn't feeling it.

"And a rabid wolf is a victim too, but it still has to be put down." I tossed my empty can across the floor, if only to see what Nik would say or do.

He heaved himself to his feet, picked it up, and went to the kitchen to throw it in the garbage. It was the same as when I was a kid, before he'd limited my mess to my bedroom. He'd cut me a good deal of slack then and I'd needed it. But then I'd grown up and I'd needed boundaries and discipline more if I was going to survive. I needed Niko to remember that and remember himself. A fifteen-year-old, emotionally and guilt-wise, wasn't going to be able to handle Jack. Nik had to know that I could more than take care of myself now. If he didn't know that, he wouldn't watch his own back and Jack . . . Jack would take advantage. Jack would kill him in a heartbeat.

Goodfellow had moved to squat in front of me while Nik was in the kitchen. "Why is he like this?" he whispered fast and low. "I understand that coping with a murderer and having to kill at fifteen would be traumatizing, but this is *Niko*—and this is not right."

I wrapped a careful arm around my ribs and dropped my chin on my chest, closing my eyes. Christ it hurt like a mother. "Sorry, Goodfellow, but it's none of your business." He was risking his life going up against Jack when he could easily walk away, knowing Jack would leave him alone. Normally that would deserve answers, but not this time.

"Cal told me about Junior and I didn't believe him," Niko said quietly. I jerked my head up and opened my eyes to see him standing behind Goodfellow. "I only had to do one thing: believe my brother. But I didn't and because of that he almost died. I might as well have held the knife instead of Junior." That wasn't true.

It wasn't, but before I could say so, he went on, relentless. "We don't talk about it. We never have. I was too much of a coward then to believe and too much of a coward after to relive it. To answer your question: that is why I'm like this. Twelve years of cowardice have come home to roost."

"Nik, shut the hell up. You know that's not right. I was a delinquent eleven-year-old kid. No one would've believed . . ." But it was too late. He'd already picked up his katana, turned, and disappeared down the hall into his room, shutting the door softly behind him. I would've preferred he slammed it. Anger was easier to deal with than blame.

"Shit." Exhaling painfully, I avoided looking at Robin as I didn't want to see whatever well-meaning emotion was aimed in my direction. Sometimes the smallest amount of empathy can break you if you let it. I kept my eyes fixed on the far wall and asked, "Can you get me up? I think I went from a cracked rib to a broken one when I tackled Nik." If it was broken, and it felt that way, it was a simple break. I could breathe, somewhat, and I wasn't coughing up blood, which meant there wasn't a shard of bone embedded in my lung. No big deal. People walked around with a broken rib all the time—it just wasn't much fun.

An arm looped around my back and under my free arm to help me once I got my legs under me. "I'm sorry. I shouldn't have asked."

I made the shrug evident in my words as I damn well wasn't going to move my shoulders to make it. "He's always thought it. Maybe it's better that he said it. Keeping it inside obviously wasn't helping, not with Jack in the picture."

"Humans, they take things so to heart. It is one of their truest—"

I cut off Ishiah without a second thought. "Just shut up with the crap about the human heart, you asshole. If your kind had actually done something about their MIA angel instead of looking under a rock or two and then giving up, none of this would have happened. Jack wouldn't have happened. Junior wouldn't have happened and Nik wouldn't be blaming himself for your mistake."

Ishiah was my boss and a former warrior of Heaven, but right then that didn't mean a thing to me. Considering all the smiting done in the Bible by his kind, I had my doubts that messing up one human's faith in himself would mean much to him. It meant the world to me though and left me in no mood for some failed pigeon's philosophy about man.

"I was only going to say it is one of the most noble things about them, to hold themselves accountable beyond any expectation I could have," he finished somberly. "I'm sorry for what was done to you and Niko. I know that means nothing now, the damage is done, but I am sorry."

Making my way to the kitchen to fish in the drawer for the bottle of codeine, I let the anger run out of me. It wasn't Ishiah's fault. It wasn't Heaven's fault if I was forced to be truthful. It was Junior's fault and he was beyond reach. It was Jack's fault and until we discovered how to kill him he was beyond reach too. I swallowed two pills, chased them with a glass of water and said, "I need to talk to Nik. I'll be back in a minute."

I made it down the hall at a speed an octogenarian with a walker would've mocked and knocked lightly on Nik's door—something I'd never done. When you've spent nearly every day of your life together, aside from that first year Nik was at college, privacy was a nonsense word. It didn't mean a thing. There were the puberty years, but that's what bathroom locks were for.

I had knocked, but I didn't wait for an invitation. That would be too far out of the ordinary and Nik needed ordinary now more than ever. He was sitting on the side of his bed oiling his katana. If positions had been reversed I'd have been under the bed sucking my thumb like an infant, but that's why Nik was Nik. He did what no one else could and then he blamed himself for not doing the impossible.

"Hey, Cyrano." I propped myself against his dresser to face him. I was afraid if I sat on the bed, I wouldn't get back up . . . at least not with anything approaching grace. My ribs were the last thing Nik needed added to his plate. "Are you really going to make me be the emotionally stable one in the room? I'm not good at it. You know that."

He raised his eyes and what I saw in them . . . Jesus, I felt like shit. He'd been the emotionally stable one our entire lives, not a single day off. My even joking about it was a crappy thing to do. "You know what? I'm a dick. You be as unstable as you need to be. If you need to kick someone's ass to feel better, I'll go hold Robin back so you can put the beat-down on Ishiah. He doesn't pay me worth a damn anyway. He deserves it."

I thought I saw a spark of amusement but it disappeared too quickly for me to be sure. He looked back down and continued to tend to the blade. "Nik, come on. So what if you didn't believe me or *want* to believe me twelve frigging years ago? You were a kid. Hell, you were a kid raising a kid, dealing with Sophia, living in a world of monsters because of me. I don't know how you weren't a drooling mess or why you didn't just take off. Anyone else would have. No one and I mean no one could've done what you did. No one could've kept me alive this long or would've even tempted to try. You gave up your life for me and you could've had a life. The best life." He could have. That's what made me want to put my fist through a wall.

"You're the fucking smartest man I know," I continued. "You could be a college professor, married, have two point five kids and a picket fence. Or you could've been the world's top mercenary living on a private island. You could have done anything and you gave it up for me. Now you're blaming yourself . . . no, you're blaming a fifteen-year-old kid who was doing it all for stumbling once when the weight went from overwhelming to impossible. How can you blame that kid when you won't blame me, an adult, for doing things I know aren't right and refusing to believe in the consequences? If you're going to be like Jack and judge someone, judge me. I do know better, but it doesn't stop me. You're the one who does that. I've screwed up so many times and you've never thrown one of them back in my face. Treat my brother the same way. We're a package deal."

Moving carefully, I nudged his foot with mine. "That fifteen-year-old kid was my hero and no one, not even you, gets to say shit about him, all right? He was a hero and there is nothing he did or didn't do that will ever change that."

This time I saw it, not amusement, but the tension. It drained out of him and this time when he looked up, I saw Nik. My brother, not the torn up, despairing kid from twelve years ago. "Is this what I get for not letting you wallow in the past, moaning about what an abomination you were?"

"I was fond of that word, wasn't I?" I tilted my head down, letting the hair fall over my eyes so that I could stare through the veil with menace and malice. "Boogety."

The corners of his mouth quirked. "Yes. Terrifying."

"Damn straight." I grinned. "Now stop picking on that kid. I loved him. He meant the world to me and he never let me down—I don't care what you or he says about that. Got it?"

"I believe I have it." It was solemn and sincere.

"Good. No more wallowing. If I don't get to, neither do you. Now get back out there and help us come up with a way to kick Jack's ass. I'm working with a horny goat and feather duster. I don't have much confidence in." Not true of course. I had a helluva lot of confidence in Goodfellow and a moderate amount in Ishiah, but nothing like I had in Nik.

"Give me a moment and I'll be there," he promised. "I'm not looking forward to it after what they saw me do."

"Hate to tell you, Nik, but they already knew you were human. Granted this is the first time they saw actual proof, but they knew."

He looked down his long nose and snorted. "Go. I'll be right there. I'd say do something annoying to distract them from my entrance, but that's a given."

"Ass," I said fondly. "Three minutes or I'll tell them about the time you stared at my teacher's breasts. The one that was a stripper? Remember her and how you—"

"Out." He pointed, but he was almost smiling now.

I levered myself off the dresser and closed the door behind me, moving as if it didn't feel as if my ribs were made of ground glass. I was proud of that.

Back in the main room, I asked Ishiah and Robin, "Jack . . . what do we do now? How do we figure out how to kill him? How do we even find him? Does knowing he was an angel help us at all?"

Ishiah, looking less like an angel with his wings tucked off wherever and dressed in a faded blue shirt and jeans, was already on his feet and had been long enough to start pacing. My question stopped him. "It does," he said abruptly. "Of course it does. How could I be so blind? Churches." He swiveled to face me. "He's trying to save sinners if in a very macabre and twisted manner. He's gathering followers. He still believes in prayer and souls. He would be most at home in a church. Abandoned ones most likely or we'd have heard about congregations going missing."

That was good. That was goddamn excellent. There couldn't be that many abandoned churches in New York. With real estate at a premium they wouldn't be empty long before they were turned into a trendy pizza place with stained glass windows of the Virgin Mary.

I was at Nik's door fast this time and I didn't think that was possible. Opening it, I said, "Nik, we know where to look for Jack. Grab your sword."

He didn't have to, and he didn't have to look for Jack. Jack had found him instead. Nik was gone.

The room was empty.

14

Niko

Twelve Years Ago

When I woke up, I felt empty. My mind blank, my skull hollow. It was a long time before a distant and misty path woven out of confused thoughts appeared. For every step on it that I took toward consciousness, I took two back. It reminded me of the dreams where I could see my room around me, but I couldn't move—the feeling of being stuck halfway between the dream world and the real one.

This was the same. Or that's what I thought, but what I was seeing wasn't my room. It wasn't any of the rooms I'd slept in, and there were many, in my life. There was the thickness of shadows and the slow swing of one dangling lightbulb. A cloud hung around the glow—a halo around a fogbound moon. It should've been peaceful. I'd spent many nights outside under the stars and moon when Sophia had worked a carnival. I'd liked that part, that feeling of floating up into the sky, the feeling of serenity.

I didn't feel serene now. I felt terrified. As one half of my mind was hypnotized by the swinging stand-in for the moon, the other half was screaming. I needed to move, I needed to go, I needed to stop him. But where and who, I didn't know. The adrenaline spiked my heart into a rhythm so fast and desperate I could hardly breathe and I didn't know why.

My eyes drifted from the light to the wall. Concrete blocks with the sheen of moisture. Farther down was a cracked concrete floor. More than cracked—shattered. I could feel the damp in my lungs and I could smell . . . I jerked in a hard breath and spasmed, the floor scraping the cheek that rested on it.

I'd been at home. I'd been with Cal.

No.

I'd been at home and Cal was gone.

I smelled it. One corner that was darker than the others, but even in the dark I could see where the floor fell away into a deeper darkness.

Cal was gone.

I vomited. Not much, only a trickle, but it tasted sharply of chemicals.

Homemade chloroform.

This time I moved with more purpose. There was pain in my shoulders as I tried to inch across the floor. Stopping, I drew in several ragged breaths and tried to sit up. It took me several tries and nearly ten minutes, but I made it and by the time I did, I knew where I was.

I was in a basement. Junior's basement and through the pounding headache the stench was stronger, making the smell of vomit nothing. Death and decomposition. I could see the blurry outline of stacked bags of quicklime against another wall. It could do only so much this close to the pit dug in the corner. The haze across my vision was fading and I saw that too clearly, but not as clearly as the rot I choked on. If it smelled this tainted and wrong to me how badly had it smelled to Cal when I'd tried to tell him this maniac was a grocery store butcher?

At that moment, choking on air that reeked of dead bodies and seeing that my hands were fastened with police-issue cuffs around a metal support pole, I realized big brothers don't get to mess up.

Not once.

Not ever.

Look what happened when you did.

"I talk to the darkness and the darkness talks to me." Junior's voice drifted down from the stairs leading up. He would be sitting on the top stair as I could see his knees folded and his scuffed sneakers. One of those sneakers had a single drop of crimson blood on it. Small and as big as the sun all at the same time. "But he's not all darkness, my master. At times he's a light that blinds. A light that's just for me when I give him an especially good offering." He seemed genuinely pleased about it. Like a dog who'd done his trick just right and got a pat from his master. "I know what he wants. What he likes."

I knew what his schizoid delusion wanted too: death.

"Sometimes he watches from above, when the lightning fills the sky."

Skylight. Attic, I thought with instant desperation.

He stood and walked halfway down. He held Cal cradled in his arms as he would an overtired, sleeping child ready for bed. If it weren't for his small chest moving, I would've thought he was already dead. His head was resting against Junior's shoulder, his hair hanging in his face, his hand fisted in the man's shirt, because he, at some level, thought it was me. He thought I'd come to save him . . . not hear him die above me while chained in a basement.

God.

"He's such a scrap of a thing. I'll bet in a year he'd have shot up like anything. Guess we'll never know about that, will we? Feisty too. Tried to stab me with a kitchen knife. Kids." Junior smiled fondly, his eyes bright, cheerful, and so happy.

So very crazy.

"I know you're close," he said with an approving tone that made my flesh try to creep off my bones. "Not all brothers are, but I've seen you watching out for him. Getting home before dark to check on him because your mama sure doesn't. A thief and a whore and worst. She would've been on my list, you know, if we weren't neighbors? You two weren't. You're innocents, but you were nosy and that's that. Looking in my windows, following me in that old biddy's giant green car. I saw you at the hospital too. They say you shouldn't piss where you live, but you wouldn't leave well enough alone. Nothing I could do for you then, nothing but this."

In all ways Junior was more than I'd thought and in the one way he was exactly what Cal had thought. "But for being innocents, for that I'll give you a gift. When I'm done with him, I won't clean the knife. I'll cut you up with the same one. Your blood will mingle. It'll be good, saving a family. Sending you on high. But first I'll sign him. I like to sign my work."

Cal murmured in his chloroform-induced unconsciousness. Junior smoothed his hair and I wanted to vomit again, but there was no time. No damn time for anything. "I like family. You'll be together always now, the two of you. It'll make me proud, the work I do, when I see that."

He started up the rough wood stairs to the first floor. "Good." He was whispering to himself or Cal now and I didn't know which made me feel more sick. "It'll be good."

I'd fucked up. I hadn't believed Cal unconditionally. I thought he might have made a mistake. I wanted it to be a mistake. I wanted to find proof first. I hadn't wanted to leave an anonymous tip and ruin a man's reputation if Cal was wrong and I hadn't wanted, more importantly, to get the police anywhere near us.

Worst of all: I'd wanted a normal life. I'd been willing to close my eyes to anything to get that.

But Cal hadn't been wrong, and because of me we were going to die. My little brother was going to die. Sliced up, throat cut, chopped to pieces, God knew what, and his body would be thrown down that dry well already brimming with death and covered in quicklime. My little brother who'd *trusted* me. There was blood seeping over handcuffs that had me trapped around the iron column in front of me. I'd already started to pull and yank at the cuffs desperately while Junior had been on the stairs and I continued to rip flesh against the metal. Blood was good. It made things slippery and once I dislocated my thumb then I could slip a cuff. I'd read that in a book. I read most everything in a book because books were easier than real life, but look where I'd ended up. Nothing is as real in life as death.

No thinking of that now. I could . . . I *would* stop Junior because that was the only choice I had.

This was not happening. I wouldn't let it.

Arms secured tight, I slammed my hand with brutal force against the pole because pain was nothing when that maniac had Cal. Pain was nothing. Pain was what I deserved. I repeated the motion again and again as blood splattered. It couldn't be that difficult to dislocate your thumb or break your hand. It couldn't be. It . . .

That's when I saw it.

The red eyes of a Grendel were peering in the narrow crack between cardboard taped to the glass and the bottom metal sill. Curious eyes, sweeping side to side looking for Cal. Always following, always watching.

They watched. They didn't stop. And for once that was all right. For once it was hope and not fear that sent acid bubbling through my veins.

"I don't know what you want with Cal," I said hoarsely. Junior was terrifyingly intelligent in his way and I hadn't seen it. Smart enough that I could taste some sort of bleach solution he had sprayed down the back of my throat while I was unconscious to keep me from screaming. I knew the Grendel could hear me, ragged whisper or not. Tapered predatory ears were made to hear fearful breaths and screams far away.

"I don't know why you wanted him born and why you watch him, but that *monster* upstairs"—the Grendel showed an improbable stretch of metal teeth, laughing; it was laughing, at the word monster—"is going to kill him. He could be killing him right now."

No. *No.*

"Whatever you want with Cal you'll never get it now. Not if he dies"—*not if he's is slaughtered*—" upstairs. Do you understand me?" I demanded desperately.

The Grendel blinked slowly but the scarlet of its eyes flared like a rising sun and it faded into the sliver of night. How pathetic was I, how much of a failure that my best hope for saving my little brother depended on siccing one monster on another? I didn't care. I'd take any hope I could get.

I felt the nauseating pain of my thumb slam one more time against the pole and pop out of the joint. There are times pain isn't pain; it's relief and it's hope and it was life. My life. Cal's life. I folded my fingers into as narrow a wedge as I could, tore them out of the metal cuff, and I ran.

I wasn't lithe and sleek as my martial arts teachers would've hoped. The one cuff still fastened to one wrist and rattling, I stumbled up the stairs, falling once with splinters ramming under my short nails and hitting my dislocated thumb. It should've hurt. It should've paralyzed me with agony, made me curl into a ball as pain exploded through me.

I didn't feel a thing.

I slipped in my own blood dripping from my wrists as I hit the cheap kitchen linoleum and kept moving. The attic I spotted in a nerve-freezing moment. The pull-down stairs in the hallway were waiting for me and I went up them as clumsily as the basement ones, but I went fast. Speed over form. Life over death. There was dried blood on them. Long soaked into the raw wood. Cleaner wouldn't get that out of the grain, would it? No, never. There was death on every step upward, but this wasn't Jacob's ladder. This trail of screams and mortality didn't raise you up—it led to Hell. I knew it.

Cal . . . God, Cal, don't be dead.

In the space above there was a skylight and it let in enough streetlights and faint painpricks, because they hurt—what they showed—hurt, of stars as well as a quarter moon.

I saw it all.

Cal's shirt was neatly folded, such a neat serial killer was Junior, on a table of knives and scalpels and other things that wouldn't leave my memory as long as I lived. My brother was there, his hands duct taped behind him and his dark head flopping loosely with chin down against his chest. He was facing the wall, slumped bonelessly in a far corner.

Limp.

Unmoving.

Rivulets of blood on the floor.

My brother.

Foulmouthed, purple handprints on the refrigerator, smart and lazy, read stacks of comic books instead of schoolbooks, who'd taken on a raging, drunk Sophia to save my money for college, who taught me the difference between shades of gray and black and white and lied to little old ladies if there were cookies in it for him. My brother who I'd seen born and who I'd let die because I didn't believe him soon enough.

I didn't look for Junior. I didn't care. Kill me, don't kill me—I did not care.

I pulled Cal up in my arms. He wasn't Sophia's, he wasn't the Grendel's, he wasn't Junior's. He was mine and I would keep him as long as I could.

Forever if I could. With my brain crumbling at the edges, fracturing through the middle, forever seemed . . . right.

I pushed his hair from his eyes, leaving my blood on his face. They were closed, black lashes against paper white skin. There was a sluggishly bleeding slice straight across his chest a few inches below his nipple line. The top slash of a J.

"I like to sign my work."

No, that wasn't right. It wasn't right. His blood should be inside him, not out. I wiped a hand frantically over the blood, trying to push it back in the wound, back inside Cal. I only ended up smearing it everywhere over Cal's stomach and thin chest, making it worse.

How could it be worse?

The thought staggered me.

Swallowing broken glass that had nothing to do with the bleach, I thought numbly . . . wait . . . no . . . the dead don't bleed. And they don't breathe. Cal was doing both. I clutched him tighter, so damn small, and all there was in my world.

Junior. Where was Junior? Where was the *dead* man?

Someone was growling savagely. It might have been me.

There was another crumpled pile in the opposite corner of Cal. This bundle was much larger. I settled Cal against the far wall, carefully making sure the blood wasn't as much as I'd thought. He wasn't bleeding out. It was a slow flow, I could see now. For a moment it could wait. Cal wouldn't mind, considering what I had planned.

I limped over and nudged clothes and muscle disguised as fat over onto his back. Junior's eyes were half open and bloody foam framed his mouth. That would be from the vicious slashes that penetrated his clothes and several inches of flesh from the base of his neck to just above his groin. I caught the faint foul smell that had to be the spill of intestinal contents. The room had a colored tint to the air, red as the blood all around us, from the crimson moon shining through the tiny skylight made of scarlet glass.

The Grendel had listened.

It had come and gone, but it had listened. It had done what I couldn't do.

I didn't know what that meant, but it was worth it. Right now it was worth it.

But it hadn't finished the job. Oh, given three minutes and Junior would be as dead as the victims in his basement, but the Grendel had left me a present.

Or it might be a reminder.

They were watching Cal. I needed to do that too and do it better.

I picked up the knife that lay across Junior's slack palm. It had blood on it, Cal's blood. Junior didn't get any of that. It didn't belong to him. I methodically wiped the blade on my pants. "I have a line, you know. It's been moving around lately, but I have one," I said cold and brittle as frost. "You, motherfucker, crossed it."

I rammed the knife through flesh and bone and into his heart.

The faint uneven beat vibrated through the metal, the handle, and into my hand before finally stopping. He touched my little brother—I stopped his heart.

It was a fair trade.

15

Cal

Present Day

It wasn't fair.

Robin and Ishiah made plans. I guessed that's what they did. I didn't pay attention. I didn't care. I had my own plan. If I could lure Jack far enough away from Niko, then I could open a gate inside him. Nik wouldn't die from the mass of moving crystal-feathered shrapnel that was the inner Jack and I'd try to gate away in time to avoid the same fate. If I made it, great. If I didn't, shit happened. I'd go down fighting. It was the best end I had hope for in my life anyway.

Life wasn't fair, childish to complain, but there you go.

I would save Nik—that was the bottom line. He

hadn't survived twelve years ago to die at the whim or hand of the same monster now.

Life wasn't fair and who told you that it was?

That's what they always said. Fine. This time I said, that's who, and I didn't care if that was childish or immature. I said it was going to be fair therefore it would be and God help you if you got in my way. But God wouldn't help, would He? God didn't interfere and that was a damn shame for you.

I knew because I did nothing *but* interfere, and I didn't work in mysterious ways. I worked in bloody ones.

At least Jack had let Niko take his katana with him; that was something. That his phone was centered in Nik's perfect anal-retentive manner on his dresser meant no tracking him by GPS, which was why I was ripping the list off the printer of the search I'd done on abandoned churches in the city. Ishiah said Jack would be in a church. I'd find that church and if I had to tear it down brick by brick to get to Nik, I would. I shoved the list in my pocket and went to my room to get a few things. Opening a gate in Jack was the only chance I had, but Nik would tell me to prepare for any eventuality. He had learned that lesson the hard way. I wouldn't do him any justice to forget that now.

"Where are you going?"

Goodfellow sounded odd, his words moving slowly as though the air was water. "To the churches. To kill Jack. To bring Nik home." It was a stupid question and he seemed to realize it.

"I think I meant more what will you do?" He chose

his words more carefully now. "To accomplish those things. Jack can't be killed."

"An Auphe can kill anything. You know that." He did. He'd seen it often enough before.

As I finished gathering my weapons, he said tightly, "If they don't care about surviving, that's true. But I know better than to have this talk with you and I don't know that I would do any differently. This once I won't play the hypocrite. Start at the top of your list. Ishiah and I will begin at the bottom. If we find them first, we'll call you."

The air was air again and I felt more human than I had in a long time. Nothing brings out the humanity in you like sheer terror. "He thinks it was his fault. I tried to help him. I think I did, some, but what if he thinks he deserves this? To be to Jack what I was to Junior? What if he doesn't fight hard enough? Shit, Robin, what if he doesn't wait for me?"

He pushed me hard enough to have the pain of my broken rib slicing through my panic but not hard enough to actually injure me. "Don't be an idiot. Yes, he feels guilty, but do you think for a second your brother would willingly transfer that guilt to you?" He pushed me again, this time in motion toward the hall and then the front door.

Robin was right. Nik wouldn't do that to me. He would do anything to be there when I showed up, still alive . . . still fighting. I glanced at the door, then back at Goodfellow. "I won't be needing that. Look for him. Find him. Call me." I pulled the gate, a gate I thought about because Nik would want me to, around myself and left this world.

I reappeared at the location of the first church. I knew it, had passed it a hundred times. It was one of the locations I was familiar enough with to travel through a rip in the world and arrive at its step. I was wearing Niko's long coat he'd left behind. It covered up enough weapons to take out the entire NRA. Nothing covered up that I'd appeared in broad daylight out of thin air surrounded by the violent purple and black oil slick of a wound that was reality torn around me. I was separated from the sidewalk by a chain-link fence, but it wasn't much of one and people saw. I don't know how many, but from the shouts and gasps it was more than one or two.

There'd be hell to pay for that later . . . if there was a later. I didn't care about the consequences. I did care about finding Nik as fast as I possibly could. If I had to reveal every hidden *paien* alive to an unknowing human world, so fucking be it.

This church wasn't that old. It was that ugly, square industrial look from the 1950s with one of those steeples that don't actually have a cross or a bell and you wonder why they stuck a steeple on it at all. What did I know though? Sophia and religion hadn't gone hand in hand. As far as I remembered, I'd never been in a church. It had nothing to do with being Rom. Rom were the same as everyone else; some were more religious than others and religious traditions varied from clan to clan.

It was amazing the shit your mind could come up with to stop the mental images of your brother being skinned alive that ran through every thought like a garrote rusted red with old blood.

Time to go.

I shot the chain and lock off the door and ran into my first church. I searched the two floors and the basement, kicking down the more flimsily locked doors. I didn't get what I was praying for. Except for rats the building was empty.

The next church called for a taxi. I had to gate back home to come out and catch it. I couldn't flag it down at the church. From inside I could hear the people gathering on the sidewalk, the disbelieving voices. If I didn't come out of the church, it was a little better. Not a lot better, but a little. They wouldn't see more proof that someone . . . some*thing* had been there to begin with.

I needed the taxi for the second church as if I'd passed that address, I didn't remember it. And if I couldn't see it, couldn't feel it, I couldn't gate there. As the cab pulled up at the second address, I told the driver to keep going and gave him a new one. This one was already half converted into condos and workers were moving inside and out. If Jack was there anywhere, there would be a good deal more screaming and slaughter or a pile of cooling dead bodies hidden somewhere inside.

The next was the same, as was the next. Nothing stayed undeveloped for long in this city. The longer I searched, the more Niko's chances declined. Unless . . . unless Jack didn't kill during the day no matter how safe his lair. Junior had his attic, his skylight . . . for Jack to watch maybe, or maybe for another reason. Jack didn't belong to Heaven anymore. At night under the stars and the moon might be the closest he could come to being home. I couldn't see the stars in the New York night sky with so much light pollution, but Jack's eyes weren't mine. Neither was Jack's mind. Jack's mind wasn't the mind he'd always had either. Maybe Jack was crazy enough to think the stars were the eyes of his fellow angels watching his work with approval.

If I wanted to lie to myself and grasp at straws, I would. In my life I'd learned one thing: the truth will kill you as often as it sets you free.

The next church was Jack's. Not his one true church, but it belonged to him. The first floor was empty, but the basement was home to fourteen fucking hoodie-wearing acolytes. If I never saw another hoodie or whoever had spread the fashion gospel on those goddamn things, I'd be happy as hell. The men had been sleeping when I came down the stairs. It was a small area, meant for storage, not a dormitory, but that's the purpose it served now. They sat up on old sleeping bags, not one of them with a knife in hand. From the direction they were reaching they slept with them under flattened, ancient pillows. It was a good place if you were smart enough to sleep with your hand under there grasping the handle. They weren't that smart. They did know me. I saw it in the set of their jaw, the disgust in their eyes. One stood up—the leader, ready to face me unarmed. That's what a brave if stupid leader would do. The rest were all still reaching for those knives when I sent Jack a message.

It was a messy one.

But sometimes you have to make a mess to get the point across.

I did think about it, Nik, before I did it, as you'd told me to. I decided if the consequences of being Auphe over human in this instance meant getting you back, it was more than worth it.

The basement was covered in gore, charred flesh, far-flung limbs when I finished walking down the stairs to jump the last stair to the concrete and moved across to the one remaining—the one I hadn't opened a gate within to turn inside out, upside down, round and round. He was still standing, the one who would know of any of them, where Jack might be. That hoodie had been white; it was Carrie-crimson now, but he was covered in a little worse than pig's blood.

I grinned at him with teeth that couldn't be as sharp and wicked in reality as they felt in my mind. "Careful. The floor's slick. I wouldn't want you to fall and hurt yourself."

That disgust in his eyes was gone. It's easy to hate an idea—that of a Godless creature—to want to destroy what was behind it . . . when it's only an idea. It's harder when that idea is a reality right in your face. Dripping down your face in this case. That's when there's only room for fear. This guy might think he was going to Heaven when he died, but God oh God, he didn't want to die like that, now did he?

I circled him. "It's funny really. When I was a kid . . . and I was once a kid, hard to believe, I know. But when I was little, one of the scariest things I came across was a jack-in-the-box. I practically pissed my pants at the sight of one." I tugged on his hood as I'd tugged on Nik's braid hours ago. "Yet now that's what I'm look-ing for. I'm looking for Jack in his godforsaken fucking box and you're going to tell me where that box is."

He did.

I didn't doubt that he would. He could barely get the words out fast enough; they tumbled over each other, a run of stones racing down the side of a mountain. That was usually a warning sign of something bigger and worse to come

This wasn't any different from that.

There may have been an assumption on his part that I'd let him live if he talked. I wasn't an idiot and I wasn't naïve. I'd dealt with the Auphe race. Jack was a poison, a disease that could spread even if he was gone. The Auphe had taught me to be a fan of the scorched earth policy. Burn it, salt it, let nothing ever grow here again.

That's what I did, and then I went to find Jack.

Jack's church was one of those I thought of as real churches. Not real in a sense of what one worshipped in an ugly church was inferior to what one worshipped in this type of church. It was just what I'd grown up seeing in movies and on TV as the epitome of the House of God. It was stone with a steeple that pierced a sky now purple and pale orange with dusk. There was a stained glass window in front that was two stories tall. There was no scene, no grazing sheep, or sunlight streaming from the sky. It was a complex mixture of rectangular and square shades of glass—a thousand windows, each leading to a better place. The doors were a dark wood and arched at least four feet over the tallest person to walk through them.

I saw all of this once I'd gotten through a fence much more secure than had been at the first church. I gated through it. I had no time for a fence this difficult. This one even came with the kind of razor wire you saw on prison fences. It was ugly and evil, an odd choice to surround a building even I thought of as beautiful. Jack was inside there though, a cancer that made all that beauty an empty shell that didn't yet know it was terminal. Didn't know there was no cure strong enough to save it.

Until me. I could save it. I could be the scalpel that cut Jack away. It wouldn't be clean but clean was overrated as long as you got to live.

The double doors weren't locked. Why would they be? Jack loved all the company he could get. As Robin had said, who among the city would Jack consider truly innocent? Not many and trespassing would be equal to thou shall not kill in his warped mind. Jack had his own commandments and ten didn't come close to numbering them.

Inside with the doors shut behind me I could still see well enough though the light was gray and dim. There was some clutter, but not as much as the other empty churches had. Jack had cleaned up. Why not? Who wanted to skin people in an untidy work area? Nik would applaud his work ethic. I swallowed with difficulty. Surprised something that automatic would be that hard to do. I swallowed again and although there was no blood in my mouth I thought I could taste it . . . because I could smell it.

The air was saturated with the scent of blood. Old, recent, fresh. I'd thought Junior's house had smelled— I'd had no idea what bad truly was. I'd fought enough over the years that the coppery tang of fresh blood had long stopped bothering me, but this wasn't the same. Old blood was a horror I couldn't explain to someone who couldn't experience it. It was something I wouldn't be rid of for at least a week. And here . . . there was an ocean of rotting blood. Jack had more victims than the police had ever found. I couldn't smell anything over what they had spilled here. I couldn't smell Nik.

"Nik!" I shouted as I limped forward. The ribs were beyond codeine now. "Niko!" I shouted again. I wasn't trying to be subtle. I wasn't looking to hide. I wanted Jack to find me. I couldn't lead him away if he didn't know I was there. I also couldn't forget how fast he was. I wasn't that fast, but for Jack I'd have to be. Whipping my head back and forth, I scanned the church and saw nothing. The basement then. I'd go . . . wait. Up. There was a paler glimmer . . . blond hair, Nik's hair in the balcony above. Through the ornate carved wood rail I could see him, a shadowed fall crowned with that rare recessive blond Leandros hair.

Above, like Junior's attic. I shouldn't have been surprised. Junior had said his master liked to watch from the sky. That could be true or it might be that Jack wanted to be either closer to what he remembered of Heaven or just free of Earth when he did his work. Angels must have wings for a reason.

Niko's form didn't move and I instantly ran to the back where the stairs would lead up because he was not dead. I could smell nothing but what soaked this place inside and out, not even Nik's normal scent, but my brother's freshly spilt blood, that I would know . . . over anything at all. Jack hadn't shown up, but he had to be here and I'd be ready for him. I reached for the handle of the door that should lead to the stairs when the blot of gloom under the balcony became something else. Knit out of the shadows, the reaped souls, and the desertion of faith that now filled this place, Jack became.

The killing gate I had planned for him took only a thought. I didn't have time for even that. A grip of ice sank into both of my temples, through flesh and bone, and I *was* the storm. I was the lightning that passed through my brain. The floor disappeared beneath me as I hung in midair, arms and legs splayed as I convulsed. Jack's incandescent glow of white-blue eyes gazed into mine. "We both come and we both go, you said." Thick with clots of flesh and blood, the phantom of them if not the actual things themselves, the words fought through. "Now I think you, Wolf-in-the-Flock, Auphe-in-the-Flock, you will go nowhere." He must have dropped me as I was now looking up at the ceiling, unable to move, unable to understand what he said next although I could hear it.

"Pray for deliverance. Pray for mercy. But they will be prayers unheard for I will not let them pass, half a soul or not."

He hovered over me, but I couldn't distinguish between the lightning-shot blackness and the electricity misfiring in the darkness of my brain. Was there a difference? I couldn't . . . think. There was the smell of freshly mown grass, the taste of metal and butterscotch, the warm sensation of Delilah's skin under my hands. I floated on it all. It seemed strange. It seemed right. It seemed . . .

I was tired.

A wolf among the sheep. Half wolf, half sheep.

There was something I needed. . . . It was on the tip of my . . . what? What was . . . now there was the smell of Oreos. Mrs. Spoonmaker's Oreos. I smiled and closed my eyes. I was so tired.

With the taste of burned butterscotch in my mouth, I slept.

DIY electroshock therapy is not an Auphe's best friend.

It was a while before I could link enough words and images in my head to come to that conclusion.

Before that I drifted. It could've been minutes. It could've been days. I didn't know. I didn't know anything. There was darkness around me and dancing lights, few and distant as the stars of a post-apocalyptic sky. That was all right, came the muzzy feeling. The world had to die sometime. It wasn't anything as complicated as a thought—it was a feeling, warm and reassuring in the futility of it all. Best to go along. Ride the light to a world better than this. Let it all go. . . .

Including Niko.

That was a thought, fully formed and capable of dissipating the fog in my brain with the force of a high noon, summertime Death Valley sun. Nik. Where was Nik? I sat up, pushing against the floor beneath me. It felt like polished wood, smooth and perfect. My muscles didn't mirror that feeling. Every single one in my body ached as if I'd run for my life for several hours, was hit by a bus, another bus, and then hit by a train before deciding to top it off with the New York City

Marathon for kicks. Tiny shivers and spasms twitched . . .
Jesus . . . everywhere as I curled into a ball, resting my
forehead on my knees until it passed.

I remembered in the fuzziest of ways cold hands,
one on each side of my head, and then a lightning
storm inside of it. Jack, friend and pal that he was, had
given me a free shock treatment. He'd zapped my
brain, and the rest of me incidentally, quickly but thoroughly. The seizures that would cause were what had
my muscles tied in what felt like unbreakable knots.

After a minute, all I had time to spare, I looked up
and around me. My muscles continued to howl, but I
told them to talk to my broken rib and get back to me.
I was in a basement from the looks of it, a fancy one.
The floor was wood, stained and polished to a high
gloss that reflected the flickering lights of the four can-
dles Jack had left me.

I thought it was to see the chains. Feeling them
around my wrists wasn't enough. He wanted me to *see*
how helpless I was as well. That was the kind of dick
he was. My hands were in front of me, the wrists
wrapped in several tight loops of thick chain that in
turn was chained around a wooden column that would
be theoretically holding up the ceiling. The chain
wasn't padlocked. That would be too easy and not
Jack's style. The ends were melted into one tangled
whole. Lightning, good for so much more than scrambling a brain.

The basement.

The imprisonment.

The symmetry of the chains.

I get it, Jack. Funny fucking ha-ha. Just like the good old days twelve years ago.

I hadn't seen what Junior had done to Niko while I was in the attic and Niko hadn't told me. He'd only said that he'd killed Junior and we were safe. I was safe. But he didn't have to tell me he'd been chained and he didn't have to tell me where. He'd had the smell on him as we sat in our own bathroom and he washed the blood from my chest and from around his wrists. He'd been with the dead . . . in the basement. I didn't know how Jack knew about that. He hadn't been there for that particular show or had and found a reason not to interfere. It could've been Junior's routine. Chain his victims in the basement, kill them later in the attic. Jack would definitely know that about his apprentice. He'd obviously known about two neighbor kids next door who'd disappeared after Junior's death. Had guessed why we'd vanished.

Jack knew more than he should.

I tried flipping that switch in my brain, starting small, a tiny gate to eat away at the chains and set me free. Nothing. There was only the creeping return of the muzzy sensation around the edge of my thoughts. If I couldn't do something so small, gating myself was impossible. Jack had seen me moving like him, if not as quickly. Jack had taken a leap of faith . . . wasn't *that* hilarious . . . that frying my brain would put a stop to that, temporarily. Permanently. Either one suited Jack.

Yeah, Jack knew way more than he should, but Jack didn't know me.

Gating didn't make me who I was. It was a part of

me, but with or without gates, I'd always be half of something that could take him out if I had to use my last breath to do it. I remember the torn flesh weeping blood that had circled Nik's wrists from his stay in Junior's basement. I'd seen him pop a dislocated thumb back into place, with a towel clamped in his mouth to keep from screaming. If my brother had the balls to do that for me when he'd been a kid, there wasn't anything that would stop me from doing the same for him as an adult.

Junior must have used handcuffs on Nik. Dislocating a thumb wouldn't help with chains. A willingness to give Jack his pound of flesh would. Or half a pound. Nik had been right. Thinking you're invulnerable makes you sloppy.

Jack had gotten sloppy.

He'd seen human weapons were nothing compared to him. They couldn't hurt him, and he hadn't bothered to take mine. He'd also left me that slack, not too bright of him either. I loved the arrogant ones. I was thinking all that when I maneuvered my hands and pulled the Mossberg Tactical shotgun out of Nik's coat. I thought on it harder than I had to. If I hadn't, I'd think about what Jack was doing to my brother right now.

I couldn't think about that. God, I . . . no. Just no.

This had happened to him when he was fifteen. When he was unarmed and had no experience with the evil in the world, other than the kind that then he had only watched. Trapped in a basement filled with the dead while Junior had been offering me to his master upstairs, he'd thought it was his fault for not believing me. The wonder wasn't that he'd had a time bomb in him. The wonder was that he hadn't given up on life then and there. The wonder was Nik himself who did not give up on me, no matter the odds, who saved my ass every last time.

I wasn't going to be any different. I was getting him out of this. Somehow. And I was going to make him goddamn proud as I did it.

If that meant that I had to take on Jack with no gating ability and no weapon that could touch him, I'd fucking come up with something. Step one: the chains. If I'd known Jack was going to turn this into a psycho high school reunion of sorts I'd have brought bolt cutters. Now, I tucked the shotgun under my arm, pressed the muzzle against the chain and fired. I then switched hands and did the same several inches over.

My hands and face burned as I reloaded and ran up the stairs.

Cuts and embedded metal fragments from the shattering of the chain in two places when I hit it with a couple of steel slugs were responsible for that. There were ugly powder burns on my hands as well to accent the blood that made me look as if I were wearing black and red gloves. I'd had to aim close to where the chain wrapped around my wrist. If the chain didn't shatter completely, I'd still have to pull my hands free of metal that wasn't completely intact, looser but still snug, and would be the new equivalent of razor wire.

That was what had happened, and that's what I'd done. I'd yanked my hands free, losing large patches of skin down to meat. Nothing I couldn't live without. Nothing I gave a damn about.

Nothing. Nothing. Nothing.

Nik, wait for me, goddamn it. You'd better fucking wait.

I kept running, limping, moving up any way I could. It was hard to breathe and if a piece of bone in your lung felt worse than this, I pitied the bastard that had that. I hit the first floor, didn't slow down as I ran for the door to the balcony and went up those too. As I staggered out onto the balcony, I was surrounded by color. Subtle but true. Moonlight washed through the stained glass of the giant window I'd seen walking into the church. The soft light wafted in a quiet drift of blue, purple, and the deep green of grass on a night shadowed grave.

This time, this close, I could smell Niko's blood and I jerked my head to the left. He was standing with his katana between him and Jack. He knew he didn't have a chance, but he was buying time, hoping I could get away and would have the sense to run.

He knew better than that, but he still tried. Nik was incapable of giving up on me, no matter how bleak the odds. Who did he think I'd learned it from? And Jack had picked up on that, was *playing* with him. "I left him his weapons," came the thick flow. "His human toys. He had knives. If he's the soulless animal I know him to be, he'll do as they do when caught in a trap. I am kind however. He won't have to gnaw his way free. He can use a knife to cut off his hand. I did chain both hands. Cutting off the second hand will be more of a puzzle without another to cut with, but Auphe are nothing if not persistent."

I leaned in the corner between wall and rail. "Nik, get down." He jerked his head toward me. I think it was the first time in my life I'd managed to appear and him not see me coming, not counting gates. But we were both caught in a past nightmare now and we were both less sharp and more desperate than we'd ever been.

There was blood on his face that started at his hairline, followed closely in front of his right ear, and ended at the tip of his chin. Superficial but messy and as Nik had told me in the beginning of this, a game, but also a start to being skinned alive if that's what Jack wanted.

Reloading on my run up the stairs, I didn't think the shotgun would work and thanks to ECT for Dummies, Jack had taken gates out of the picture. Chances were that both Nik and I were going to die here, but I wasn't going to make it easy for Jack. When he looked back on taking us down, if it couldn't be with fear, then I'd settle for vast annoyance. "Nik, down!" I repeated as I fired the first slug into the swirling mass of every nightmare come to life that coiled between us and instantly pumped the shotgun for the next round.

Nik didn't get down, because Nik knew I had no plan. He would fight the same as I would and if we survived, kick my ass for suggesting he wouldn't.

"I neutered your mutt of an Auphe. I filled his head with the light of the storm. He can't leave. He can't walk through doors not meant for him. He can't save himself and he can't save you either," Jack gloated, the slug having disappeared in the shadows around him before it dropped to the floor coated in ice. "He cannot do anything. He may as well be human now, weak and ready for judgment, but he still won't have it. Death is all that's for him. Redemption is beyond him, neutered or not." The glitter of his eyes focused on me, disappeared—toward Nik, and then back to me. "But who shall first give up his skin to the priest that is Jack? Who is the first offering?"

Nick slashed with his katana in a movement as quicksilver fast as Jack's lightning. He was aiming for the eyes, but it was the same as with anything we'd tried. The blade bounced back and Jack laughed. The son of a bitch laughed. "You then, with a skinning tool of your own. I think I shall use it on you and then use your skin to choke your soulless sibling to death. A fitting end for the talented apprentice you took from me. Hammersmith gave me many of the wicked. Now you die in my pet's name."

Not happening.

This was fucking not happening.

I was about to fire again, then take on Jack with my hands and teeth when I saw them.

Through those squares of color, I saw, blurry and lit only by streetlights, but it was enough. This time when I shouted, "Niko, get the fuck down!" he listened.

The stained glass window exploded behind him. As glass flew through the air, Ishiah, Samyel, and four other peris from the Ninth Circle hung in the air, white and gray and copper wings beating the air into a storm that rivaled the one that was Jack.

"You are sick, brother," Ishiah said as they circled him. "Pyriel, you are Fallen and this cannot go on."

Jack's eyes faded to the barest glimmer for a moment. "Brothers." He sounded confused. "No, no, I am not with you any longer. I am my own creation. I am judgment and redemption. I am not of you but I am sanctioned or I would've been punished long ago."

"This," Ishiah said with a grim twist to his mouth. Sadness. Resignation. It was time to put the rabid wolf down. "This is your punishment and it is long overdue." He arrowed in, a hawk stopping on a rabbit. Samyel and the others followed. They covered Jack and buried hands in the blue and white flaring mist around him. Immediately a lightning storm exploded on the balcony, at least fifty bolts. I had gone down as quickly as Nik when the window had burst and I was grateful for that now. Ishiah and the others were thrown back, glowing and *burning*. But as quickly as they'd been tossed aside, they were back and every time the lightning threw them away they returned. Jack tired and the lightning became jagged and intermittent. The peris were on him then and stayed on. They began to peel back pieces of . . . something—ragged chunks of darkness that bled in the sizzle of faint bolts of electricity. They were removing the storm spirit from Jack— Pyriel—tearing it to pieces to free what it had latched on to hundreds of years ago.

They were peris, retired angels with limited powers, but it was enough to kill a parasitic storm spirit and without that spirit, Pyriel was frozen. He might not want to fight his brothers. He might be all but powerless himself now that the spirit that had fed on him and channeled his life force all those years was gone.

I didn't give a rat's ass either way.

The peris, each trailing a limp drapery of dead or dying storm spirit with them, soared higher. They'd done their part, nothing I'd expected, nothing I'd hoped, but now it was my turn. Jack, when the darkness had flowed away like the outgoing tide, was revealed to be a glass statue, one that had been shattered and glued back together by a senile, blind man. Angles, knife-sharp edges, jagged shards that cut not only skin but the air itself solidified. You could almost picture that there had once been wings that could lift him into flight, but now were melted together into a crippled caricature—layered with the same fractured glass that made up the rest of him.

Yet . . . I could see what he once had been before he changed. Something awe-inspiring. Something beautiful.

Crystal and cut glass, each feather on his wings a knife blade of diamond made to slash and fly. He would've been something. Hell, a glory. Now he was the ice over a winter lake and if I looked hard enough I thought I might see the eyes and mouths of his victims wide open with terror as they drowned trapped beneath the frozen barrier.

The parasite was gone, but what had been beneath it, the angel, his eyes, the same blue-white, were as insane as they'd ever been while he'd been Jack. Angels went mad too. It wasn't as much a surprise as I'd thought. All that power, all that judgment—there'd be no Hell if angels hadn't gone mad or bad in the first place, would there?

Who better than me—something darker and more deadly than any demon—to kill an angel?

He'd thought himself judge, jury, and executioner. Now it was my turn to play that part. I aimed the Mossberg at him. It didn't matter if you were from Above or Below or somewhere in the middle; you touched my brother and you died.

"You're wicked, Jack," I said without emotion. "You're wicked and wrong and I damn sure am not here to save you."

I shot him in the head and then the chest, shattering him to hundreds of pieces falling as tears from Heaven. Niko was at my side as Pyriel—no, Jack, he'd always be Jack to me—continued to rain down on the floor with the soft ringing of bells. You know how the movie goes: when you hear a bell ring, an angel gets his wings. Or gets a slug in the head. Choose whichever version you like.

"My turn," Niko said firmly, the rope he'd escaped easily enough still in tatters around his wrists. Jack had left him his weapon as he'd left me mine. Jack had made sure he could escape to stand and fight. Jack who'd wanted a challenge from the one who'd killed his worshipper twelve years ago. Jack—who'd gotten exactly all that. I wished he'd had longer to enjoy it. I wished we all had. Sick or not, Jack had been far beyond the grace of a mercy killing.

Wordlessly I passed over the shotgun and Nik used the barrel to beat those pieces of Jack, glittering bright as a crop-killing frost, to a fine, crystalline sand. The metal flew up and thundered down more times than I cared to count. With every blow the sound of rotten ice breaking beneath careless feet echoed. Gone, but it didn't matter. You could hear the death in him the same as before I cut him down. Finally a wind blew in through the destroyed window and Jack—his presence and fatal song—simply blew away.

Gone, just like that. As if he'd never existed at all. I'd have killed all the angels in Heaven to have made that true.

"Feel better?" I asked, moving to stand beside Nik as he dropped the shotgun to the floor.

He wiped at the trickle of blood running down his jaw and bumped my shoulder. "You know, little brother, I think that I do."

We were at home . . . surprising me as I hadn't thought we'd live to come back. The start of the plan, if not the rest of it, had worked out—color me all kinds of fucking surprised. I'd started at the top of the list of churches, Ishiah and Robin at the bottom and we'd met, more or less in the middle. Fortunately, Ishiah had a plan of his own he hadn't told me about, one he hadn't had much faith in—that the peris from the bar could kill and remove the storm spirit from Jack. Peris were forbidden from killing *paien* in New York, parasites included. He doubted he could get all of the crew from the Ninth Circle to risk expulsion from the city or that they'd be able to accomplish it if they did agree. That spirit had been riding Jack a long, long time. Fortunately, Ishiah had been wrong on both counts. For an ex-angel he had less belief than I'd have thought.

In the end, it was what Robin had suggested. Without each other, the spirit and Pyriel weren't even the halves of a whole. Easy prey.

Promise was with Niko in his bedroom, taking care of the cuts on his face and his wrists. As the door was closed, she could be taking care of other things, but I doubted it . . . this time. My hands looked like they'd been through a meat grinder, my ribs told me breathing wasn't on the menu for supper today, and my face was peppered with tiny fragments of metal chain. All of which Goodfellow was working on, but it wouldn't be long before Nik was out to take over.

"It's difficult to believe Jack would go to those lengths to relive Junior's favorite scenario. He was the master after all. Junior was only the apprentice . . . or the worshipper. I'm not certain what label to put on that wretched bastard," Robin said. "Putting you in the basement instead of Niko. Niko in the closest thing to an attic instead of you." Nik had mentioned it was the same setup from twelve years ago when we left the church, the things I'd already known but as always hadn't talked about, what Junior had done to us both, which was a good thing. Not talking about it all those years, trying to protect each other, that had been a mistake.

Or mostly a mistake.

"Either he hated losing an apprentice or he was the dramatic sort. Or both," he continued. He was right about one thing: it had been as close to being exactly the same as Jack could make it. Robin was bathing my hands in peroxide diluted with sterile water. After that he'd follow with antibiotic cream, loose bandages, and we'd hope there wasn't any scar tissue that was bad enough to limit my range of motion. Pulling a trigger was important in my business.

"The light was different," I murmured. I couldn't tell Nik. I'd sooner eat my gun. But I needed to tell someone or I'd end up having a meltdown the same as my brother. There'd be no avoiding it. Some secrets eat you from the inside out until nothing is left.

"The light?"

"The skylight in the attic was red. Everything looked red there. Everything looked bloody before it actually was." I flexed my fingers under the loose gauze and winced. That was not good. That put the ribs into perspective.

"Nik used to call me a rubber ball when I was a kid. All the time. He said I could bounce back from anything. He said I was amazing that way." That was a warm memory. I'd keep that one. "Then the Auphe took me when I was fourteen."

"And you didn't bounce back," Goodfellow said quietly.

"No, I'd stopped bouncing a little earlier, when I was eleven. I stopped after what I saw in the attic. What I heard really." I flexed my other hand, and, damn, that was worse than the first one. "I pretended. Fake it until you make it, right? I faked it with the best of them. But no more bouncing, not the real kind. That's when I knew I was right not to tell him. I didn't want him to be like me."

Resigned to fate.

"Tell him? Tell him what?"

"I was awake part of the time, in the attic. Nik doesn't know. Nik can't know," I warned. "I was awake when Junior cut me with his knife, telling me I was an innocent. I had no sin in my blood to drain, but he *liked* that part. Loved it. He knew I wouldn't mind." I'd still been confused and half out of it from the drugs but I remembered him holding me close, with an arm wrapped around my bare back as he dragged the point of the knife through my skin to watch me bleed.

Robin rested his elbows on his knees and folded hands against his mouth. "*Gamisou*. The monster."

I almost laughed, but Nik could've heard. I held it back, but it wasn't easy. "Monster. That's what he thought he was, but then a Grendel opened a gate into the attic and Junior found out how wrong he was. The Grendel . . . fuck, the Auphe, I mean, slashed him to pieces. Left him dying on the floor. I'd never seen anything like it. It tore Junior apart with no more effort than it took to breathe." Vicious and predatory and fucking murder made of moonlight and blood. "Before they'd only watched me. I didn't know. I had no idea what they could do." I'd had no idea how outside of the world and everything in it they were. How alien and how fucking *unstoppable*. "And then it came over and whispered in my ear. I was on the floor, trapped in a corner. I'd never seen one close up, only through windows. I didn't know they could talk. . . .

"It had bent down and pressed those metal teeth to my ear and hissed possessively, 'You belong to us, little cousin. One day we will come for you. Next year, the year after, the year after. You will not know, but we will come and take you through that.' A black talon pointed at the roiling mass of ugly, tarnished light that had torn a hole in the world and hung there, waiting. 'We will take you home to your true family. Wait for us. Watch for us.'

"Then it and the gate were gone. Nik had pounded up the stairs just as I'd let my eyes shut. I'd heard him talking urgently to me, but I wasn't hearing words anymore. I did hear the meaty thump that was the knife ramming into Junior's heart, Nik finishing him. For all that the Auphe had half killed him, Nik had completed the job. Nik had killed to save me."

"How could you not tell him?" Robin had his hand on my shoulder squeezing. It was the same one Nik gave me when he knew I needed reassurance, but not the embarrassment of the words.

"How could I? Nik was meant for college, meant for a real life. If I'd told him the Auphe would be back for me anytime, he never would've tried those things. He wouldn't have gone to school and it wouldn't have made a damn bit of difference. Even at eighteen Nik wasn't a match for all the Auphe." I'd known that and I'd thought I was doing the right thing. "You know, Robin. It took four of us and a suicide run that never should've worked to do that." I slumped back in the couch and let my head fall to stare at the ceiling. "Three years before they came for me. It was a long time. It was so fucking long knowing every night might be the night. But it was worth it. Niko didn't get all the college he wanted or that real life, but he got a taste and that's better than nothing, right?" I believed that. I had to, but for one other person to tell me so, for one other person to know—that would be good.

Secrets are so goddamn heavy.

"It *is* worth that." Robin moved from the coffee table to sit next to me. "You're a hero, Caliban. I know you refuse to believe that about yourself, but you are. You say how Niko raised you, how he saved you. What you don't let yourself see is that you saved him as well—more than he knows. You let him see there was more to life than abusive mothers and life on the run. It didn't last long, but it lasted long enough for him to know it was possible and build the same thing for you both now. And, no, I won't tell. You each have far too impossible heights of guilt. It's like an unholy competition. I refuse to add to that."

I lifted my head and let the corners of my mouth twitch into an honest smile. "Thanks. And thanks for letting me get it out. I have mental graves all over the place and I get tired of reburying that particular one."

There was silence; then Robin asked one more question. "Do you think Jack shorted out your gating abilities for good?"

I tilted my head back again, this time with my eyes shut. "I don't know. With Grimm out there and all, I should care, but right now, I don't."

And while it wasn't a practical feeling, it was a good one.

That was enough for me.

I'd seen enough holes in the world to last me a lifetime.

16

Niko

Twelve Years Ago

"It made a hole in the world."

They were the first words Cal had said since he'd woken up two hours ago. I'd bandaged the cut on his chest, which wasn't close to as bad as I thought it would be. It would scab over by tomorrow and be gone in a week. Junior had liked to play before he truly got started. Bastard. I gently scrubbed the duct tape residue from Cal's face and lips and wrists with soap and warm water. He woke up halfway through the process and let me dress him in pajamas without helping or trying to stop me. He stared at me with blank eyes, then past me. Rain sluicing down the empty windows of an abandoned house. He would bounce back. Cal didn't fail to bounce.

Unless his brother slapped down that ball and crushed it underfoot because he didn't want to believe.

I smoothed hair I'd already combed out into his usual straight sheen. He let me fold him up on his mattress as I climbed in behind him, pulled his blanket over us and wrapped arms around him.

"I'm here, Cal."

Silence, and it went on.

"You're not alone. I'm staying.

"Junior's dead." I swallowed, but said it. Cal didn't trust anything I hadn't done myself and I had done it. "I killed him. He's not coming back.

"We'll leave tomorrow, away from that house and the police, but we need the rest tonight, okay?

"I won't, I can't make it up to you. From the first time you told me, I should've said screw Junior's good name and the police. With some things your instincts are better than mine and I fucked up."

None of my uncustomary cursing got through to him either.

"Cal . . ." I tightened my grip on him, wrapped around him as I hadn't since he was six and had nightmares every night—clowns, evil reindeer, and Grendels. "I'm sorry."

I didn't know if he would say anything, if he *could* say anything, but I heard the faintest of whispers, the barest of exhalations against the skin of my hand tucked under his small chin when he said those first words.

"It made a hole in the world."

Once he started, he didn't stop, his voice much younger than eleven. "It made a hole in the world. It made a hole in the world. It made a hole in the world. It made a hole in the world. It made a hole. . . ." He turned his head to bury it in the pillow.

I didn't know what he meant. He could've been awake for a few minutes and seen the Grendel start what I finished on Junior, but a hole in the world? I didn't know. I ran fingers through the long strands of his hair. "I'll stop it. Whatever it is, I promise I'll make it go away."

Pressing a light kiss to the top of his head, wishing he'd punch me for that as he normally did, I murmured, "Love you, little brother."

There was a shudder and a promise more determined than I could've asked for. "Love you, big brother. Forever." Ferocious in its way, *protective* almost when that was my job. It was enough to worry me more.

What had he seen?

God, what hadn't he?

We moved the next day. Packed what little we had and took the bus several states away. We didn't leave a note for Sophia, but she would find us. She always did. She was like a Grendel that way.

The apartment was cheap and dirty and not fit to live in, which is why it was more or less abandoned until maintenance got around to it. We could squat for a while. It had been three weeks and Cal was back to normal—as normal as my little brother ever was. We'd slept in the same sleeping bag for two weeks before he decided he was eleven and only babies slept with their brothers. I was surprised it took him that long to move to the sleeping bag right next to mine. For all that had happened, Cal was never one to admit he was afraid . . . of Grendels, of anything. Two weeks for him was the same as two months for someone else.

It worried me, but he didn't mention that night in the house, in the attic, and neither did I. I tried. It wasn't healthy, all the books said, to bottle up that kind of trauma. But when I did make an attempt, it was as if Junior was back with the bleach spray scorching my throat, banishing my voice.

I'd almost gotten Cal killed by not believing him. I couldn't live with that—so I put it away. What Cal did with it I didn't ask. I couldn't without tasting bleach, feeling his blood on my hands, and reliving the terribly satisfying crunch of knife through bone.

I couldn't talk about it. If I did, I couldn't be who I needed to be for him. I wouldn't be strong. I think it would've broken me . . . for good.

So that's what I did. Put it away. I wouldn't take it out again, not as long as I lived.

I hoped.

As for Cal, he seemed fine, not quite cheerful, but . . . functional. His ball was bouncing, if not as high and wild as normal. I didn't know how that could be, that he was walking and talking at all, but that was Cal. I should be grateful and I was. I was more than grateful; I was proud. The deck had been stacked against my little brother since before he was born. He never let that stop him and he never let it beat him. One little boy and he had the strength of a hundred men. I loved him, but I was also . . . humbled by him. He was an amazing boy now and he'd be a man to be reckoned with when he grew up. I was fortunate I was the one who would see that. Of all the people in the world, somehow I'd been chosen, and hard as it could be, this life, I'd never give it up. Make it better, yes, but never give up the miracles I got to see on a daily basis. Even on the days I stumbled and didn't know what to do, I was the luckiest person alive.

I came in the apartment door, ignored the smell of mold from the ceiling that no amount of scrubbing had done away with. It didn't much matter anyway. The black-green of it matched the carpet. "We start the new school tomorrow. Have you been catching up on what you missed?"

Cal looked up at me from the same math book from a table with the same wobble and, terrifyingly, wearing the same casual expression. The déjà vu was a punch in the stomach. "Mrs. Kessler is a cannibal."

Mrs. Kessler? Who had painted her door cotton candy pink, who was seventy at least and baked cookies for everyone on the floor? That Mrs. Kessler? Yet, she *did* eat a lot of what looked like pork sandwiches in that rocker on her tiny balcony. I headed immediately for the scarred baseball bat propped in the corner.

Cal laughed. "Sucker." It was his first real laugh since Junior's attic. His first true laugh, first true grin, and it was worth being fooled for that. Of course he still had to pay. That was how brothers did it. I chased him out the door and down the hall. I echoed his laughter, my first too, and continued racing after him out of the building and down the sidewalk. Of course I let him think he could outrun me, giving him the glee and the hope.

Hope is the second most important thing in the world.

Trust is the first.

When Sophia finally caught up with us, the bruise from her thrown whiskey bottle had almost faded from Cal's chest. I was checking it for the last time, the pale tinge of yellow, and smiling, relieved. That's when I heard the first door open. I recognized the particular click of our mother's picklock at work. "It looks good," I told him as he pulled his shirt down. "I've got a new Wolverine comic book I've been saving for you. It's under my sleeping bag. Have fun." While he dived for it, I went to meet Sophia.

I met her in the living room with her last full bottle of whiskey I'd brought with us when we packed. It was poetic justice. I liked poetry and I liked justice. I hefted the bottle. I didn't say anything. What was there to say? I'd made a promise to myself. It was time to keep it.

Cal was my line, I'd told Junior. This was what happened when you crossed it.

I swung the bottle and broke her arm.

As she screamed, I did regret one thing . . .

That I hadn't done it sooner.

17

Cal

Present Day

"We should've done this sooner."

"I think waiting until you could use your hands was the better notion," Niko commented. "Not that I didn't enjoy unzipping you every time you needed the bathroom."

"*Did* you enjoy it?" Robin had his chin propped in his hand at the table.

"No," Niko replied with a sigh that he made far grimmer than it had to be. "I would've paid you a hundred dollars a day to do it if I'd thought Cal wouldn't have sooner pissed his pants at the thought."

"You've seen Goodfellow naked. Hell, we both have." Accidentally or catastrophically, both adjectives applied to that occasion. "I don't want him or the Godzilla that doubles as his dick mocking Cal Junior and he would, the bastard." The Ninth Circle was closed, empty . . . of patrons and peris. I was behind the bar, pulling two bottles of wine and one of Scotch. The Scotch was for me and the wine for Goodfellow and Nik. Normally Nik didn't drink. This was not a situation anyone could define as normal. I tossed him a corkscrew. "I don't think we need glasses. Buckets maybe, but glasses are too small for what I have in mind."

I turned the chair, straddled it, and sat with them at the table in the far corner. It had been three weeks, but it was always a night where "back to the wall" was an adult monster-killer's security blanket. I opened the Scotch with only some awkwardness with my healing hands and took a swallow. It wasn't the cheapest Scotch in the place but it wasn't the best either and I didn't bother to savor the taste. It would be good on stubborn household stains though.

Taking a look at Robin's shirt, a radical departure from his Italian suits that cost more than the gold toilets in the Vatican, I groaned at the eye-searing colors and slick polyester blend. "Disco is dead. If it hadn't died before I was born I would've killed it myself. Burn the damn shirt."

"This is vintage, I'll have you know," the puck said, the wounded pride evident in the way he ran his hand down the front of an era that rivaled the Dark Ages for inventive tortures: visual and auditory. "I have a friend in Miami, Saul. He sends me only the best. I save them for special occasions."

"This is a special occasion?" Niko inquired, appearing more relaxed than he had since Jack had shown up.

"I thought Ishiah and the others cleared out to give us a night to finally decompress and, I don't know, not rip them a new one for being lying dicks every day since we've known them?" I took another swallow.

Robin spread his arms wide, the wine bottle swinging in punctuation. "Angels. Please. It was a white lie. Barely a lie. If you both weren't so naïve you would've immediately caught on and it wouldn't have counted as a lie. Basically you have no one to blame but yourselves."

"It was for our own good," I snarked in an echo of my brother, not happy with it yet, but then again I did love my grudges and putting Nik in his place as it happened usually only once a decade.

"Yes, we've both been hearing that quite a bit lately," Niko said wryly. "Let it go, Cal." He was looking down his nose at the wine he'd just tasted. I'd tried to pick something expensive, but when your palate is accustomed to grass clippings and soy husks there isn't much a person can do. "We know why they lied. Why Robin did as well. They had their reasons. We have issues."

I snorted at that and drank again. Issues. That was a word for it, but not the right one by a long shot. Our issues should've come with radioactive warning labels, sealed in hazardous waste drums, and tossed into the

Mariana Trench or Mount Doom if anyone had the upper body strength to carry them that far.

"Yes, they had their reasons. I had my reasons. We were trying to protect two babes in the woods. We were watching out the best we could for our friends." Goodfellow drank half his bottle in one long swallow. It was an impressive and kind of filthy skill if you thought about it. I didn't want to think about it.

"And, yes, Cal, this is a special occasion. To friends. Value them." He lifted his bottle. He had an oddly indecipherable glint in the mossy green of his gaze. His bottle was held stiffly as if the toast was almost ceremonial. "They go and they come."

Nik's fingers clenched around his bottle as his face went blank. He echoed slowly, "They go and they come. That's what you said before. I *remember* you. You were at our house. You were the man with the flat tire." As he said it, I remembered it too, in a barely there haze, but I remembered Goodfellow . . . no, Goodman he'd called himself, standing on our porch and no doubt looking absolutely identical to how he looked now. My memory wasn't clear enough to see it, but that didn't mean I didn't know it.

"Yes, the first time we met—this time around. I'd always thought of myself as unforgettable but six years later you show up at my car lot, which was your idea by the way, Niko—I opened one at your suggestion, and neither of you remembered. But considering what happened after that with Jack's apprentice, I cannot say I'm surprised that you did everything you could to forget that entire year altogether. Now, toast for the love of Priapus's ever-upright phallus. This is the first time I've been able to tell you, in all your lives, without being beat over the head with a club or the jawbone of an ass or a wine amphorae for blasphemy against the gods. Leave it to Niko to be a Buddhist before Buddha himself. To be that for all his lives and not know it."

Not life. *Lives.*

Numbly I clinked my bottle against theirs and watched Niko go from shaken to intrigued, then rueful in less than a second flat. "And I the Buddhist—in this life at least—never caught on."

My brother believed in life after death, many lives. I believed in nothing. It looked like I might be wrong.

"What the hell are you saying? You knew us? You've always known us? That we were your friends, comrades in arms, buddies, whatever, reincarnated over and over throughout history? That we knew you and hung out with you on *purpose* God knows how many times? Reincarnation I'll buy. Maybe. But choosing to spend all of history listening to your egomaniacal ass sounds more like Hell to me." I grinned at Robin because at the moment he appeared as if he could really use it. After the angels, telling us another truth was bound to be nerve-wracking. He couldn't know how we'd take it.

On the whole, I thought we were damn lucky.

Life after life? I had no religious beliefs or philosophies, but if Niko wanted to drag me behind him through reincarnation after reincarnation, I did owe him, didn't I? In this life and most likely every other one.

"Yes, because you've been such a delightful companion throughout the ages. Of the six hundred and seventy-eight times I've nearly been killed, six hundred at minimum have been your fault." He turned to Niko to say one word, one name actually, "Achilles."

Niko, the alcohol shall not profane my holy temple having gone out the window with Boris and now this, Niko, took another quick swallow before saying with disbelief, "Last month, when my father was here"—late father, for which I happily took full credit—"and you told him that you were there when Achilles cut his hair to mourn his cousin Patroclus, you were actually saying *I* was Achilles?"

"Simply because of how I, and even Cal, whose entire knowledge of history could be collected in a comic book, compare you to Achilles on a monthly basis? Oh, and the legend in your clan that your blond hair and exceptional genetic tendency toward lethality in a fight comes from a descendant of Achilles playing hide the *loukaniko* with a winsome Rom maiden when your clan was in Greece a few centuries ago?" Robin snapped, rubbing his forehead with the heel of his free hand. "Zeus's golden shower, you're as thick as your brother. *Of course* you were Achilles."

"And I'm guessing I was the dead guy, Patroclus," I muttered. "Great. Just my luck." I had a feeling that history did love to repeat itself. But at the same time . . . once I'd been human. Not Auphe, not monster. I'd been human. That was worth knowing.

"Live by the sword, die by the sword. That little Jewish fellow with the big feet knew what he was talking about there. The two of you were mortal and warriors—always. Soldiers, mercenaries, fighters of all stripe, with nothing save a vulnerable human body to keep you alive. The combination makes for short life spans." This time he finished the bottle rather than face us. "And shorter friendships."

He peered at the empty bottle and sighed, bereft and despairing. That meant he was too lazy to get a replacement. I groaned and fetched one for him. "How'd you even figure this out? We looked different, right? We probably weren't always brothers, were we?" A feeling of loss, icy and sharp, spiked in me at that thought.

"Strangely enough, you are brothers most often. Sometimes cousins. Occasionally, as I told you when you were younger, friends bonded by blood and battle. As for me noticing, it started when I kept crossing paths centuries apart with a string of humans of foul and sarcastic attitude. These were the days when there was little law, rare enforcement, and a smart-ass mouth was reason enough for someone to be beaten to death, anyone would agree. That I kept running into this same nonsurvival-prone personality type began to make me somewhat suspicious. Nature should've weeded this strain out hundreds of years after I first encountered it for the sake of the species."

That was harsh. I didn't think my personality was species dooming. Not necessarily.

"That this annoying persona was invariably accompanied by another saner character who kept him from being beaten to death as he deserved, I began to think

I'd gone insane. Older pucks do once you've lived a
million or so years. Then after sharing a meal and a conversation with Buddha, the thin Indian version, that
conversation we had about sex—enlightenment is very
overrated—I think I've mentioned this story before. Ah,
yes, by the constipated look on Cal's face I have told this
one. Irregardless we discussed other things as well and
I knew. I was cursed"—he coughed—"ah . . . blessed
with eternal companions to fill the long years of an eternal life. One way or the other fate draws us together
time and time again."

When we'd first met him, or when I'd thought we'd
first met him, at the car lot, Robin had seemed the most
unwillingly solitary person or creature I'd known. Sex
partners he had in plenty—he'd made certain we knew
that in the first five minutes, but with the majority of the
paien hating pucks and pucks absolutely despising each
other, friends were definitely a seller's market. He'd
seized on us like a life preserver. For a moment I wondered how he could've been lonely if we'd been there
all along and then I knew. We'd been mortal and he was
not. We were seemingly eternal but present for a handful of years at a time. How many times had he seen
Niko and me fall to that sword? How many times had
he seen us die? How long were the stretches when we
weren't around? Tens of years, hundreds, thousands?
Was he lonely or was it truer to say he was abandoned?

Now I felt guilty for dying—repeatedly—instead of
feeling as if I'd fallen through the rabbit hole, which
would be a far more normal reaction. Fuck. I gave him
a light shove. For once, I'd try not to make everything

about me. "Short, but apparently we always eventually turned back up . . . like a bad penny, the kind coated with the supernatural Ebola of rotten luck."

"True." His smile was solemn enough to make the unspoken words etch themselves in the air as sharp as diamond-cut crystal: although sometimes it took a very long time before you did.

There was nothing to be done about it—except taking it up with Niko's Buddha and universe-at-large and I had a feeling that wasn't an option. That meant I did with it what I did with all problems I couldn't solve: I ignored it and moved on. "So since we met you at the car lot. No, hell, since you showed up on our porch when we were *kids*, you thought . . . knew who we were to you and you didn't bother to say anything? Didn't think we'd like to be clued in?"

"Naturally I didn't tell you when you were children. First, you kept calling me a pervert." He glared. I might have forgotten most of it but he hadn't. Neither forgiven nor forgotten. "And second, it would've interfered with your development."

Niko picked up the thread of conversation. "Who we'd become, who we were meant to be. A person has the same basic core of personality in each life, but there are some differences based on environment, genes, the paths we choose, things such as that."

In this life, yeah, genes were in the driver's seat on that one. In this life, for once, I wasn't mortal, but I was as likely to have that short life span. More likely in fact.

"Did you know I was Auphe . . . when I was a kid?"

I asked abruptly. I didn't stop with one swallow of Scotch on that question.

"No." Goodfellow sounded . . . hell, sounded as if he'd thought about this more nights than I'd care to consider and found himself guilty every time. "*No*. If I had known about them, if I'd known about Sophia, if I'd known how bad it truly was, I would've interfered and *gamisou* personality development. I could see you were poor, but I didn't see the rest. I am sorry for that. You don't know how sorry."

He turned his attention to his wine. "When years later, at the car lot, when we met for what you thought was the first time, you hadn't seen all that you've seen now. You wouldn't have believed me, the things that I knew. You didn't trust me either, not then. You didn't know me." And the wine was gone again. He was like a camel, storing wine for the long trek across the desert. "Finally, after six years, the time seemed right. Last month I started dropping more hints than the number of hair extensions Rapunzel threw out her tower window and you didn't catch on. Achilles, the bacchanalia when we were in Greece, the life*times* you've dragged my ass through the fire and on and on. I expected that from Cal. He's oblivious in any life, but I was disappointed in you, Niko."

"As there were three creatures trying to kill us then, including my own father," he said dryly, "and Jack now, I've been a shade distracted. Forgive my unmindful ways."

"Were we anyone else famous besides Achilles and Patroclus?" I asked curiously.

Goodfellow rolled his eyes upward. "The wonder of the afterlife revealed to you, your personal afterlife, mind you and that is the question you ask. How vain. If you're good, I'll tell you later. However, *I* was Robin Hood and my john was anything but little."

On that somewhat horrifying note, Niko held up his bottle and Robin joined in, ignoring the fact his was empty. I raised mine to meet theirs and Niko said soberly, "To friends. They go and they come. The going must be difficult, but know we will always come back."

Personally, I wasn't a big fan of history repeating itself, but in this one case . . .

I made an exception.

18

Cal

Nine Years Ago

It came when I was in bed for the night.

A tap at the trailer window, harmless. It could've been one of those giant summer beetles. They were everywhere this month. Then one more tap, soft, like the beating of a moth against the glass. They were out this summer too, some as big as your hand. They left a shimmering dust against the glass every night.

I looked up from where I'd been pounding my pillow into submission, not worried. As the years pass, you forget the things you should remember. Forget promises made. It wasn't a moth, but it hung in the window all the same—the Grendel outlined by a bright full moon, its skin scrubbed even whiter by the lunar glow. The narrow face, the slanted red eyes, the thousand needle teeth bound by the same gleeful grin I remembered from Junior's attic. This time it wasn't here to only watch. It tapped again and it spoke, the voice the same too, the gargle of glass wrapped in a serpent's complacent hiss. "Mine."

Three years was a long time.

Nik had saved his money. He had college now and his plan for our future. The wheels were in motion and finally we were leaving Sophia. He was the happiest he'd ever been and I'd gotten to see that. That was something to be grateful for. I'd gotten to fucking see that. He would be all right eventually. I hoped. He'd miss me, more than anything—I knew that. I knew my brother. But afterward, in time, he'd have a life, a real one. Normal. That was something he wouldn't have with me in it. No goddamn way. That's the way it was and I'd known that long before I was eleven. Long before I was fourteen.

A hand with spidery fingers and black talons exploded through the glass, the nails hooking into my flesh. It hurt and I was scared. I was so damned scared, but I held on to it: three years was a long time. Three years had been long enough for Nik to be happy.

"Time to go home," the Grendel crooned.

Three years.

I'd had my big brother for three more years.

A serial killer had almost taken that from me. A Grendel had given it back, but nothing is free. I'd known that all my life.

"Time to go home," it reminded me with a laugh as

it snatched me through the window, all my struggling and screaming less than nothing to it.

Three years.

I hung in the night air, terrified, my sweatpants wet with piss, feeling the sanity pour out of me like water out of a pitcher, but despite it all . . .

I thought it was worth it.

It had to be worth it.

It was for Nik.

Two years later when I escaped the Grendels to come back through my own hole in the world and found my brother still waiting, I *knew* it was worth it. And the years we had coming to us after that, each one we'd take for our own no matter how hard we had to fight for them, run for them, rip the world apart for them, they'd be worth it too. We'd find that life I'd wanted for Nik. We'd have friends we could trust with the truth someday. We'd have the not quite normal but normal enough for us. We'd have all of that, no matter what we had to do to take it for our own. That's what we did, Nik and me. That's what we always did.

We survived.

And that was worth everything.

Lions didn't play to win. Lions didn't play at all. Lions survived.

—Niko Leandros

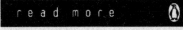

ROB THURMAN

NIGHTLIFE

'There are monsters among us. There always have been and there always will be. I've known that since I can remember, just like I've always known that I was one ... Well, half of one anyway.'

Cal Leandros is nineteen. He eats junk food, he doesn't clean up after himself and he fights with his half brother Niko. It's a fairly normal life, but for the fact that Cal and Niko are constantly on the run. Cal's father has been after him for the last four years. And given that he's a monster whose dark lineage is the stuff of nightmares they really don't want him and his entire otherworldly race catching up with them. But Cal is about to learn why they want him, why they've always wanted him - he is the key to unleashing their hell on earth.

Meanwhile the bright lights of the Big Apple shine on, oblivious to the fact that the fate of the human world will be decided in the fight of Cal and Niko's lives ...

ROB THURMAN

MOONSHINE

'I was born a monster. Although truthfully, I was only half monster. Half monster or whole, in the end it didn't matter. I had my weaknesses, same as anyone else. And I was facing one of them now.'

Cal and his half-brother Niko's lives are settling back to normal after preventing their bloodthirsty relatives from bringing about the apocalypse. They've found a new apartment and even gainful employment by starting an investigative agency in partnership with a glamorous Upper East Side vampire. Of course, their clientele tends to be a little . . . unusual, but their money spends just the same.

Their latest job is undercover work for the Kin - New York's werewolf mafia - to sniff out proof of a set-up by a rival. The location is Moonshine, a gambling club for the otherworldly and Cal figures it will be an easy in-and-out sort of job. But as Niko likes to point out, nothing is more dangerous than overconfidence and when a brawl gets out of hand, it looks like he's right. Are Cal and Niko being set up themselves? And by people whose bite is much worse than their bark . . .

ROB THURMAN

MADHOUSE

'My brother had spent a lifetime - mine, at least - telling me that I was normal, that I wasn't a monster. With his help, I'd finally realized that as long as I could remain who I was, I could survive what I was. It was only bad genes . . .'

Half-human Cal Leandros and his brother, Niko, aren't exactly prospering with their preternatural detective agency. Who could have guessed that business would dry up in New York City, where vampires, trolls, and other creepy crawlies are all over the place?

But now there's a new arrival in the Big Apple. A malevolent evil with ancient powers, dead set on making history with an orgy of blood and murder, is on a human killing spree. And for Cal and Niko, this is one pay cheque they're going to have to earn . . . if they survive to collect it.

Praise for Rob Thurman

'Supernatural elements put this in the company of Jim Butcher and Charlaine Harris' *SFRevu*

'A roaring rollercoaster of a read, with supernatural highs and lows . . . it'll take your breath away' Simon R. Green

ROB THURMAN

DEATHWISH

'How I felt the mental stirrings of a bloodthirsty heritage when I passed through the gray light wasn't my favourite topic . . . the Auphe nature wasn't mine. I wouldn't let it be. And if I said that to myself over and over and sprinkled around enough frigging fairy dust, maybe it would be true.'

Half-human Cal Leandros and his brother, Niko, are barely getting by with their preternatural detective agency when the vampire Seamus hires them. He's being followed, and he wants to know by whom. But the Leandros brothers have to do more than they had planned when Seamus turns up dead (or un-undead).

Worse still is the return of Cal's nightmarish family, the Auphe. The last time Cal and Niko faced them, the Auphe were almost wiped out. Now they want revenge. Cal knows that before the Auphe get to him, they will try to destroy everything and everyone he holds dear. Because for the Auphe, Cal's pain is a pleasure.

And they're feeling good.

HUNGRY FOR FRESH

BLOOD ?

Then come and join us at
www.facebook.com/BerkleyUK,
where we're dedicated to keeping you
fully up to date on all of our SF, fantasy
and supernatural fiction releases.

- Author Q&As
- Exclusive cover reveals
- Exclusive competitions
- Advance readers' copies
- Guest blogs from our authors
- Excellent reading recommendations

And we'd love to hear from you, email
us at **berkleyuk@uk.penguingroup.com**